Praise for *New York Times* bestselling author

SUSAN MALLERY

"There's a little fun, a little sizzle
and a whole lot of homespun charm."
—*Publishers Weekly* on *Summer Nights*

"Mallery infuses her story with eccentricity,
gentle humor and small-town shenanigans, and readers...
will enjoy the connection between Heidi and Rafe."
—*Publishers Weekly* on *Summer Days*

"If you want a story that will both tug on
your heartstrings and tickle your funny bone,
Mallery is the author for you!"
—*RT Book Reviews* on *Only His*

"When it comes to heartfelt contemporary romance,
Mallery is in a class by herself."
—*RT Book Reviews* on *Only Yours*

"An adorable, outspoken heroine and an intense hero...
set the sparks flying in Mallery's latest lively,
comic and touching family-centered story."
—*Library Journal* on *Only Yours*

"Mallery...excels at creating varied, well-developed
characters and an emotion-packed story gently infused
with her trademark wit and humor."
One of the Top 10 Romances of 2011!
—*Booklist* on *Only Mine*

"Mallery's prose is luscious and provocative."
—*Publishers Weekly*

"Susan Mallery's gift for writing humor and tenderness
makes all her books true gems."
—*RT Book Reviews*

"Romance novels don't get much better than
Mallery's expert blend of emotional nuance,
humor and superb storytelling."
—*Booklist*

Also available from Susan Mallery and Harlequin HQN

Halfway There (ebook novella)
A Christmas Bride
A Fool's Gold Christmas
All Summer Long
Summer Nights
Summer Days
Only His
Only Yours
Only Mine
Finding Perfect
Almost Perfect
Chasing Perfect
Hot on Her Heels
Straight from the Hip
Lip Service
Under Her Skin
Sweet Trouble
Sweet Spot
Sweet Talk
Accidentally Yours
Tempting
Sizzling
Irresistible
Delicious
Falling for Gracie
Someone Like You

Watch for more Fool's Gold romances, coming soon!

Two of a Kind
Three Little Words
Christmas on 4th Street

SUSAN MALLERY

JUST *One* KISS

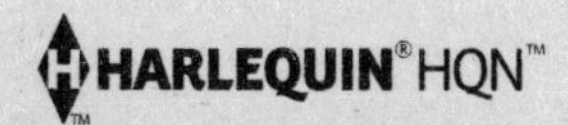

Recycling programs for this product may not exist in your area.

ISBN-13: 978-0-373-77760-0

JUST ONE KISS

This edition published by arrangement with Harlequin Books S.A.

For questions and comments about the quality of this book, please contact us at CustomerService@Harlequin.com.

Printed in U.S.A.

This one is for 2011 Fool's Gold
Co-Head Cheerleader Michele,
whose energy is surpassed only by her heart.
Thanks, Michele, for everything!
You're incredible!

JUST
One
KISS

PROLOGUE

Fifteen years ago...

PATIENCE MCGRAW COULDN'T breathe. She placed her hand on top of her chest and wondered if it was possible to have a heart attack and die from fear. Or maybe anticipation. Her mind raced and her throat was tight and here she was, on possibly the most *significant* day of her life, and she couldn't catch her breath. Talk about lame.

"The snow's melting," Justice said, pointing toward the mountains just east of town.

Patience looked up and nodded. "It's getting warmer."

It's getting warmer? She held in a groan. Why did she have to sound so stupid? Why did she have to be so nervous? This was Justice, her best friend since he'd moved to Fool's Gold at the beginning of October last year. They'd met in the school cafeteria and they'd reached for the last cupcake. He'd let her have it; she'd offered to share. She figured because he was older, he would refuse, but he'd smiled instead and that day they'd become friends.

She *knew* him. They hung out together, played video

games together, went to the movies together. It was fun. It was easy. Or it had been until a few weeks ago when she'd suddenly looked into Justice's dark blue eyes and felt something she'd never experienced before.

Her mom had reassured her it was normal. Patience was fourteen, Justice was sixteen and it was unlikely they would stay friends forever. But Patience wasn't sure she liked the change. Before, she hadn't had to think about everything she said or worry about what she wore, or how her hair looked. Now she was always *thinking,* which made it hard to just hang out.

After two months of sweating every word, every thought, every action, she was done. She was going to tell Justice the truth. That she liked him. That she wanted him to be more than her best friend. If he liked her back, well, she didn't know what would happen then, but she was sure it would be wonderful. If he didn't, she would probably die of a broken heart.

They walked through the quiet residential neighborhood of Fool's Gold. The small town was nestled in the foothills of the Sierra Nevadas. With spring chasing away winter, there were buds on trees and the first daffodils and tulips of the season swayed in the afternoon breeze. All of which had nothing to do with the fact that she was seriously scared. Because while *talking* about dying of a broken heart was very *Pride and Prejudice*—her mother's favorite book and movie—it might be painful and a little gross.

But she had to know. Had to stop wondering. She should just tell him and get it over with. There was a school dance in two weeks and she wanted to go with Justice.

She was pretty sure he didn't like anyone else. Although he was two years older than her, he didn't have a girlfriend and they always hung out together at lunch. Not that he'd tried to kiss her. She wasn't sure how she felt about kissing, but if she was going to have a boy kiss her, she wanted it to be Justice. Oh God, why did her stomach hurt so much?

"Patience?"

She jumped. "Huh?"

"Are you okay?"

She came to a stop and clutched her books to her chest. "I'm fine. Why do you ask?"

"You're quiet. Is something wrong?"

His eyes were so beautiful, she thought. Dark, dark blue. They crinkled a little at the corners when he laughed, which wasn't that often. He had a great smile. He was still kind of skinny, as if he'd grown too fast, but cute. And sweet to her.

"Justice, I need to ask you something."

He nodded and waited, facing her. "Sure. What?"

She opened her mouth, then closed it. Words disappeared as she got lost in fear and panic and—

"Hey, Justice."

They both turned and saw Ford Hendrix crossing the street toward them. Patience exhaled, both relieved and frustrated by the interruption.

Ford was one of six kids. Dark hair and eyes. All the girls thought he was hot, but Patience only saw Justice.

"Could you believe that history test?" Ford asked. He and Justice were the same age and had a lot of classes together. "Hey, Patience."

"Hi."

They all fell into step together, walking toward home, the moment lost.

"Man, why do we have to know that stuff?" Ford asked. "World War One was like a hundred years ago or something. That essay question..."

"Brutal," Justice finished for him.

Patience glanced at him and saw he was watching her, his expression questioning. She swallowed as she realized he might ask her what she'd wanted to talk about and she couldn't possibly say anything in front of Ford. He was a nice enough guy, but no way!

"I, um, need to get home," Patience said. "I'm going to cut through here. See you tomorrow."

"Patience, wait."

But she ignored Justice and hurried away, ducking around a house and through a backyard as she made her escape.

THE NEXT MORNING, Patience was determined not to wait another second to tell Justice the truth. She'd spent a horrible night tossing and turning, feeling a little sick to her stomach. She couldn't keep doing this to herself. She was going to be brave. She was going to be honest. If things went really bad, she was sure her mom would be willing to move.

She walked from her house to Justice's, as she had

every school morning for months now. He lived a couple of blocks closer to town so he was on her way. As she walked down the sidewalk, she looked at the small two-bedroom house he shared with his uncle. Normally Justice would be sitting on the porch steps, waiting for her. Only he wasn't there this morning.

Did he know? Had he figured out what she wanted to tell him? Was he disgusted? Did he think she was a complete dork and was so embarrassed he couldn't speak to her?

Anxiety propelled her up the stairs. If it was bad, she wanted to hear it fast. He should just tell her the truth so she wouldn't hope. Then her heart would break and she could get over it and…

She paused on the porch as she realized the front door was partially open. As if someone had left it that way in a hurry. She frowned as she moved forward.

"Justice? Are you okay?"

She knocked once and the door swung open.

She'd been in the small house dozens of times. There was a living room with a tiny dining room and kitchen beyond. There were two bedrooms and a single bathroom in the back. She remembered a sofa and a couple of chairs, some kind of coffee table.

Only all of that was gone now. The living room was empty, as was the dining room beyond. There was nothing. Not a cushion or a box or a scrap of paper. It was as if no one had ever lived here at all.

Patience slowly walked through the house. Her

breathing sounded loud in the stillness. She didn't understand. How could everything be gone?

The kitchen was as vacant as the rest of the place. The cupboards stood open, the shelves bare. The sink was empty, as were all the drawers. In Justice's bedroom, there was no hint he had ever lived there.

She returned to the living room and blinked away sudden tears. She turned in a slow circle, fear growing inside her.

This wasn't right. People didn't just disappear in the night. Something had happened. Something bad.

She darted out the front door and ran all the way home. She burst in the back door and yelled for her mom.

"Justice is gone! He's gone and his uncle's gone and all their stuff."

Her mother hurried into the living room. "What are you talking about?"

Patience told her what had happened. Ava grabbed a jacket, then followed her out the back door. Ten minutes later she was gazing at the empty interior. Fifteen minutes after that, the police had arrived.

Patience watched the activity and listened to the conversation. No one knew what had happened. No one had heard anything or seen anything. But they all agreed it was very strange. Justice and his uncle had disappeared. It was as if they'd never been there at all.

CHAPTER ONE

"TRIM UP my eyebrows," Alfred said, wiggling his white, bushy brows as he spoke. "I want to look sexy."

Patience McGraw held in a smile. "Big night planned with the missus?"

"You know it."

A concept that would be romantic, if Alfred and his lovely wife were a tad younger than, say, ninety-five. Patience had to keep herself from blurting out a warning that, at their age, they should be careful. She supposed the more important lesson was that true love and passion could last a lifetime.

"I'm jealous," she told her client as she carefully trimmed his brows.

"You picked a piss-poor excuse of a man," Albert told her, then shrugged. "Excuse my French."

"I can't complain about you telling the truth," Patience said, wondering what it would be like to live in a bigger city. Where everyone didn't know every detail of your personal life. But she'd been born in Fool's Gold and had grown up with the idea that there were very few secrets between friends and neighbors.

Which meant the whole town knew that she'd gotten pregnant when she was eighteen and the "piss-poor excuse for a man" who'd been her baby's father had walked out on her and her daughter less than a year later.

"You'll find someone," Alfred told her, gently patting her arm. "A pretty girl like you should have them lined up for miles."

She smiled. "You're very sweet. If I didn't know better, I'd say you were flirting with me."

Alfred gave her a wink.

Despite his compliments, she managed to find herself amazingly man free. Fool's Gold wasn't exactly swimming with prospects, and as a single mother, she had to be especially careful. There was also the fact that most of the men she met weren't interested in other men's kids.

As Patience picked up the scissors to clip a couple of errant hairs, she told herself that she was very comfortable with her life. Given the choice, she would rather open her own business than fall in love. But every now and then, she found herself longing for someone to lean on. A man to care about, who would be there for her.

She stood back and studied Albert's reflection. "You're even more handsome than before," she said, putting down her tools and unfastening his cape.

"Hard to believe," Albert said with a grin.

She laughed.

"Patience?"

She didn't recognize the male voice, but turned anyway. A man stood in the entrance of the shop.

Her mind registered several things at once. Albert was her last appointment of the day. If the guy was a walk-in, he wouldn't call her by name. The man was tall, with dark gold-blond hair and deep blue eyes. His shoulders were broad and he had the kind of face that would be happy up on a movie screen. Nice, but she had no idea who he…

She felt the cape flutter to the floor as she really looked at the man moving toward her. He was a few inches taller, a lot more muscular, but his eyes… They were exactly the same. They even crinkled when he smiled at her.

"Hello, Patience."

She was fourteen again, standing in that empty house, more scared than she'd ever been in her life. There hadn't been any answers. Not then or since. No solution to the mystery. Just questions and a gnawing sense that something had gone terribly wrong.

"Justice?" she asked, her voice more breath than sound. "Justice?"

He gave her a slight shrug. The familiar gesture was enough to send her flying across the shop. She flung herself at him, determined to hang on this time.

He caught her against him and held on to her nearly as tightly as she held on to him. He was warm and solid and real. She pressed her head against his shoulder and inhaled the scent of him. A clean, masculine smell that had nothing to do with the boy she remembered. This wasn't happening, she thought, still dazed. Justice couldn't be back.

Yet he was. But the man was very different from the boy, and the moment got awkward quickly. She stepped away and put her hands on her hips.

"What happened? You left me! Where on earth did you go? I was so scared. The whole town was worried. I called the police and everything."

He glanced around the salon. Patience didn't have to follow his gaze to know they were the center of attention. She was used to the friendly interest of the shop, but Justice might find the attention uncomfortable.

"When can you take a break?" he asked.

"Five minutes. Alfred is my last client of the day."

"I'll be outside."

He was gone before she could stop him, moving with a combination of power and purpose. The second the door closed behind him, the other stylists and half the clients descended.

"Who is he?" Julia, her boss, demanded. "What a handsome man."

"I've seen him around town before," another woman said. "With that ballet dancer. He was her bodyguard."

"Has he moved here?"

"Is he an old boyfriend?"

Alfred cleared his throat. "Back away, ladies. Give Patience some room to breathe."

Patience smiled at him gratefully. He paid her for the cut and gave her a fifty-cent tip. She was so not getting rich working here, she thought as she walked him to the door and kissed his cheek.

With Alfred gone, she returned to her station and

quickly cleaned up. Julia watched with unconcealed interest.

"You'll have details tomorrow?" she asked.

"Of course."

Sharing was as much a part of the culture of Fool's Gold as showing up with a casserole when there was a birth, death or serious illness. She might not want to reveal every detail of her upcoming encounter with a man from her past, but that wasn't her decision.

Patience made a quick stop in the restroom to make sure she hadn't spilled anything on her black T-shirt. She released her long brown hair from its ponytail, thought briefly that she should have gotten highlights, and worn makeup and hey, maybe been something more exciting than ordinary, then shrugged. She was who she was, and nothing short of serious plastic surgery and/or a makeover was going to change her now.

She applied lip gloss and brushed the front of her "Chez Julia" T-shirt one last time. Two minutes later she had her purse and was walking out onto the sidewalk.

Justice was still there. All six-two of him. He wore a dark suit, blinding white shirt and a smoky-gray tie.

"You weren't this stylish a dresser fifteen years ago," she said.

"Occupational hazard."

"Which begs the question, what occupation? But that can wait." She looked at him, trying to reconcile the man with the teenager she'd known and loved. Well, maybe not loved, but liked a lot. He'd been her first crush. She'd wanted to tell him, to have him for her boyfriend and then he'd been gone. "What happened?"

He glanced around. "Can I buy you a cup of coffee?"

"Sure." She pointed down the street. "There's a Starbucks this way."

They started down the sidewalk. A thousand questions filled her mind, but she couldn't seem to grab any one to ask it. She was both curious and shy—a combination that didn't make for easy conversation.

"How long have you—"

"I would have thought you'd—"

They spoke at the same time.

She sighed. "We've lost our rhythm. That's just so sad."

"It'll come back," he assured her. "Give it a minute."

They reached the Starbucks and he held open the door. She paused before stepping past him.

"You're here for good?" she asked. "Or at least a while?"

"Yes."

"No disappearing in the night?"

"No."

She nodded. "I didn't know what to think. I was so scared."

His dark blue gaze settled on her face. "I'm sorry. I knew you'd be worried. I wanted to say something, but I couldn't."

She saw a couple of older women approaching and

ducked into the store. As she walked to the counter, she pulled out her Starbucks card, but Justice waved it away.

"I'm buying," he told her. "It's the least I can do after what happened."

"Ha. Sure, bring me out for coffee instead of a steak when you're doing apology buying."

He flashed her a smile that was so familiar she felt her heart constrict. At the same time, she experienced a very distinct "wow—handsome guy" tingle in the area just south of her belly button. It had been so long it took her a second to recognize sexual attraction.

She was pathetic, she thought as she ordered her usual grande skinny vanilla latte. This was the closest she'd come to dating in the past five or six years. She really needed to get out more. And just as soon as she had a little free time, she would work on that.

"Tall drip," Justice told the girl.

Patience rolled her eyes. "Very masculine. I'm not even surprised."

He flashed her another smile. "I don't strike you as the soy-chai-latte type?"

"No, but I'd pay to watch you drink one."

"Not enough money in the world."

They moved aside to wait for their orders, then took them over to a table in the corner.

"You probably want to sit with your back to the wall, right?" she asked, taking a seat that would allow him to do just that.

"Why would you think that?"

"Someone said you're a bodyguard. Is it true?"

He settled across from her, his broad shoulders and large frame seeming to challenge the space around them.

"I work for a company that provides protection," he admitted.

She sipped her coffee. "You can't just say yes?"

"What?"

"The answer is yes. Wouldn't that be easier than telling me you work for a company that provides protection?"

He leaned toward her. "Were you this much of a pain in the ass when we were kids?"

She grinned. "I've mellowed with age." She raised her latte. "Welcome back, Justice."

PATIENCE'S BROWN EYES danced with amusement, just as Justice remembered. She'd gotten a little taller and had filled out in fascinatingly female ways, but otherwise she was the same. *Sassy,* he thought. Not a word he would have used as a teenager, but one that suited her perfectly now. The Patience he recalled had been all attitude and blunt talk. It looked as though that hadn't changed.

She glanced around the coffee place and sighed. "There are, what, five million of these across the country? We need something different."

"You don't like Starbucks?"

"No," Patience said as she sipped on her latte. "I adore Starbucks. We own stock and everything. But don't you think a town like Fool's Gold should have a local place, too? I would love to open my own coffee place. Silly, huh?"

"Why is it silly?"

"It's not a big dream. Shouldn't dreams be big? Like I want to end world hunger?"

"You're allowed to dream for yourself."

She studied him. "What do you dream about?"

He wasn't much of a dreamer. He wanted what other people took for granted. The chance to be like everyone else. Only that wasn't going to happen.

"Ending world hunger."

She laughed. The happy sound took him back in years to when they'd been kids together. He'd been forced to lie every second of every day. He'd been discouraged from making friends and fitting in too much, but he'd defied them all, claiming Patience as his own. Even then he'd known he was different, but he'd still wanted to belong. Being friends with her had been the only "normal" part of his life. He'd needed her to survive.

His choice had been selfish and she'd paid the price for his decision. When he'd had to leave, he hadn't been able to tell her why. Later, he'd known getting in touch with her would bring her into his world. He'd liked Patience too much to sully her with that.

So what was his excuse now? As he stared into her eyes, he knew he'd again chosen what *he* wanted rather than what was right for her. But he'd been unable to resist the call of his past. Maybe he'd secretly been hoping she wasn't as good as he remembered. Now he had to deal with the fact that she was even better.

She leaned toward him. "You've stalled long enough, Justice. What happened all those years ago? One second you were there and the next you were gone."

She still wore her brown hair long. He remembered the slight wave and how her hair had moved as she walked, swinging back and forth. Sexy.

He'd been too old for her then. At least that's what he'd told himself every time he'd been tempted to kiss her. An eighteen-year-old masquerading as a sixteen-year-old, to outwit the man who wanted him dead.

"I was in the witness protection program."

Her eyes widened and her mouth dropped open.

He let the words sink in and took a moment to study the cartoon hairstylist on the front of her black "Chez Julia" T-shirt. The drawn hairdresser was wielding scissors with comical intent.

"Are you kidding?" Patience asked. "Seriously? Here?"

"Where better than Fool's Gold?"

"That can't be real. It sounds like something from the movies."

"It was plenty real." He sipped his coffee and thought about his past. He rarely talked about it. Even his closest friends weren't privy to the details.

"My father was a career criminal," he said slowly. "The kind of man who believed the world owed him a living. He went from one scheme to the next. If he'd put half as much effort into working a steady job, he could have made a fortune, but that wasn't his way."

Patience's eyes widened as she held on to her cup. "Please don't make me cry with your story."

He raised one shoulder. "I'll do my best to stick to the facts."

"Because they won't make me cry?" She drew in a breath. "Okay, bad father. And then what?"

"When I was seventeen, he and a couple of buddies held up a convenience store. The owner and a clerk were killed and my dad was the one who pulled the trigger. The friends were caught and gave up my dad. Bart. His name was Bart Hanson." Justice had been born Bart Hanson Jr., but he'd rejected that name years ago. Had it legally changed. He'd wanted nothing that had belonged to his father.

"The local SWAT team came to take him in. Dad wasn't going without a fight. He'd planned everything and was going to take out as many officers as he could. I figured out what he was going to do and jumped on his back. I distracted him long enough for the police to get him. He wasn't happy with me."

An understatement, he thought. His father had cursed him, vowing to punish his son, no matter what it took. Everyone who knew Bart Hanson had believed he was more than capable of murdering his only child.

"That's so horrible. Where was your mother in all this?"

"She'd died years before. A car accident."

He didn't bother mentioning that the car's brakes

had been cut. Local law enforcement had suspected Bart but had been unable to make the charges stick.

"When I testified against my father, his anger turned to rage. Right after sentencing, he broke out of jail and came after me. I was put into a witness protection program and brought here. That's when we met."

She shook her head. "That's amazing, and scary. I can't believe you went through all that. You never hinted or..." She looked at him. "Seventeen? You were seventeen? I thought you were fifteen. We celebrated your birthday when you turned sixteen."

"I lied."

"About your age?"

"It was part of me being in the program. I was two years older than you thought. Still am."

He could see she wasn't amused by the joke. "I was only fourteen."

"I know. That's why I never—" He picked up his coffee. "Anyway, my dad was spotted in the area. I was living with a marshal at the time. The decision was made to get me out of town immediately. I wanted to tell you, Patience. But I couldn't. By the time my dad was caught and put away, so much time had passed. I wasn't sure you'd remember me."

Or that he should get in touch with her. Even now, telling her the sanitized version of his past was a lot for her to take in. She looked dazed. He'd lived it and he still had trouble believing it had happened.

"What happened to your father?" she asked. "Is he still behind bars?"

"He's dead. Died in a prison fire."

Burned beyond recognition, he thought. Bart had been identified using dental records. A hell of a way to go, Justice thought, still aware that he felt nothing for the old man. Nothing except relief he was gone.

The question of how much of his father lived within him wasn't anything he was going to discuss with her. That was for the late nights when he was alone and the shadows pressed in. Patience wasn't a part of that. She was light to his dark, and he didn't want that to change.

"My head is spinning," she admitted, then put down her coffee. "You know what's really twisted? I'm actually still more surprised that you were eighteen when I thought you were sixteen than the fact that you were in a witness protection program because your father wanted you dead. I think that means there's something wrong with me. I apologize for that."

He smiled at her. "At least you have priorities."

She studied him for a second, then ducked her head. "I can't imagine what you had to go through. Here I was, feeling sorry for myself because I had this crazy crush on you. I wanted to tell you. In fact, I was going to that last day, but Ford walked up."

He told himself the information was interesting but not important. Even so, he felt a sense of satisfaction, quickly followed by a sense of loss. He'd often wondered what would have happened if he'd just been a regular kid who happened to live in Fool's Gold. Unfortunately his luck had never been that good.

He knew if he were a halfway-decent guy, he would

walk away now. That a man like him had no place in her life. But he couldn't leave, just as he'd never been able to forget.

"I remember that day," he admitted. "You were acting like there was something on your mind."

"There was. You. At fourteen, my girlish heart trembled whenever you were around."

He liked the sound of that. "That bad, huh?"

She nodded. "I took hope in the fact that you didn't seem interested in anyone else, but was worried you only saw me as a friend. I was determined to tell you the truth. I was also terrified. What if you didn't like me back?"

"I did like you. But I was too old for you."

"I see that now." She grinned. "Eighteen. How is that possible? I'm totally freaked. I'll recover but I'll need a moment." Her smile faded. "Justice, when you were just gone it was... Well, we all missed you and were worried about you."

He reached across the table and lightly touched the back of her hand. "I know. I'm sorry about that."

"It was like you were never there in the first place. I used to walk by the house and hope you'd show up as mysteriously as you'd left."

He'd hoped she had done that, he admitted, if only to himself. He'd often thought of her, wondering if she remembered him. Some days memories of Patience were all that had gotten him through.

"Were you really here last fall?" she asked.

"Briefly. I had a client."

"Dominique Guérin. I know. I'm friends with her daughter." Patience tilted her head. "Why didn't you look me up then?"

Before he could figure out an excuse that sounded better than he'd been apprehensive—which was, he admitted, a fancy way to say "scared"—a girl walked into the store. She was maybe ten or eleven with long brown hair and familiar brown eyes. She glanced around, then skipped over to their table.

"Hi, Mom."

Patience turned and smiled. "Hey, baby. How'd you know I was here?"

"Julia told me you were going for coffee." Her gaze slid to Justice. "With a man."

Patience sighed. "This town does love to gossip." She put her arm around the girl. "Lillie, this is Justice Garrett. He's a friend of mine. Justice, this is my daughter, Lillie."

CHAPTER TWO

AS SOON AS Patience said the word *daughter,* she knew there was a problem. How was she supposed to casually mention she wasn't married in front of her daughter and while Justice's gaze slid directly to her left ring finger? Just as complicated was the burning need to cut to the chase and blurt out "I'm single." A need she resisted. Giving him information was one thing. Sounding desperate was another.

"Hi," Lillie said, leaning into Patience, her expression both shy and curious. "How do you know Mom?"

"I knew her when she was only a little older than you."

Lillie turned to her. "Really, Mom?"

"Uh-huh. I was fourteen when I knew Justice. He lived here for a while. Then he had to move away. We're old friends."

More friends than old, she thought. At least that was her hope.

She kept her arm around her daughter. "Lillie is ten and the smartest, most talented, beautiful girl in all of Fool's Gold."

Her daughter giggled. "Mom always says that." She

leaned toward Justice and lowered her voice. "It's not really true, but she loves me so she believes it."

"That's the best kind of love to have."

She was about to go for it and say she wasn't married when it occurred to her that she didn't know anything about Justice's personal life. She sucked in a breath and fought against the heat she felt burning on her cheeks. What if he was half of a happy couple with a dozen or so charmingly attractive children?

Why, oh why had she admitted she had a crush on him without getting a few facts? She really had to start practicing thinking before speaking. The evening news was always showing great stories about some eighty-year-old getting a high school diploma or learning to read. Surely she could teach herself to self-edit.

"Justice has moved back to Fool's Gold," Patience said. "He's going to..." She paused. "I have no idea what you're going to do here."

"Open a bodyguard training facility. My partners and I haven't worked out the details yet, but we're going to offer security training for professionals along with corporate team building and survival training."

"Stuff you do outside?" Lillie asked.

"Uh-huh."

"Mom doesn't like going outside."

Justice turned to her and raised an eyebrow.

"I'm not a huge fan of weather and dirt," Patience explained. "It's not like I have to live in a plastic bubble." She offered a weak smile. "So, um, you'll be moving your family here?"

"You have a family?" Lillie asked. "Any kids?"

"No. It's just me."

A score for the home team, Patience thought with relief. "Lillie is the only one I have," she said, hoping she sounded casual. "Her dad and I split a long time ago."

"I don't remember him," Lillie offered. "I don't see him." She looked as though she was going to say something else, then stopped.

Patience had hoped for some reaction from Justice at the news of her not being married. A fist pump would have been perfect, but there wasn't any hint as to what he was thinking. At least he didn't bolt out of the building. She supposed she could take that as a good sign. And he *had* looked her up on his own. It wasn't as if she'd gone looking for him or they'd run into each other.

On the other hand, he'd probably left the witness protection program years ago and he'd never bothered to get in touch with her. The men in her life tended to leave. Her father. Lillie's dad. Justice. A case could be made that Justice hadn't chosen to leave, but he also hadn't chosen to reconnect. At least not until now.

She drew in a breath. She needed a bit of distance to gain some perspective. Justice was an old friend. She didn't have to make any assessments of his character at this very second. She also had errands to run and a thousand life details to take care of. She wanted to spend more time with him, to get to know the man he'd become. Just not here in the middle of town.

"Come to dinner," she said before she could stop herself. "Please. I'd like to catch up more and I know my mom would love to see you."

His expression softened. "She still lives around here?"

"We all live together," Lillie told him. "Mom and me and Grandma. It's a house of women."

Patience laughed. "Obviously a phrase she's heard before." She shrugged. "I'm back at home. I moved out briefly while I was married, then came back with Lillie. It works out for all of us." Ava had company, Patience had support so she could feel less like a single parent and Lillie had the constancy kids craved.

His dark blue eyes didn't seem to judge, for which she was grateful. "How's your mom doing?"

"Pretty well. She has good days and bad days."

"It's lasagna night," Lillie told him. "With garlic bread."

Justice gave her an easy smile. "Well, then. How could I say no?" He turned his attention to Patience. "What time?"

"Six work for you?"

"It does."

She stood. "Great. We'll see you then. You remember where the house is?"

He rose and nodded. "I'll see you at six."

PATIENCE FORCED HERSELF to walk at her usual pace. She wanted to run, or at the very least, skip or jump. But that would require an explanation and probably some nervous phone calls from neighbors to local law enforcement.

Lillie chatted about her day at school. Patience did her best to pay attention, but she had a difficult time. Her mind kept wandering back to her unexpected encounter with Justice. She couldn't wrap her mind around the fact that he'd shown up without warning. Talk about a blast from the past.

They turned up the walkway leading to the house. She paused, looking at it with a critical eye, wondering what Justice would see.

The color was different. Pale yellow instead of white. The winter had been late with the first snow not arriving until Christmas Eve, but then hanging around for weeks. Daffodils, crocuses and tulips had arrived in mid-March to brighten up the garden. The last of them were making one final effort before disappearing in the warming days of spring. The lawn wasn't too bad and the front porch looked inviting. She'd put out the bench and two chairs just the previous weekend.

The house itself was two stories. Like many homes in this part of town, it had been built in the 1940s and was a Craftsman style with big front windows and lots of little details like built-ins and moldings.

Lillie led the way up the stairs and through the front door.

Inside there weren't many changes. A different sofa, a couple of new appliances in the kitchen. When Patience had moved back shortly after her divorce, her mother had made a few modifications: The three bedrooms upstairs had become two, with the smaller rooms being combined into a decent-sized master suite. A second master had already been added off the main floor. It jutted out into the oversized backyard. A necessary addition, given Ava's condition.

When Patience was thirteen, her mother had been diagnosed with MS. If there was a "good" kind, Ava had it. The disease progressed slowly and she was still mobile. But there were hard days and climbing the stairs had become too difficult. With the additional master downstairs, that wasn't necessary.

"Grandma, Grandma, guess who I met today?" Lillie asked as she burst into the house.

Ava was in her home office. An open area with a desk, three computer monitors and keyboards. A technological marvel that could make NASA envious. Apparently computer smarts skipped a generation. Lillie could do almost anything on a computer, while Patience had trouble working her smartphone.

"Who did you meet?" Ava asked, holding open her arms.

Lillie ran toward her and retrieved her afternoon hug. They hung on to each other for several seconds, a daily ritual Patience always found gratifying.

"Justice Garrett," Patience said, standing in the doorway to the study.

Her mother stared at her. "That boy who disappeared?"

"That's the one. He's back in town, and he's not a boy anymore."

Ava smiled. "I would hope not. As it is, he has plenty of explaining to do. What happened? Did he say where he'd been?"

"He was in the witness protection program."

Ava's eyes widened. "Seriously?"

Patience glanced at Lillie, a signal that she didn't want to go into the details right then. Her ten-year-old didn't need to know there were parents awful enough to want to kill their own children.

"We invited him to dinner," Lillie said. "He said yes after I told him about the lasagna."

"Of course," her grandmother said. "Who could resist lasagna?"

Lillie laughed.

"He'll be here at six." Patience glanced at her watch. That gave her barely enough time to shower, put on makeup and obsess about what to wear.

Ava's brown eyes twinkled. "You probably want to go get ready."

"I thought I might change my clothes. It's not that big a deal."

"Of course not."

"He's just an old friend."

"Yes, he is."

Patience grinned. "Don't make this more than it is."

"Would I do that?"

"In a heartbeat."

AT TWENTY MINUTES to six, Patience was in her bedroom. She'd showered, blown out her long, wavy hair until it was straight, traded in her work T-shirt for a light green twin set in a fine-gauge knit and her black jeans for a dark blue fitted pair. Then she'd put on a dress, followed by a shirt and blouse before settling on jeans and a long-sleeved T-shirt that proclaimed her the queen of everything. She was the single mother of a ten-year-old who also happened to live in the same house where she'd grown up, with her *mother.* There wasn't an outfit on the planet that could disguise the truth. Not that she wanted to change anything about her life. Or apologize. She'd made a good life for herself and her daughter. It's just that thinking about Justice made her nervous. He would either respect her choices, good and bad, or he would go away.

She went downstairs and found her mother and Lillie in the kitchen. The table was set. The last of the tulips in the garden had been cut and placed in a glass vase. The smell of lasagna and garlic filled the house.

"Relax," her mother told her.

"I'm relaxed. Shrill and relaxed. It's a great combination."

Ava smiled with amusement. "So, is Justice coming alone?"

"Yes. He said he wasn't married."

"And he doesn't have kids," Lillie offered. "He should have a family."

Patience turned to her mother. "Don't you start anything."

"Me? I'm happy to welcome one of your school friends back to town. Nothing more."

"Uh-huh. Let's keep it that way."

"I am curious about his past, though."

Patience held in a groan. "Please, Mom, you can't."

"I'm the mother," Ava reminded her with a wink. "I can do just about anything."

JUSTICE STOOD ON the sidewalk and stared at the familiar house. Very little had changed. The color, maybe the garden, but nothing else. Off to the side, he could see a wheelchair ramp, but it led to the back door rather than the front. For Ava, he thought.

As he walked up the stairs, he braced for what he might find. Patience's mother had always welcomed him into their home. She'd been kind and motherly. As a kid who'd grown up surrounded by a lot of fear, he'd soaked up the affection she'd offered. She provided an emotional haven and he'd missed her nearly as much as he'd missed Patience when he'd had to leave.

He didn't know a lot about her disease, but he knew it was relentless and cruel. He told himself he'd seen worse. That his job was not to react. Then he rang the bell.

Lillie opened it seconds later and smiled at him. "Hi," she said cheerfully. "I'm glad you're here. I'm starving and the garlic bread smells so good." She stepped back to allow him entry, then turned to yell, "Mom, Mr. Garrett is here."

Patience walked into the living room. "Indoor voice, remember?" She glanced at him. "Hi."

"Hi, yourself. Thanks for the invitation to dinner."

She looked good. Her hair was long and sleek with the kind of shine that invited hands to touch. She wore jeans and a T-shirt with a girl in a crown on the front. "Queen of Everything" was written underneath. She was curvy enough to keep things intriguing, and when she smiled, he felt as if he'd been kicked in the gut. Fourteen-year-old Patience had made his voice crack. Grown-up Patience was physically beautiful, emotionally sweet and intellectually challenging. A lethal combination.

He'd always tried not to be like his father. When in doubt he thought about what Bart would do and did the opposite. Now he realized that the decent thing was to walk away. Only he didn't want to.

"You're welcome," she said. "It'll be fun to catch up."

He passed her the bottle of wine he'd brought. A nice California Cabernet the store owner had promised would go with pasta. Their fingers brushed and he felt a jolt of attraction. Swearing silently, he took a deliberate step back. No way. Not with Patience. He refused to screw up one of the few decent memories he had in his life. She was his friend, nothing more.

"There you are. All grown up."

He shifted toward the voice and saw Ava walk into the room.

She looked the same, he thought, accepting the relief as both truth and a statement that he really had to work on his character. But it was a flaw he was willing to accept. He needed Ava to be okay, not just for herself, but for him, as well. To keep his connection to the past.

She was a couple of inches shorter than Patience, with the same brown hair. Hers was in tight curls that brushed her shoulders. She had big brown eyes and an easy smile. When she held out her arms, he moved into them instinctively.

She hugged him close. He'd forgotten what it was like to be hugged by Ava. To be engulfed in a circle of acceptance and affection. She held on as if she would never let go, as if she would always be there. She hugged like a mom who genuinely loved all kids and wanted you to know. When he was a kid, Ava had been something of a revelation. The marshals had done their best to give him a stable home, but they'd been employees on the clock. Ava had been his best friend's mom. She'd made him cookies and talked to him about going to college. Just as if he was a regular kid.

"I was nervous about seeing you," he admitted, speaking softly so only she could hear.

She squeezed tighter, then released him. "I have good days and bad days." She tilted her head.

He followed her gaze and saw the wheelchair folded up in the corner of what was clearly her home office.

"This is a very good day," she told him, still holding his gaze. "We were so worried about you."

"I know. I'm sorry. I would have told you if I could have."

"You came back. That's what matters." She turned to her granddaughter. "You're hungry, aren't you?"

Lillie danced in place. "Yes. Very. I'm *starving*."

Ava held her hand out to the girl. "Then let's get the salads on the table. Patience, why don't you have Justice open that bottle of wine he brought?"

Patience waited until they'd walked into the kitchen to lean close. "She's still running the world, as you can see."

"She's great and looks terrific. With her disease..." He wasn't sure what he wanted to ask.

Patience nodded and led him to a hutch in the formal dining room. She pulled open a drawer and removed a wine opener.

"She's had a couple of bad episodes, but then she went into remission. It came back, but it's not aggressive right now. Most days she can't do stairs. Technically she probably could, but it takes so much out of her. The issues have mostly been in her legs, which means she can still work with no problem."

Ava was a software designer. She'd started back when computers were novelties. Her job allowed her to work from home—a plus considering that her husband had walked out when she'd been diagnosed. When Patience had told him that, he'd realized that a father didn't have to pull a gun or use his fists to hurt his family. Pain came in all forms.

He went to work on the wine bottle. Patience collected glasses from the hutch.

"She's the bravest person I know," she continued. "She's always so cheerful and caring. I would want to scream at the unfairness of it all, but she never does." She smiled. "I want to be like my mom when I grow up."

"She inspires me, too," he admitted. "When I was in a tough spot, I would think about Ava and remind myself I had it easy."

Patience blinked several times, as if fighting emotion. "You're very slick, Mr. Garrett. You could have flattered me with meaningless compliments, but instead you slip right past my defenses by saying that about my mother."

"I meant it," he said, looking into her eyes and inhaling the scent of something clean with a hint of flowers. Not perfume, he thought, remembering. Essence of Patience. "I'm not slick. I'm telling the truth. I've seen what it takes to be brave, and your mom has it." He knew the danger of getting close, but couldn't help reaching out and lightly touching her cheek. "It's me, Patience. I know it's been a long time, but no defenses required."

Although as soon as he said the words, he realized he should have kept his mouth shut. Patience was right to be wary of him.

Something clattered to the floor in the kitchen. Patience turned toward the sound. Justice used the distraction to pick up the wine, thereby putting distance between them.

Fifteen minutes later they were all seated at the table. Lillie had sniffed her mother's glass of wine and wrinkled her nose, declaring the smell "icky." The lasagna was sitting on the counter, ready to be served, and they had their salads in front of them.

Patience raised her glass. "Welcome home, Justice," she said.

"Thank you."

They all took sips of their drinks. Lillie put her milk down and turned to her grandmother.

"Mr. Garrett is a bodyguard." She wrinkled her nose. "Like on TV, right?"

Patience had called him Mr. Garrett to make a point. Lillie was doing it because of how she was raised. "If it's okay with your mom, you can call me Justice."

Lillie beamed. "Is it, Mom?"

"Sure."

Lillie sat a little straighter and cleared her throat. "*Justice* is a bodyguard, Grandma."

"I heard." Ava glanced at him. "That sounds dangerous. Is it?"

"Sometimes. Mostly I protect rich people who travel to hazardous places. I make sure they're safe."

"What are you doing in Fool's Gold, then?" Patience asked. "We're about as far from hazardous as you can get and still stay on the continent. Is it part of your new business?"

He nodded, then glanced at Ava. "I want to open a

business with a couple of buddies of mine. We'll provide training for security firms."

Ava looked interested. "A bodyguard school?"

"We think of it as more comprehensive than that. We'll provide instruction on strategy, weapons and other equipment. Up-to-the-minute reports on various conflicts in different parts of the world. In addition, we want to offer corporate retreats. Team building through activities. Obstacles courses and other physical challenges."

Patience blinked. "Wow. That puts my idea of a coffeehouse to shame. I mean, I got as far as having a book club and maybe an open-mike comedy night, but that's it."

"My partners and I have been working on the plan for a while. We've been waiting to find the right place. Ford suggested Fool's Gold, so when I came here last year, I checked it out."

Ava's surprise was evident in her voice.

"Ford? Ford Hendrix?"

He nodded. "We've been friends awhile now. We reconnected in the military. Our third partner is a guy named Angel Whittaker."

"I'd heard Ford was returning," Ava said, "but no one knows when. He's been serving in the military for years."

"He gets out in the next couple of months. He should be back then."

Angel didn't care where they started the business, and once Justice had come back last year, he'd lobbied for Fool's Gold. He'd thought about looking up Patience then, but he had enough self-control to avoid her. This time, not so much.

"Who's Ford?" Lillie asked.

"You know the Hendrix triplets and Mrs. Hendrix," Patience said. "Ford is the youngest brother in the Hendrix family."

"Oh. He's old."

Ava smiled. "He's in his thirties, Lillie."

The girl looked confused. "That old?"

"Ah, to be young again." Ava picked up her fork and speared a piece of lettuce. "So, Justice, tell me what you've been doing for the past fifteen years. Did you get married?"

CHAPTER THREE

PATIENCE SILENTLY VOWED she would never complain about her mother again. Not that she did it very much, but sometimes it was difficult sharing a house. Tonight, though, Ava had proved herself to be a master at getting information from anyone at any time.

By the time the dinner plates had been cleared and the dessert served, Justice had spilled nearly all his secrets. He'd spent a decade in the military before going into private-sector security. He had never been married and had no children. He'd come close to getting engaged once, he'd lived all over the world, but didn't call any place home and had put off finding a house or an apartment in Fool's Gold, preferring to live in a hotel until the business was up and running.

Patience had simply settled in to listen. Her mother's gentle grilling had been better than live theater and she'd been able to enjoy both the floor show and the view.

Since their earlier encounter in the salon where she worked, Justice had traded in his suit for jeans and a long-sleeved shirt. She liked the way he'd filled out— all muscles and strength. No doubt a result of excellent physical conditioning. She would suspect that the bodyguard business required that sort of thing.

Watching him talk, she noticed the odd line or two around his eyes and that his expression was more guarded than she remembered. She was also very conscious of the fact that the last man to walk into their house had been a plumber and before that, the guy who had upgraded their cable TV. Ava hadn't dated much after her husband had left. Patience hadn't meant to follow in her mother's footsteps on that front, yet here she was, pushing thirty and chronically single.

Justice was the kind of man to set the most chaste of hearts to fluttering, and Patience had to admit that any chastity on her part had been due to circumstance, not choice. If her handsome, slightly dangerous former childhood crush made a move, she would cheerfully agree. Justice seemed like the type of man to cure nearly any female ill. As long as she was careful to keep things emotionally casual.

She supposed that in today's modern age, she should be willing to make the first move herself. To self-actualize. But that wasn't her style. She'd never been especially brave and now, walking Justice out onto the front porch, she didn't experience any sudden surge in courage.

"Still adore my mother?" she asked as she closed the door behind them. Just in case he had the idea he should kiss her good-night. Which he should. She was doing her best to send that message telepathically. Not that she had any psychic talent.

Justice sat on the porch railing and nodded. "She's good. I'm going to talk to Ford and Angel about hiring her to teach the interrogation classes."

Patience smiled. "It's a gift and she uses it. I think people believe that I was a pretty decent kid naturally, but that's not true at all. It's because I knew my mother could make me confess if she suspected I'd done anything wrong." She leaned against the upright support and smiled. "It helps keep Lillie in line, too."

Justice grinned. "Lillie's great. You're lucky to have her."

"I agree."

His smile faded. "Can I ask about her dad?"

"You can, and I'll even answer." She shrugged. "Ned and I got married because I got pregnant. I was young and stupid."

"Lillie's ten?"

"Uh-huh. I'll do the math for you. I was nineteen when she was born. Ned was a guy I was dating. I was bored and confused about my life, and one thing led to another. I got pregnant, he did the right thing and we were married. Six months later, he ran off with a fortysomething redhead who had more money than sense. Lillie was three weeks old."

Justice's expression hardened. "Does he pay his child support?"

She allowed herself the brief illusion of believing that Justice would rush to take care of Ned if he didn't. The fantasy was very satisfying.

"He doesn't have to. He signed away all rights in return for not having to support her financially. I think I got the better deal. He wouldn't have been consistent, and that would have hurt Lillie."

"You could have used the money."

"Maybe, but we get by. I'll never be able to save enough to open Brew-haha, but I can live with that."

He straightened. "What?"

She laughed. "Brew-haha. It's what I would call my coffee place. I've actually designed the logo. It's a coffee cup with little hearts on it. Brew-haha, Ooh, la-la is the part in writing."

His mouth twitched.

She put her hands on her hips. "Excuse me, but are you making fun of my business?"

"Not me."

"You think the name is silly."

"I think it's perfect."

"I'm not sure I believe you." She glared at him. "I'm playing the lottery most weeks, and when I win, you're going to see just how great the name is."

"I hope that happens."

Maybe it was her imagination, but she would swear Justice was moving closer to her. His dark blue gaze locked with hers. The night got quiet and she suddenly found it difficult to breathe.

Kiss me, she thought as loudly as she could.

He didn't. He just stared at her, which made her nervous. And being nervous made her talk.

"It's great to have you back," she mumbled. "Here in Fool's Gold."

Ack! Really? As opposed to just in the state or country?

"I'm glad to be back," he told her. "Your friendship meant a lot to me."

"It meant a lot to me, too."

He moved closer and closer…and stood up.

"I should head back to the hotel," he said, stepping to the side and starting down the stairs. "Thanks for dinner."

Patience watched him go. She supposed some socially correct response was called for, but all she could think was Justice Garrett owed her a kiss and she was going to find a way to collect.

THE NEXT EVENING Patience climbed the stairs to the house. It was her day to work late, so it was already close to seven. Her mom took care of Lillie's dinner and helped with any homework, which made the later shift easier. She knew that she was lucky—a lot of single moms didn't have the built-in support she did.

She opened the front door and was about to call out she was home when she saw her mother talking on the phone. Ava looked intense and concerned, neither of which was good. Patience dropped her purse onto the table by the door, then headed up the stairs to her daughter's room.

Lillie was curled up on her bed, reading.

"Hey, baby girl," Patience said as she walked over and sat on the mattress.

"Mom!" Lillie dropped the book and lunged forward for a hug. "You're home."

"I am. How was your day?"

"Good. My math test was easy. We're watching a video on gorillas tomorrow and we had tacos for dinner."

Patience kissed her daughter's forehead, then stared into her eyes. "I noticed you slipped in that bit about the math test."

Lillie grinned. "If I study, the tests are easier than if I don't."

"Uh-huh. Which means I was…"

"Right." Her daughter grumbled. "You were right."

Patience squeezed her. "That never gets old."

"You love being right."

"I love it more when you say it." Patience glanced toward the stairs. "Do you know who Grandma's talking to?"

"No."

Patience supposed she would get the story when her mother hung up. "I'm going to make a salad. Do you want anything?"

"No, thanks." Lillie picked up her book.

Patience went back downstairs and into the kitchen. She could hear her mother's voice, but not the conversation. She opened the refrigerator and pulled out leftover taco meat. By the time her mother had hung up, she'd assembled a salad and was carrying it to the table.

"Sorry," Ava said as she walked into the kitchen.

"That was my cousin, Margaret." She took the chair across from her daughter.

Patience took a bite of her salad and chewed. "She lives in Illinois, right?" she asked when she'd swallowed.

Her mother had some family in the Midwest. Patience vaguely remembered a few of them visiting when she'd been little, but there hadn't been much contact in years. There were the obligatory cards and letters at the holidays and not much else.

"Yes. Margaret and her mother, who is my step-aunt. It's complicated." Ava paused.

Patience watched her, aware that something had happened. Ava was flushed. She shifted in her seat and couldn't keep her hands still.

"Are you okay?"

"I'm fine." Her mother started to smile, then shook her head. She half rose, then collapsed back in the chair. "Great-Aunt Becky died."

"Who?"

"Great-Aunt Becky. My step-aunt's mother. She's not technically a relative—at least I don't think so. She and I wrote the occasional letter. You met her once. You were four."

"Okay." Patience put down her fork. "I'm sorry she died. Are you upset?"

"I'm sad, of course. But like you, I only met her a few times. She visited us when you were little." Her mother smiled. "You took to her. From the second you first met her, you couldn't stand to be away from her.

You wanted her to hold you. You wanted to be on her lap. When she got up, you followed her from room to room. It was very sweet."

"Or annoying, if Great-Aunt Becky wasn't into kids."

Ava laughed. "As it turned out, she was as charmed by you as you were by her. She extended her visit twice and you both cried when she left. She always meant to come back, but never made it."

"I wish I could remember her." Patience had vague recollections of a tall woman, but that could have been anyone. "Do you want me to send a card?"

"If you'd like. The thing is, Great-Aunt Becky left you some money. An inheritance."

"Oh." That was unexpected. "Didn't she have children of her own?"

"One daughter. Great-Aunt Becky was very wealthy, so her immediate family is taken care of. You don't have to worry." Ava leaned forward and took Patience's hands in hers. "She left you a hundred thousand dollars."

Patience stared at her mother. She heard a rushing in her ears and if she'd been standing, she would have surely fallen to the floor. The space-time continuum seemed to shift just a little to the left.

"A hundred…"

"Thousand dollars," her mother said. "You heard that right."

The number was too big. No. It was too huge. Impossible to grasp. That was all the money in the world.

"Margaret wanted to let me know that the lawyer in charge of Great-Aunt Becky's estate will be calling you in the morning. He has the check written and ready to overnight to you."

Patience pulled one hand free to press it to her chest. "I don't think I can breathe."

"I know."

"We can pay off the mortgage."

"I don't want you to worry about that."

Patience shook her head. "Mom, you've been there for me all my life. I want to pay off the mortgage. Then I'll fund Lillie's college account." She bit her lower lip.

Even after all that, there would still be money left over. Maybe as much as twenty-five thousand dollars. Assuming she put some away for a rainy day, there was still enough to…to…

Ava nodded. "I know. I thought of that, too."

"The coffeehouse."

"Yes. We could do it."

Patience sprang to her feet and raced upstairs. When she reached her bedroom, she pulled open the bottom drawer of the small desk under the window and removed a file. It was her business plan—the one she'd been working on for years.

She returned to the kitchen and spread out the papers.

Everything was there. The cost of the lease, money for minor renovations, equipment, supplies and some promotions. There were cost projections, income estimates and a profit-and-loss statement.

"We could do it," she breathed. "It would be tight."

"I have some money I've saved," Ava told her. "I'd want to invest in the business. That way we're really partners."

"We're partners no matter what."

"I want to do this, Patience. I want you to open the business and I want to help."

Patience returned to her seat. "I'm terrified. I'd have to quit my job with Julia to do this." Which meant giving up the security of a regular paycheck. She would also have to take on the lease and hire people.

Her stomach churned. Somehow dreaming was a whole lot easier than facing the possibility of trying and failing. Yet even as she wondered if she *could,* she knew there wasn't really a choice. She'd been given a once-in-a-lifetime opportunity. Great-Aunt Becky's gift deserved more than her being afraid.

"You want to do this?" she asked.

"Absolutely."

"Then we will." She drew in a breath. "I'll call Josh about the building I have my eye on and get an appointment to see it as soon as possible. Once we figure out if that's the right space, we can move forward."

She stood and her mother did the same. They faced each other.

"We're really doing this," Patience said, laughing.

"We are!"

They hugged each other and started jumping up and down. Lillie appeared on the stairs.

"What's going on?"

"We're opening the coffeehouse," Patience said, holding out her arm so her daughter could join them.

"Really? Are you going to call it Brew-haha?"

"I am."

"Can I help?"

"Yes."

They hugged and jumped and screamed and danced. When they were all exhausted but still grinning, Ava motioned for them to follow her.

"This calls for ice cream," she said. "Let's all go get hot fudge sundaes."

Patience laughed. "I've always admired your style, Mom."

"JUSTICE?"

Justice turned at the sound of his name. Patience stood on the other side of the street, waving at him.

The sight of her—worn jeans hugging curves, a T-shirt featuring a white cat with a martini in one paw, long, wavy hair fluttering in the light breeze—hit him in the gut. And lower. Her smile made his mouth curve up, and her enthusiastic wave drew him.

In the fifteen years they'd been apart, he'd never forgotten her, even as he'd wondered if he was remembering more than there was. Now, watching her practically dance in place as he crossed the street to get closer, he knew he'd missed out on the main point. Patience in real life was far more vibrant than any of his recollections.

"Guess what?" she asked as he stepped onto the

curb. She grabbed his arm and literally bounced in place. "Guess! Guess!" She squeezed his biceps and grinned. "You'll never guess, so I'll tell you."

Her brown eyes glowed with excitement and her skin was flushed. She looked like someone who had just won the lottery. Or been thoroughly kissed. He found himself fervently hoping for the former and thinking he would have to have a serious talk with someone if it was the latter.

"My great-aunt Becky died!"

"And that's a good thing?"

"Oh." The bounce slowed. "You're right. Of course I'm not happy she's dead. It's sad. Apparently she lived a long and happy life, though."

"You didn't know her?"

"I met her when I was four. I don't remember, but apparently I liked her a lot. She liked me, too, and was a fabulously generous woman." She paused expectantly. "She left me a hundred thousand dollars!"

He smiled. "So that's what all this is about?"

She started bouncing again. "Can you believe it? A hundred thousand dollars! That's so much money. My mom and I were talking last night. I can pay off the mortgage and put money aside for Lillie's college."

She leaned toward him, the scent of vanilla and something floral drifting to him. "I'm a hairstylist. I love my customers, but some of the guys tip me fifty cents. There was no way I could have saved for Lillie's college. My mom does well as a software programmer, but her medical insurance is hugely expensive. Some of her medications aren't covered. She helps, but she has to take care of herself. This money means security for us. I never thought I'd have that."

Patience released him and spun in a circle. "But you know the best part?"

He shook his head, grateful he didn't have to speak. Because with her dancing around him, he found his brain wasn't actually in working order. And other parts of him were starting to take over. Need began to pulse in rhythm with his heart, and had they been anywhere but on a public corner in the middle of Fool's Gold, he would have pulled her close and kissed her. Then he would have done a whole lot more.

"There's going to be money left over."

It took him a second to catch up. "From the inheritance?"

She nodded vigorously. "Look."

She pointed across the street to a vacant storefront. "Isn't it perfect?"

The building wasn't all that remarkable. A door, windows and space inside. But he knew that wasn't the point. To Patience, this was her dream.

Justice was also going to open a business. It seemed the next logical step. He was sure it would be successful and that he would enjoy the work, but it wasn't a dream. He didn't allow that much wanting in his life.

"It's perfect," he told her, enjoying the way she gazed at the building—as if it were magical.

"I know exactly how it's going to look," she told him. "I already have my business plan. I worked so hard to get my plans together and to save, but honestly I never thought I had a chance."

He reached out and squeezed her hand. "I'm really happy for you. Congratulations."

"Thank you." She laced her fingers with his. "Come with me. I'm meeting Eddie right now. She's going to let me in so I can check out the space."

Her sparkling brown eyes compelled him to agree. "Sure."

She drew in a breath and leaned into him. "I'll try not to make high-pitched girlie sounds. I live with a ten-year-old and know how shrill they can be."

"You can squeal all you want. This is exciting."

"I know."

She hung on to his hand with both of hers. He would guess that if he pointed out what she was doing, she would pull back and be embarrassed, which he didn't want. Her enthusiasm reminded him there was plenty of joy left in the world, and that was a lesson he needed.

She tugged him along as she crossed the street. "Obviously the location is fabulous," she said, practically vibrating with enthusiasm. "Look. We're right across from the park and on the parade route. That means we're easy access for tourists and locals. I'd love to be closer to Morgan's Books, but he's just around the corner from you-know-where."

Justice stepped up on the sidewalk. He was familiar with "you-know-who" from the times he'd been guarding families with *Harry Potter*–reading kids, but this was a new one.

"You-know-where?"

Patience glanced around, as if making sure no one was nearby and listening. "The other coffee place," she said in a whisper. "I love them and I sort of feel guilty about what I'm doing."

"The other coffee... You mean Starbucks?"

"Shhh." She waved her free hand at him. "Don't say it."

"Why not?"

"I don't know. I don't want to hurt their feelings."

"You think the store is sad about this?" He gentled his tone. "You know they're a multibillion-dollar corporation. They'll be fine."

She paused for a second, then nodded. "Good point. I'll let my guilt go." She touched one of the bare windows. "What do you think?"

"It's very nice."

She laughed. "I know. It's an empty store, right? But there's so much more here. Once Eddie lets me in, I'll show you."

"Eddie?"

Before Patience could fill in the details, an older woman rounded the corner. She had to be in her seventies, with white, short, curly hair. She wore a brightly colored velour tracksuit and athletic shoes.

"I'm glad you didn't keep me waiting," she said as she pulled keys out of her large handbag and started fitting them into the lock. "I have to help Josh with interviews. That man can't keep staff. He's forever talking about dreams and doing what matters. Then the staff gets bugs up their butts about joining the peace corps or working for a nonprofit. Sure, they're saving the world, but I have to train the new people."

She paused and eyed him. "We haven't met."

"Justice Garrett," he said, stepping away from Patience and holding out his hand.

She fluttered her lashes at him. "Eddie Carberry. You're very handsome."

"Thank you."

"Single?"

Before he could process the question—the woman couldn't mean what he thought she meant—Patience stepped between them.

"Sorry, Eddie, he's with me."

Eddie sighed. "The good ones are all taken." She turned the lock and opened the door to the business.

"Take your time looking around. I'm going back to the office. Just give me a call when you're finished. I'll come back over and lock up." She glanced back at him. "If you change your mind…"

He cleared his throat. "It was nice to meet you, ma'am."

She lightly touched his arm. "Call me Eddie." She turned back to Patience. "Josh wants you to have the place. He'll give you a good deal on the lease. You know how he supports new businesses in town. He's such a softie, it's something of a miracle he got as rich as he did." She leaned into Patience. "Did you check out his—"

"Yes," Patience whispered back, cutting her off. "You should probably get back to the office."

"I should. Call me when you're done."

"I will."

Justice watched the old lady leave. There weren't many circumstances when he felt uncomfortable, but this was one of them.

"Was she trying—"

"To suggest she'd like to have her way with you?" Patience asked, her eyes bright with amusement. "Oh yeah. Eddie and her friend Gladys consider themselves connoisseurs of handsome men. Especially unfamiliar handsome men. So if you're interested, let me know and I'll get you her number."

"Very funny."

She grinned. "I acted without thinking before. You know, when I said we were together. Because I can let her know we're just friends. Eddie's really sweet. She's worked for Josh for years."

He figured the unknown man was a safer topic. "Josh?"

"Josh Golden. He's a former cyclist. Very famous."

"I've heard of him. He won the Tour de France a few times."

"Among other races. He's a great guy, lives here in town."

Suddenly Justice found himself disliking the other man. "You know him?"

"Everyone does. He's a big part of the community. He got married about three years ago. He and Charity just had their second child a couple of months ago. A boy." She turned to face the open space. "This is it. What do you think?"

He turned his attention to the store. The main room was maybe fifteen hundred square feet. He would guess there was a bit more in the back, for storage. Floor-to-ceiling bookshelves dominated one wall. Big windows let in plenty of light.

"I love the flooring," Patience said, pointing to the hardwood covering. "It's in great shape. I wouldn't change that. Obviously the bookshelf stays. I thought about having doors put on the bottom for storage."

"You'll need to change locks."

She wrinkled her nose. "Probably." She crossed to the back of the store. "This wall is where the magic happens. We'll have a long, wide counter, with three sets of sinks. The dishwasher goes in the back."

She turned and walked forward three steps. "The main counter here. Pastry display, sandwiches, that sort of thing. Mom and I have picked out the most fabulous cold case." She spread out her hands, as if demonstrating where it would all be.

"We've been looking online for months. We know what fixtures we want." Her smile widened. "I spent the morning finding out what was in stock. It was so surreal. When I'm done here, I'm going to talk to a lawyer about the lease."

She clapped her hands together and spun in a circle. "I can't believe it. We're going to do this. We're going to open Brew-haha."

Her whole body personified happiness. Her hair swung as she moved, her eyes drifted closed. She was completely in the moment, excited, hopeful and sexy as hell.

When the side of her foot hit an open box, she staggered a little. Justice instinctively reached to steady her. The second his fingers closed around her arm, he knew he was lost and there was only one way to be found.

CHAPTER FOUR

PATIENCE OPENED HER eyes as she tried to regain her balance. Warm, strong arms came around her. Justice pulled her so close she had no choice but to settle against him. One second she was in danger of falling, and the next she was staring up into his dark blue eyes. Her head was still spinning, but this time for a very different reason.

She rested her hands on his shoulders because it seemed the most sensible place for them to be. She saw sunlight streaming through the bare windows and tiny dust motes floating in the air. Felt her heart beating too quickly and the intensity of Justice's gaze.

Then he was lowering his head. She had only a second to catch her breath before his mouth brushed against hers.

His lips were firm. Not unyielding, exactly, but determined. He was taking charge, and under the circumstances, she was good with that. She'd had enough responsibility in her life, thank you very much.

He moved his mouth slowly, gently, exploring, testing, as if he enjoyed what he was doing. She sank into him, giving herself up to the delicious pressure.

She hadn't been kissed by a man in a long time. Years, actually. She'd nearly forgotten the thrill of the closeness, the quivering in her belly, the hint that there could be more and that the more could take her breath away.

She was aware of the smoothness of his shirt beneath her fingers, and the honed muscles under that. Of the way he was so much taller and broader and how she could picture herself leaning on him in more ways than this.

Then his mouth moved a little more—back and forth, as if he was figuring out how it all was going to be. The first tingles began deep inside her, and thinking became more difficult. She could only feel. Feel his hands on her waist, his mouth on hers. Feel the rapid beating of her heart and the way her blood seemed to race faster and faster.

He moved, kissing first one cheek, then the other. He kissed her nose and her chin before returning his attention to her mouth. She wasn't sure if he asked or she offered, but suddenly she parted her lips and he swept his tongue inside.

With the first stroke, she had to hold in a whimper. On the second, her knees went weak. With the third, she wanted to beg. Her wanting wasn't subtle. It exploded in her breasts, then went about sixty miles an hour to the very center of her. She got so aroused so fast she started to ache.

She wrapped her arms around his neck and silently urged him to take inappropriate advantage of her. Seriously, didn't he want to put his hands on her breasts or maybe between her thighs? The idea of him pushing her up against the wall while he had his way with her caused her to shudder. The image was so clear she began breathing harder.

Now, she thought almost frantically. He should make his move now.

He drew back and gave her a faint smile. "I should probably let you get to it."

She had no idea what he was talking about. It? What it?

Justice cleared his throat. "You have a lot to do."

He took another step back and headed for the door. Before she could figure out what was happening, he was gone. Just like that. A couple of hot kisses and he was out the door.

Patience had a feeling she looked as shocked as she felt. How could he have left like that? He'd kissed her. Passionately. Didn't he want to do something else? Something more? Something that required them getting naked and sweaty?

As she was standing alone in the empty store, she would have to say the answer to the question was obviously no.

Disappointment replaced excitement. Reality intruded. Justice was one hot guy. He had been when they were kids, and that hadn't changed today. She'd liked him then and she still liked him. Which made her vulnerable.

While she couldn't blame him for being whisked

out of her life all those years ago, he'd done nothing to get in touch with her since then. He'd managed to find Ford, but not her. She could come up with a hundred reasons to explain his actions, but she couldn't avoid the truth. If he'd wanted to see her earlier, he would have. So he hadn't wanted to.

He was back now and more tempting than should be legal. But tempting wasn't safe. She wasn't that fourteen-year-old girl anymore. She was a single mom with an impressionable daughter. She knew how caring about Justice could break tender hearts. She had to be strong and resist. For her sake, but also for Lillie's.

JUSTICE STOOD IN the center of the old warehouse on the edge of town. The building was a whole lot less fancy than the place he'd seen the previous day with Patience. The floors were concrete, there weren't any walls or windows and the ductwork was exposed. But the building had been built to last and was well insulated. Putting up walls would be easy. If they added some windows, set aside half the building for various workout rooms, it could work. There was land outside, as well. Enough for target practice and an obstacle course. The location was good and the price better. If they picked this building, he would have to find a place in the mountains for a more advanced obstacle course, but that would be easy.

He walked around, the only light coming from the overhead fluorescents and the open double doors where he'd entered. He knew he didn't have Patience's enthusiasm for his new business, but that was okay. He didn't like emotional highs or lows. He'd learned a long time ago to accept things as they happened and keep moving forward.

He, too, had a business plan, along with the cash to make it happen. His friend Felicia had emailed him that morning, asking if he'd made up his mind. If he had settled on Fool's Gold, he needed to let her know. If he hadn't, it was time to go look somewhere else. After all, this wasn't just about himself. He had business partners who wanted him to make a decision.

As far as Felicia was concerned, she would go anywhere normal. Small-town America appealed to her, and Fool's Gold fit the definition. She would be there to set up the business, and if she ended up hating Fool's Gold, she would move on. But the others would be stuck.

Ford Hendrix had also emailed two days ago to tell Justice to pick Fool's Gold already, and yesterday to say anywhere but there. Ford's ambivalence came from his close-knit family. There were days the former SEAL wanted to reconnect and others when he needed to head into some wilderness and never be heard from again. It was the kind of ambivalence Justice could relate to. With Patience…

He shook his head. He wasn't here to think about her.

His third partner, Angel, fell into the neutral category. He'd never been to the town. When he'd read the description, he'd been intrigued by the nearby mountains. Angel enjoyed the outdoors and getting away from the world. The rugged topography offered plenty of both. So the decision fell to Justice, who, honest to God, didn't have a clue.

Except he did. There was a part of him that had always wanted to come back here. To the one place he'd felt welcome.

Patience was a big part of the pull, he admitted, if only to himself. He'd never forgotten about her and had often wondered where she was and what she was doing. With his resources, it would have been easy to find out. He could have had a complete dossier on her in less than six hours. Only he never had.

Now he knew she was in town and single, which made her a temptation. Their kiss the previous morning had only fueled the fantasy. He wanted more. He wanted her in his bed, pulling him close, taking him with as much passion as he wanted to take her.

Which meant the best solution for both of them was for him to walk away.

He knew who he was and the type of man he could become. Patience deserved better. He wanted to think he could be better, do better, than his father. That Bart Hanson's DNA wasn't his son's destiny. But he couldn't be sure. When his father had finally been captured and sent back to prison, Justice had been free to choose. He could have been anything, gone anywhere. The fact that he'd joined the army wasn't noteworthy. His choice of occupation was.

He'd become a sniper. Not a cop, not a technician.

The son of a murderer had chosen to kill others. It was the ultimate proof of the darkness in his soul. Which meant leaving made the most sense for Patience and her family. They deserved better than him. The problem was he didn't *want* to go. And that made him the biggest bastard of all.

He heard footsteps on the concrete and turned to see a well-dressed older woman walking into the warehouse. Like Eddie from the day before, she had white hair. But the similarities ended there. This woman had on a well-tailored suit, pumps and pearls. She smiled as she approached and held out her hand.

"Welcome back, Justice Garrett. I'm Mayor Marsha Tilson. You probably don't remember me."

"No, I don't. But it's nice to meet you, again."

They shook hands.

The mayor studied him. "You've grown up. I remember when you were a tall, skinny teenager. You were friends with Patience McGraw and Ford Hendrix. It was always the three of you, but I thought you had special feelings for Patience."

He stared at the older woman. She was talking about relationships that had played out fifteen years ago. While the events had been important to him, he couldn't imagine a woman in her fifties paying attention to the lives of a group of teenagers.

Her smile widened. "I can see my observations are startling. I confess I was intrigued by you from the very beginning. Your guardians did an excellent job of fitting in, but there were inconsistencies in their story.

When you first arrived, it was obvious you'd suffered some kind of trauma."

"You knew I was being protected?"

"No. I never figured that out. I thought maybe the man who claimed to be your uncle wasn't a relative and that you didn't want anyone to know. There could be many reasons for the subterfuge. So I watched to make sure you weren't being abused, and when you began to settle in and make friends, I knew all would be well."

He shifted slightly, uncomfortable with the idea that she'd been watching out for him. "I was fine."

"Until you had to leave so mysteriously. We were all worried. Patience especially. Under the circumstances, you had to go. We see that now. But at the time, we were concerned."

Obviously the mayor knew the story of what had happened. He shouldn't be surprised. News traveled fast in a town this small.

"Now you're here to open a business. Some kind of bodyguard school, I hear?"

He chuckled. "Is that what they're saying?"

She laughed. "It is, although I'll admit I had my doubts about that. What's the real story?"

"The business will provide advanced security training of all kinds."

"Not for your average mall cop?"

"No. We're interested in the security forces who travel to the dangerous parts of the world. We'll cover basic evasion techniques, hand-to-hand combat, along with weapons expertise. In addition, we'll train security forces to understand the safest way to travel to and through the trouble spots. Most of that is about planning."

They were also going to be offering workshops on dealing with local terrorists and hostage negotiations, but he doubted the mayor wanted to know the details about that.

"We'll also be providing corporate retreats," he added. "A facility where they can practice their team building."

She nodded. "A nice steady source of income." She paused. "Has Ford decided if he's willing to move back to Fool's Gold?"

Justice stared at her. How in hell did she know what Ford was thinking? "Not yet."

She nodded. "He's been gone a long time. The transition to civilian life is bound to be difficult for any soldier. But with what Ford has seen…" She sighed. "He has family here, which he probably considers both a blessing and a curse. I can't help thinking he'll need their support. There are other considerations, as well. What about Mr. Whittaker?"

"You know about Angel?"

"I've heard a few things. We haven't yet met, although I'm looking forward to that."

She moved toward the doorway. He found himself following, although he couldn't say why.

"You'll have some kind of physical-fitness facility?" she asked.

"Yes. And an outdoor obstacle course."

"You're very close to Josh Golden's cycling school." She handed him a business card. "You might want to speak to him about using the facilities. Cycling provides overall conditioning."

He took the card. "You came prepared."

"I'm always prepared, Justice. This is my town and I take care of my citizens."

He got the message and braced himself for the warning. He told himself she was just an old lady who made smart guesses, but he didn't believe it. She knew things and that meant she could easily have figured out his issues. She was going to warn him off, and he couldn't blame her for that.

"You'll find the city is very supportive of your venture. If you need anything, contact me directly and I'll get you in touch with the right person. You belong here, Justice—I have a feeling about that."

He'd been captured once. On a mission. Held and beaten for a few hours. He'd barely begun to prepare himself for the ordeal when his team had broken in and rescued him. He'd been as shocked by their arrival then as he was by the mayor's words now.

"You'll want to provide some community outreach," she continued. "Maybe self-defense classes, something for children. You'll be welcome in the community regardless, but it's nice to give back. You'll feel better about yourself, and the transition will be easier for all your staff."

She smiled again. "I doubt your employees are just regular folks, are they?"

"Not really."

"I thought not. They'll need to find their footing, as well. Some of them will believe that's not possible. You and I know otherwise. It's up to us to show them what Fool's Gold has to offer."

"I hadn't thought of classes for the community," he admitted.

"That's why I'm here. To offer possibilities." She lightly touched his arm. "Welcome home, Justice. I'm glad you found your way."

He wanted to tell her he wasn't sure he was staying, but even as he thought the words, he knew they weren't true. He had decided the second he'd returned. Seeing Patience had sealed the deal. He might not be able to have what he wanted with her, but he couldn't seem to walk away, either. An uncomfortable dilemma.

Mayor Tilson wished him the best and walked out of the warehouse. Justice reached into his pocket and pulled out his cell phone.

"Is it Fool's Gold?" Felicia asked by way of greeting.

"It is."

"Great. It's going to take me a couple of weeks to wrap everything up. Maybe three. I'll let you know when I'm on my way. In the meantime I'll notify Ford and Angel and get going on the plan. Send me pictures of the building and the outlying area. I'll coordinate with the lawyer on the purchase and investigate leasing options, as well."

Felicia wasn't one for pleasantries. She got right to the problem and in a matter of seconds, had sixteen solutions. She could list them in order of success ratio, danger or cost. She was the smartest person he knew, and probably one of the ten most intelligent people in the world. At times that made her challenging to work with, but she was never boring.

"How are you?" he asked, mostly to mess with her.

She sighed. "Really? We have to do that every time we speak?" There was a pause. "I'm fine, Justice. Thank you so much for asking. How are you enjoying Fool's Gold?"

"It's very nice." He grinned. "Are you calculating how much work you could have gotten done if we hadn't wasted time on that exchange?"

"No. I'm trying to be more social. I'm going to be living in a small town and I want to be like everyone else."

He didn't have the heart to tell her that would never happen. She was many things, but "just like everyone else" wasn't one of them.

"Did you see her?" Felicia asked. "Your friend?"

He'd told her a little about Patience—that they'd known each other back in high school. But not that she'd haunted him and that the memories of her had kept him anchored and strong.

"I have."

"Is she how you remember?"

He thought about the feel of her in his arms. How she'd kissed. He remembered her laughter and her spinning in the middle of an empty storefront.

"She's better."

JULIA HELD OUT her arms. "Congratulations, Patience. This is everything you've wanted."

Patience hugged her boss. "I know. I'm so excited." She'd gotten the lease from Josh and had taken it over to an attorney that morning for a quick review. The next order of business was telling the woman she worked for that she would be leaving.

"What's your time frame?" Julia asked, releasing her.

"Six weeks," Patience said. "Maybe eight. I thought I could work part-time for a while, if that's okay with you." She held up her hands. "I feel like I'm leaving you in a lurch."

"You are, but so what? This is like winning the lotto. You can't turn your back on opportunity. We'll talk about who would do best with each of your clients. After we do that, you can call all your regulars and let them know what's happening." Julia's good humor faded slightly. "Just don't let them go over to Bella's place."

"Yes, ma'am," Patience murmured, eager to avoid that particular conversation.

Bella and Julia were sisters. Estranged sisters. They owned competing salons in town, which required the good citizens of Fool's Gold to be careful if they wanted to keep the peace.

Patience promised to contact her clients within a couple of days and left the office. She'd come in on her day off to tell Julia what had happened. Now she had a thousand things to do and no idea of where to start.

As promised, Great-Aunt Becky's lawyer had sent the check overnight. The money was currently sitting in her checking account. Ava had already researched where to put the money for Lillie's college fund, and they would pay off the mortgage at the end of the week. Once the lease was signed, they would start ordering the equipment and talking to a contractor about remodeling the store.

Patience stepped into the salon, prepared to get her purse and move to the next item on her list. She was stopped by a tall blonde waiting by her station.

"Your mom said I'd find you here."

Patience saw her friend Isabel and laughed. "No way. When did you get back?"

"Yesterday."

They hugged.

"Did I know you were scheduled for a visit?" Patience asked, excited to see her friend.

"No. It was kind of unexpected."

Isabel lived in New York and worked in marketing. Like Patience, she'd grown up in Fool's Gold and still had family here.

Patience glanced at the clock on the wall. It was nearly eleven-thirty. "Want to get an early lunch and catch up?"

"I was hoping you were going to say that," Isabel admitted. "I have so much to tell you."

"I can't wait to hear it."

They took the short walk to Margaritaville and were shown to a quiet booth by the window. After ordering diet soda and guacamole, they pushed aside the menus and looked at each other.

"You first," Patience said.

Isabel tucked her long blond hair behind her ear and shrugged. "I'm not sure where to start."

Patience had known the other woman all her life. Isabel was a couple of years younger, so they'd never hung out in school, but shortly after Ned had walked out on Patience, leaving her with a newborn, Isabel had flunked out of UCLA and returned to Fool's Gold. They liked to joke that their moments of disgrace had brought them together. They'd been friends ever since.

"Before I tell you my sad tale," Isabel said, "I want to see pictures."

Patience laughed and handed over her phone. Isabel flipped through the photos. "She's getting bigger by the minute. She's so pretty. Tell Lillie I can't wait to see her."

"I will."

Isabel passed the phone back. Their server appeared with drinks, chips, salsa and guacamole. Isabel waited until they were alone to put her left hand on the table and wiggle her fingers.

"I'm getting a divorce."

Patience stared at the bare ring finger. "No. What happened?"

"Nothing dramatic," Isabel said, her wide blue eyes filled with sadness, but no tears. "Eric and I are still friends, which is pretty sad. I think the truth is we were always friends. We got along so well we wanted to believe friendship was enough, but it wasn't."

"I'm sorry," Patience said, studying the other woman. There was more, she thought. Something Isabel wasn't telling her. Not that she was going to push. When her friend was ready, she would get to it.

"Me, too. I feel stupid and lost. My parents have been married something like a hundred and fifty years." She gave a rueful smile. "Okay, more like thirty-five, but still. Maeve has been married twelve years and keeps popping out babies. I'm the family failure."

Patience pushed the guacamole toward her. "Is that why you're visiting? Because of the divorce?"

"Some of it. My parents have decided it's time for them to follow their dreams. Maeve and I are grown and they don't want to wait until they're too old to travel. So they took their 'rainy day' fund and bought themselves tickets on a cruise around the world."

"You're kidding?"

"No. They leave in a couple of weeks. They also want to sell Paper Moon."

Patience stared at her, a chip raised halfway to her mouth. "No way." Paper Moon was the local bridal shop in town. It was an institution. Isabel's great-grandmother had opened the store.

"I know," Isabel said. "I was shocked, too. But my mom is tired of running it and Maeve isn't interested. She has too many babies even if she was."

"I can't picture the square without Paper Moon Wedding Gowns."

"It will still be there. I'm sure we'll find a buyer."

"But it won't be the same."

Isabel glanced out the window. "Everything changes, even when we don't want it to." She grabbed a chip. "Anyway, that's why I'm back. I'm going to work in the store for the next eight months and get it ready to sell. In return I get a cut of the sales price. Good news for me because I'm going to need the money."

She leaned forward, her expression more animated. "I have a friend in New York. Sonia. She's a brilliant designer. We're going to go into business together. Working in my folks' store for a few months will give me the retail experience I'll need and some extra cash for start-up costs."

"You sound excited."

"I am. My plans mean I can stand living here for a little while."

"It's not so bad here. You'll do fine," Patience told her.

"I can't believe you never left."

"I didn't want to. I like the town."

"I do, too, but come on. There's a whole world out there."

Patience knew that was true, but she'd never been all that interested in it.

The server returned and they placed their orders. When she was gone, Isabel looked at her friend. "So, I've done all the talking. What's new with you?"

"For once, I have actual news." Patience told her

about Great-Aunt Becky and the money and the coffeehouse she and her mom were going to open.

Isabel laughed. "That's fantastic." She raised her glass of diet soda. "To all your dreams coming true."

They clinked glasses.

"I'm terrified," Patience admitted. "I don't know anything about retail. I've taken some classes, but it's not the same."

"I know what you mean. I worked in the bridal shop when I was in high school and college, but that was just for the money. I wasn't paying attention to how things were run. If I don't do well, we can't sell it for as much and there goes my nest egg."

"We'll be learning together," Patience said.

"I like the sound of that. We'll support each other." Isabel picked up another chip. "Have you heard anything about Ford Hendrix lately?"

The question was casual enough. To someone who didn't know Isabel's past, it would be seen as a thoughtful inquiry. But Patience did know her friend's history. Instead of answering, she raised her eyebrows.

"Really?"

Isabel rolled her eyes. "Don't look at me like that. I'm just curious."

"Because you're getting a divorce?"

"No. Of course not. I'm back and that's making me think about the past."

"And how he was your 'one true love'?"

Isabel winced. "Please don't say it like that. It makes me sound like a crazy stalker."

"You were a fourteen-year-old with a crush. I'm not sure there's a difference." Patience grinned. "You were wild about him."

"Like you're one to talk. You had a serious thing for that guy who left. What was his name?"

"Justice."

"Right. It was all so mysterious. Did you ever find out what happened to him?"

"Yes."

"Really? When?"

"A few days ago. He's back."

Isabel glared at her. "You didn't tell me? You let me go on and on about my boring life when you have that kind of news? Have you talked to him? What's he like? Where did he go? Why is he here?"

Patience sipped her soda. "As unbelievable as it sounds, he was in the witness protection program." She quickly outlined the details. "He was here last year as a bodyguard and decided he wanted to return. So he and a couple of other guys are opening a business. They're calling it something different, but it's basically a bodyguard school."

"A dangerous man. Is he good-looking?"

Patience did her best not to blush. "Yes."

"So you've seen him."

"He, uh, came over to dinner the other night. You know, to see my mom and stuff."

Isabel pressed her lips together. "It's the 'stuff' that's so interesting. You still like him."

"No. Maybe." She squirmed on her seat. "Okay,

yes. I do. He's *that* guy and now he's all grown up and when I'm with him, I have trouble breathing."

Something flickered in Isabel's eyes, then faded away. "That's an impressive description. And I'm sensing a but."

Patience nodded. "But why now? While he was in the witness protection program, he couldn't tell me who he was. Then his dad was captured and sent back to prison. Which meant Justice could do whatever he wanted. Obviously he didn't want to get in touch with me."

"Oh." Isabel straightened. "That's an excellent point."

"He did find Ford. They're friends. Now he's back and my hormones are singing praises, but I'm telling myself I need to be careful."

"Yeah, you do. Men aren't always who they seem." Isabel reached for another chip. "It's never easy, is it?"

"No. I'm trying to be calm and adult about the whole thing." She thought about the kiss and how it had left her weak in the knees. "If he's opening a business, it's not like he's going to disappear again, right?" Because that's what she couldn't get past. Him leaving. Every man she'd ever cared about had left.

"It's a very good sign."

Patience drew in a breath. "I hope so. And while we're on the subject of hope, I do have something to tell you about Ford."

Isabel looked at her. "Which is?"

"He's going to be here soon. Apparently he's leaving the military and coming back to Fool's Gold."

Isabel opened her mouth, then closed it. "He'll be in town?"

"That's the rumor. I don't have any details or dates."

"Oh God. No. I can't face him. I wrote him for years. Not that I'm sure he got my letters or if he did, if he read them, but still."

"He would have liked your letters."

"You can't know that. He probably does think I'm a stalker." She covered her face with her hands. "I knew coming home would be complicated, but I didn't think I would have to face Ford." She dropped her hands to the table. "Is he married?"

"I don't know."

"He's probably married. With six kids, right? And a dog. So I don't have to worry. He won't even remember me."

Patience reached for another chip. "I want to make fun of you, but I can't, because I know exactly what you're going through."

"That makes me feel better. You'll tell me if you learn anything?"

"Every detail."

"I'll do the same for you. Not that I'm expecting to be in the middle of gossip central. When people come to the bridal shop, they tend to be past the dramatic stage of their relationship." She picked up her soda. "You really think Ford's married?" She sounded both horrified and hopeful.

"He could be. And I'm sure he's not nearly as good-looking as he was."

"Right. He's old now and uninteresting." She paused. "You said Justice is hunky."

Patience held in a sigh. "The hunkiest."

"Good. One of us should get the great guy."

"It's too soon to know if he's great or not," Patience said. She wanted to believe he was, of course, but she had no actual evidence.

CHAPTER FIVE

"YOURS IS bigger than mine," Patience said, walking around the warehouse.

Justice chuckled. No matter the circumstances, she could always make him laugh. "I thought women liked to say size doesn't matter."

She looked at him, blushed, then turned away. "I meant your business."

"I know what you meant. I'm going to be doing different things here. We'll need the space."

She walked around the open area. "I guess the good news is you can do anything you want."

"That's what I thought. Frame in the walls, build some offices and meeting rooms."

"A bathroom," she added. "If your clients are going to be working out, you might want to think about showers."

He did want to think about showers, but not in the way she meant.

He followed her as she walked around. She wore jeans and another of her decorated T-shirts. This one was pink with rhinestone flamingos sitting at a table, sipping martinis. He wasn't sure what it meant, but it was pure Patience.

She turned to face him. "You've decided? You're staying?"

He wondered if the truth was that since seeing her, leaving wasn't an option. "I'm staying."

"And you're opening this business with your partners?"

"Ford and Angel."

"Angel?"

"You haven't met him yet."

She raised her eyebrows. "Have you warned him what he's getting into, coming to a town like this one?"

"He'll be fine."

She walked toward him. "You've obviously stayed in touch with Ford."

He nodded, then wondered if her interest was personal rather than general. They'd all been friends together. Ford had spent years in town after he had left. Had they dated? Ford had never said anything, but he didn't share all that much. Tension tightened the muscles across the back of his shoulders.

"You looking forward to seeing him?" Justice asked.

"Sure." She paused. "Is he married?"

He didn't like the question and liked the answer even less. "No. Is that good news?"

She smiled. "It's always fun when a hometown hero returns. I think his mother and sisters will be more excited." Her smile turned mischievous. "As for the married thing, you can't tell anyone, but my friend Isabel is totally freaked out about Ford coming back."

His muscles relaxed. "She had a thing for him?"

"Big-time. Ford was engaged to her sister. Maeve cheated on him with his best friend and Ford was understandably pissed. He took off and joined the army. Maeve married the best friend. They're still together. But Ford almost never comes back to visit. When he sees his family, he meets them somewhere else and not very often. Isabel was only fourteen when Ford left and she wrote him for years. Now they're all grown up and she's moved back to town. She's very nervous about seeing him again." Patience paused. "Is this too much information?"

"No. It's confusing, but not too much."

She looked around at the warehouse. "Are you scared?"

"About?"

"Starting a business. I'm terrified. If I think about it too much, I start to doubt myself." She looked back at him. "My dad took off when I was only a couple of years older than Lillie. He never bothered to stay in touch with me. After he left, it was my mom and me. Then I met Ned and that was a disaster. I was alone and I had Lillie, and my mom invited me back home."

She folded her arms across her chest. "She was always there for me. The inheritance will help pay the mortgage off. That's security for both of us. But I have Lillie, and if the coffee shop fails, I will have wasted all that money. Am I being irresponsible, taking on the risk?"

He moved toward her and put his hands on her shoulders. "No. You get to be happy, too."

"I'm happy working at Chez Julia."

"Is being a hairstylist your dream?"

"No, but…"

"Is Brew-haha?"

The corners of her mouth turned up. "Yes, but—"

"No buts. You get to have your dream, Patience. You've taken care of your mom's house and your daughter's college. You get to have a little something for yourself, too."

"Opening a business isn't a little thing."

"You deserve to have one of your dreams come true."

"What if I fail?"

Her eyes darkened as she said the words, and he knew she'd just spoken her greatest fear. But before he could tell her she wouldn't and list all the reasons why, someone spoke his name.

"There you are. You're a very difficult man to find."

Patience stepped back and he dropped his hands to his sides. The woman walking purposefully toward him was probably close to fifty, with blond hair and a familiar face. He searched his memory and came up with a name.

Denise Hendrix. Ford's mother.

PATIENCE WATCHED THE big, bad bodyguard back up when faced with his business partner's mother. She settled in to watch what she knew would be an excellent show.

Denise Hendrix had six children. Patience was sure she loved them all equally, but five of them were living in town with the sixth risking his life serving his country. Any mother would get a little intense about that.

Denise stopped in front of Justice.

"You're the reason my son is finally coming home."

Justice swallowed. Patience would swear something very close to fear invaded his eyes. He held up both hands in a gesture that looked two parts protection, one part surrender.

"I, uh—"

Denise nodded, blinking back tears. "I've been praying for this. He was so upset when he left. Of course he was." She glanced at Patience. "I blame Maeve. I've forgiven her, of course. Still, did he have to stay gone? It's been years and years. I know his work is dangerous—he won't talk about it. He emails. Because an email is as good as a visit?"

She turned back to Justice. "Then you came here and decided to open your business. I can't thank you enough."

"We, uh, thought—"

She nodded and wiped her cheeks. "I know. It wasn't all you. But I was starting to think he would never come back and now he'll be here. I have to make sure he never leaves again."

Poor Ford, Patience thought. She hoped he knew what he was getting into by returning to his hometown.

"Thank you," Denise said, then lunged forward.

Patience was sure Justice knew a dozen moves to ward off his friend's mother. But instead of using any of them, he simply endured the long hug.

When he was finally free, he managed a strangled "You're welcome."

Denise sniffed. "I remember when you were just a teenager, Justice. You were a good friend to Ford. I'm glad you found your way back here." She smiled at Patience, waved and left.

Patience turned to Justice. "Always the hero."

He tugged at the collar of his shirt. "Mrs. Hendrix is very enthusiastic."

"We're all adults and you just had a significant body press from her. You should probably call her Denise."

He winced. "I think Mrs. Hendrix is more appropriate."

She grinned, delighted with his obvious discomfort. She liked knowing the very together and powerful Justice Garrett could be rattled by a middle-aged mother of six. "Uh-huh. She terrifies you."

"Just a little."

She started to laugh. "It's always fun when a tough-guy facade cracks."

His gaze narrowed. "You know a lot of tough guys?"

"You're my first, but it's way more appealing than I thought it would be. Just so you know—later I'm going to ask you to show me how to disarm someone with a Q-tip."

"Why are you afraid of someone with a Q-tip?"

She crossed to him and put her hands on her hips. "Very funny. You know what I mean."

"I do and a Q-tip is a pretty silly weapon."

"A spoon, then."

"You can do a lot with a spoon."

As he spoke, he put his hands on her waist, drawing her against him. She went willingly, aware of the sudden interest from her girl parts. She was conscious of the danger, but the possibility of being left seemed less significant now that they were standing so close. And the possibility of him kissing her again seemed so much more important.

They weren't touching anywhere good. At least not yet. But she was close enough to feel the heat of him.

He was tall and broad and strong and should be someone who made her nervous. Only he didn't. It was probably their past. Because she'd adored the boy, she trusted the man. She'd been predisposed to like him from the second he'd returned to her life. She could only hope he wouldn't prove to be yet another romantic mistake.

She gazed into his eyes, noting the various colors of blue that made up his irises. His lashes were slightly darker than his hair. With his chiseled chin and high cheekbones, he was handsome but still masculine. All in all, an impressive package.

"What on earth are you doing in this tiny town?" she asked. "Shouldn't you have settled down in Paris or New York?"

"My French sucks and Angel hates New York."

Good information but it didn't answer the real question. Probably because she hadn't asked it.

Are you going to break my heart? That's what she really wanted to know.

Apparently Justice was a mind reader in addition to his other bodyguard-based skills, because his gaze intensified.

"I'm not one of the good guys. You have to know that."

She wasn't sure if he meant the information was common knowledge or that it was important for her to realize the fact. In the end, she supposed it didn't matter.

"Does it occur to you by saying that, you're proving the opposite?" she asked.

He moved his hands to the bottom of her T-shirt. He pulled on the fabric, studying the design. "Flamingos?"

"They're fun birds who love a good martini."

"I can see that."

His gaze locked with hers. He raised his arms and slid his fingers through her hair. "What the hell am I going to do with you?"

She supposed she should be quiet and let him work through the problem on his own. However, the answer seemed obvious and she couldn't help saying, "Kiss me."

One corner of his mouth turned up. "Why didn't I think of that?"

Still cupping her head, he leaned in and pressed his lips to hers. She rested her hands against his chest and let her eyes sink closed. The feel of his mouth—soft, yet firm, anchored her in place. In the space of a single heartbeat, she knew surrender was inevitable. Maybe not today, but soon. When he asked, she would say yes. Not because of how long it had been but because this was Justice and she'd felt connected to him for half her life.

There would be consequences. There were always consequences. She would figure out a way to keep her heart safe. But that was for later....

She tilted her head, then slid her hands up to his shoulders. He dropped his to her hips and drew her against him. Even as his tongue slipped inside and brushed against hers, his fingers settled on her rear and squeezed.

She sank against him, letting his body cradle hers. The deep kisses stirred her senses. She traced his shoulders, then moved down his arms, wanting to feel all of him. Need took on a frantic edge.

He moved his head so he could press his lips to her jaw, and then he eased down to her ear where he bit on the lobe. Jolts of need and hunger burned through her and he licked the sensitive spot right below her ear.

At the same time he shifted his hands to her waist and began to move them higher. Her breath caught in anticipation. He kissed his way down her neck. She let her head fall back and waited for his fingers to touch her—

He straightened, dropping his hands to his sides. Her eyes snapped open. Passion darkened his eyes, but along with the desire was a determination. The question was a determination about what? To avoid the obvious next step? Because she was ready. More than ready. She was eager.

She dropped her gaze and saw what looked like a very impressive erection straining against the front of his jeans. Okay, that was good. She wasn't the only one panting here.

"I'm not who you think."

The statement came out of nowhere and took her a second to process. "Because you used to be a woman?"

The tension in his face eased. He gave a raw laugh. "No. Because of my past. What I've done and seen. It's complicated."

She wanted to argue with him. To say it was simple. So simple they should take off all their clothes and just get to it. But advice from friends suddenly popped into her head. Something along the lines of when a guy tells you he's flawed, it's important to listen.

A man admitting he had never been faithful or that he wasn't interested in a commitment was probably telling the truth. So when Justice said things were complicated, she should pay attention.

"Is there someone else?" she asked.

"No."

"Are you playing me?"

He touched her cheek. "No. I give you my word."

"It's because you didn't come back before now, right? This is about why you stayed away?"

She saw the truth in his eyes and took a step back.

"Okay," she said slowly. "Tell me now. Why didn't you? Why was it okay to see Ford and not me?"

"Because I can't hurt Ford."

"And you can hurt me." She raised her chin as she spoke, determined to be strong.

"I don't want to." He seemed to struggle for words. "Dammit, Patience, I know what's right and I can't resist..."

Her? Them? Sex? This was not the best time for him to be unable to finish a sentence. She waited, hoping he would say more. Maybe admit she'd haunted him. Because she would love to be thought of as the kind of woman who haunted a man rather than one who wore fun T-shirts and did hair.

He cupped her cheeks and lightly kissed her mouth. "Complications. Come on. I'll buy you a cup of coffee at you-know-where."

She should probably refuse. Walk away and pretend none of this had ever happened. She had enough going on in her life without dealing with Justice. But she couldn't seem to summon the strength to resist.

"I may want a couple of pumps of mocha in mine," she told him.

"I think I can handle that."

JUSTICE STARED AT the spreadsheet on his computer screen. Felicia had done her usual excellent job of sorting through the numbers and breaking them down into relevant relationships. If she went into a little too much detail, it was a small price to pay.

He was about to read the income projections when he heard a knock on the door.

He rose and crossed the living area of the suite at Ronan's Lodge. Eventually he would have to get an apartment or rent a house, but for now, the hotel suited his needs.

He opened the door, prepared to tell housekeeping that he didn't need any more towels. But instead he found himself staring at a ten-year-old girl.

"Hi," she said. "I'm Lillie McGraw. Patience's daughter."

"I remember."

Lillie had obviously come from school. She had a backpack over one shoulder and a book in her hand. She gave him a tentative smile.

"Can I talk to you?"

"Sure." He grabbed his room key and stepped into the hallway. "Let's go down to the lobby. I'll buy you a soda."

She smiled. "That would be nice. Thank you."

They took the elevator down to the spacious lobby. Justice settled Lillie on a sofa in the corner.

"What would you like?" he asked, glancing toward the coffee cart in the lobby.

Lillie shook her head. "I'm okay. I'd like to just talk, if that's okay."

"Of course it is."

Her eyes were the same brown as her mother's. He could see a lot of Patience in her, as well as a few features he didn't recognize. Her father's influence. Patience had said things hadn't gone well, but hadn't provided any details.

He took one of the club chairs across from the sofa. "How did you know where I was staying?"

Lillie smiled. "There aren't that many hotels in town and when Grandma was talking about you the other night she said you weren't a B-and-B kind of guy." She paused. "That's a bed-and-breakfast. We have a couple here in town."

"I saw."

Lillie leaned forward and unzipped her backpack. She pulled out several bills and thrust them toward him. "I want to hire you."

Justice hadn't been expecting that. "What's the job?"

"I need a bodyguard. There's this boy at school. Zack." She wrinkled her nose. He's always around and he watches me. It's creepy, you know? I don't know what to do about him and I don't want to say anything to my mom because she might take it wrong. Maybe talk to my teacher. That would be embarrassing. But you're a guy and I thought if you talked to Zack it would be better."

Justice watched her carefully. "What exactly has he done? Has he hit you? Pushed you?"

Lillie frowned. "No. He doesn't even speak to me. He's— Oh!" She shook her head. "No, he's not bullying me. We study that in school and watch movies and talk about it. I'm not being bullied. He's just there all the time. I can't figure out what he wants. I did ask, but he ran away. Boys are very strange. Mom says I'm going to like them someday, but I don't think so."

He relaxed a little. "Okay."

"I don't want her to worry. You can't tell her."

"I have to tell her if something is going on in your life, Lillie."

The girl sighed. "Can you tell my grandma instead?"

She was a good negotiator. "Sure. I'll tell Ava if I find anything, and I'll report to you." Because if someone was bothering Lillie he wanted to make sure it stopped.

"Great." She held out the money again. "Is this enough?"

"You don't have to pay me. The first one is free."

She smiled. "Thanks." She put the money in her backpack and withdrew a piece of paper. "Here's his name and where he lives and stuff. So you can find him."

He took the information. "I'll look into the situation and get back to you." He wasn't sure what was going on with Zack, but he would sure find out.

"Thank you for helping me. Mom's busy with her new store. She's really happy and I knew this would upset her. Grandma's excited, too. So I didn't know where else to go. Maybe it would be different if I had a dad." She put her elbows on her thighs and rested her chin in her hands. "I mean, I *have* a dad, but I never see him."

"I'm sorry."

"It's okay. I don't remember him at all. He left like when I was born or something. He doesn't see me."

She spoke without emotion—because this was all she knew. He wondered what kind of man could walk away from his child, then told himself the question was stupid. Parents walked away from kids all the time. Or did worse. Look at his own father. Justice had lived the nightmare of parental abuse. Having Bart abandon him would have been a kindness.

"If you have questions about him, I'm sure you can talk to your mom," he said.

"I know. Or Grandma. They tell me that. But what am I supposed to ask?" She straightened and stood. "Thanks for helping me."

"You're welcome. I'll get back to you in a couple of days."

She grinned. "Can we set up a secret meeting place, like we're spies?"

"Sure."

"I'd like that. But it's okay if you just come to school, too. Mom says you're busy with your business."

She picked up her book and her backpack and walked to the main entrance to the hotel. Justice followed her to the door and watched her walk away. Then he took the stairs back to his room. He returned to his computer, but instead of seeing Felicia's detailed spreadsheet, he saw the past. A much-younger Patience and how she'd smiled at him.

She'd only been about four years older than Lillie. A pretty girl who had grown into a beautiful woman.

He stood and crossed to the window, then stared out at his view of the mountains.

If things had been different, he thought, even though he knew it was a waste of time. Things couldn't have been different. Not with who he was and how he'd been raised. Bart Hanson had liked living on the wrong side of the law, liked the risk and flirting with death. His sociopathic tendencies had kept everyone around him on edge.

Justice remembered his last night in Fool's Gold all those years ago. How the phone call had come, warning them Bart had escaped from prison and been spotted in the area. Justice had been whisked away in a matter of seconds. Less than an hour later, a team had arrived to clean out the house. By morning it was as if they'd never been there at all.

He'd raged against being taken away. Had tried to bargain to be allowed to at least phone Patience and tell her what had happened. One of the marshals had explained if she knew, she was in danger. Justice had known that was true and had stopped asking.

After Bart had been captured, Justice was finally free. The murder conviction along with his other crimes had ensured that he would die behind bars. But he hadn't gone quietly and his final screams as he was led away had been a vow that his son would die. That Bart would hunt him down and kill him.

Even now, long after his father's death, Justice couldn't shake the sense that Bart was still out there. Waiting. Watching. That if Justice went too far, got too close to being like everyone else, too close to being happy, his father would pounce and destroy it all.

He glanced down to the street below and saw Lillie walking along the sidewalk. She was joined by a couple of girls her age and they talked and laughed together.

He couldn't risk it, he thought grimly. His father haunted him. There was no way to know that he could keep anyone he cared about safe. Especially if the enemy was him.

PATIENCE STOOD LOOKING at the floor in her newly leased space. She'd swept and cleaned in preparation for her meeting with her contractor. But before she handed over the deposit for the remodeling, she wanted to be sure. So she'd shown up, armed with a plan, a tape measure and masking tape.

So far she'd taped in the back and front counters, along with several tables and chairs. She walked back to the front door to confirm the flow, then wandered over to the empty area by the far window. What exactly was she going to put there? She had a cold case she was eyeing, or she could put in some kind of shelving and keep it for small meetings. Like for a book club. Ava kept suggesting a karaoke machine, but Patience wasn't thrilled about that idea.

She pulled out her phone and took a picture of the taped outlines on the floor, then looked at the next hand-drawn design. Maybe if she moved the tables to the right of the door, she thought.

"Patience?"

She turned toward the sound of her name and looked at the man standing in the open doorway to the store. With the sunlight behind him, she couldn't see him clearly at first. As he moved inside, she saw the features of an older man. He had green eyes and nearly white hair.

Her first thought was that she'd never seen him before in her life. Only there was something about him. Something familiar. They must have met somewhere and…

Her body stiffened as her brain filled in the blanks. She instinctively took a step back.

"Hello, Patience."

"Steve."

He gave her a slight smile. "I wasn't sure you'd recognize me. We only met that one time."

"Right. Two weeks before the wedding. You took us out to dinner and promised you'd see us at the ceremony."

Ned's father had made other promises. He hadn't kept those, either. Instead he'd disappeared. She'd been shocked, but Ned had shrugged it off. He wasn't used to anything better from his father.

"Why are you here?" she asked, her voice cold and stiff.

"I wanted to talk to you."

"I'm not loaning you money."

Steve's expression turned rueful. "I suppose I deserve that. I haven't been a very good grandfather."

He'd been just as bad as a father, she thought. When

she'd met Ned, one of the things they'd had in common was they'd both been abandoned by their fathers. She hadn't seen hers in years, while Steve had drifted in and out of Ned's life. When they'd talked about what they'd been through, Patience thought they had learned the same lesson. That it was important to follow through. To commit.

Instead, Ned had learned how easy it was to walk away.

Maybe it wasn't fair, but she blamed Steve for that lesson. On a personal level, she wasn't sorry to have Ned gone and had no interest in having him back. But this wasn't about her. Lillie was the one who suffered without her father.

He glanced around at the empty storefront. "I heard you're opening a coffeehouse."

"Something like that."

"Congratulations. That's very exciting."

She crossed her arms over her chest and watched him. "That's not why you're here."

"No, it's not."

He wore a white shirt tucked into jeans. Not the least bit threatening. Still, she couldn't help thinking she could make a dash for the back door if she had to.

"I'm not the man I was," he told her. "For years, I had lousy priorities. I lost my wife and my son because of that."

"You didn't lose your son," she told him. "You walked away. There's a difference."

"You're right. I take responsibility for what happened with Ned. I've tried to see him, but he has no interest in me." His green eyes grew thoughtful. "I can't blame him for that, but I do wish things had been different."

She tensed. "You're here because of Lillie."

"I'd like a chance to get to know her."

She wanted to tell him no. To scream at him to get out of here and never come back. Lillie didn't need another male relative breaking her heart.

"I'm retired now," he went on. "I have been for a few years. I took stock of my life and realized I'd focused on the wrong things." He gave her a slight smile. "I went into therapy and figured out what I'd done wrong. I want to do better, be better, for my granddaughter."

"Can you think of a single reason why I should trust you?"

Steve shook his head. "Not one."

She could feel herself getting angry. She wanted to scream that nothing about this was fair. Instead, she spoke the truth.

"I blame you for Ned's behavior. He did what you taught him. He walked away. Do you know he never sees Lillie? He signed away all rights to her so he wouldn't have to pay child support. She's a sweet, smart little girl and I'm the one who had to explain why she doesn't have a daddy anymore. For now she accepts what I've told her, but what do you think is going to happen when she's older? When she figures out that her father simply wasn't interested in her? How much do you think that's going to hurt?"

"I'm sorry."

"Being sorry isn't good enough. It's bad enough that Ned left me, but he also abandoned my daughter and I'll never forgive him for that. There is absolutely no reason for me to trust you with Lillie. Not ever."

He held out his hands, palms up. "You're right. There is no reason to trust me. But that doesn't change the fact that I'm Lillie's grandfather and I want to get to know her. I want to be a part of her life. I'm asking for a chance with her."

"What's the plan? Are you going to show up a few times, get her to like you, then disappear and break her heart?"

"No," he said quietly. "I've moved nearby. I want to be close to the only family I have left. I'm willing to do whatever it takes to earn your trust." He hesitated, as if he had more he wanted to say, then shook his head. "Please think about it," he added.

Patience hated that an outright no wasn't an option. While there was nothing he could say that would make her trust him, that wasn't the point. If Steve wasn't a complete jerk, then Lillie deserved to know her grandfather. She deserved to have more family, more people to care about her.

Steve pulled a business card out of his shirt pocket. "Here's my cell number. I'll be around. You can limit my visits, supervise them or make me post a bond." He gave her a quick smile. "Whatever it takes, Patience. I'm sorry for how my actions affected you. If I could change them, I would. Believe me."

He handed her the card, then left. She shoved the card into her back pocket and did her best to forget about it. Having Lillie's grandfather show up like that was one thing she didn't want to have to deal with.

JUSTICE KNOCKED ON the house's front door. A couple of minutes later, Ava opened it and smiled at him.

"Patience isn't here," she said by way of greeting. "She's working at the salon this afternoon."

"You're the one I came to see."

Ava laughed and invited him in. "I will take that comment in the spirit in which you meant it and not infer any other motive."

Justice grinned. "Thank you."

She led the way to the sofa. Today her steps weren't as steady as they had been before and she was using a cane. The disease, he thought, wishing there was a way for her to get better.

When they were both seated, she turned to him. "How can I help?"

"Lillie came to see me." He explained about Zack and how Lillie was uncomfortable around the boy. "She wants me to find out what's going on and make it stop. She says she's not being bullied, but I'm less sure. Under normal circumstances, I'd confront the guy myself. But he's a ten-year-old kid."

"I can see how that would make you uncomfortable," Ava told him. "I didn't know Lillie was concerned about anyone."

"I think she came to me because I'm a professional. But this is out of my area of expertise."

"I understand." Ava thought for a second. "I'm going to call the school and arrange a meeting with the counselor and the teacher. Maybe we can get an answer that way. I'll tell Patience, but ask her to let you and me handle this. That way if Lillie asks if she was there, you can say no."

"I appreciate your help."

Ava smiled. "You've always been very sweet to my girl. Even when you were much younger. I'm happy to help now."

He wasn't sure he would define his feelings as "sweet," but that wasn't a conversation he was going to have with Patience's mother. He wasn't sure he would even have it with Patience herself. He didn't know what was happening between them. He knew what he wanted, but going there meant inviting danger. His need to protect Patience was more important than his desire for her. Which left him with something of a dilemma.

CHAPTER SIX

"THANKS FOR meeting me," Patience said as she slid into a booth at the Fox and Hound. "I'm sure I sounded mysterious on the phone."

"There was a James Bond element to your request," Justice told her. He mumbled something suspiciously like "It runs in the family." But that didn't make sense, so she shrugged it off.

She'd called him that morning and asked if he was free for lunch. She had a million things she needed to be doing, but this was too important to put off. Plus, who could complain about having lunch with an attractive man, even if that man confused the heck out of her?

Wilma, the sixtysomething, gum-snapping waitress, peered at Justice.

"I don't know you, but you have the look of my Frank. That's a compliment, in case you were wondering."

"Thank you," Justice said.

Wilma turned to Patience. "He with you?"

"Sort of."

Wilma's penciled-in brows rose. "Well, isn't that the cat's pajamas? What'll you have?"

"Diet Coke," Patience said, knowing she could no more stop the town from paying attention to her and her personal life than she could stop the rotation of the earth.

"Coffee for me," Justice told the waitress. "Black."

She wrote down their orders. "There was a small accident in the kitchen earlier. Nothing to worry about, but I'd get one of the wraps if I was you."

Patience held in a groan. Obviously they should have gone somewhere else. "Thanks for the information."

Justice looked at her. "Is there a wrap you recommend?"

"The London wrap is the best," Wilma said. "With fries. You'll like it."

He passed her his menu. "I'm sure I will."

"The same for me," Patience said weakly.

"Smart girl."

When Wilma had left, Patience risked a glance at Justice. "She can be a little forceful."

He looked more amused than irritated. "I'm okay with that. Part of the town's charm."

"You say that now," Patience muttered. "Just wait." She drew in a breath. "Thanks for helping with the Lillie–Zack situation. My mom filled me in on everything. I agreed with her theory that I should stay out of it so Lillie doesn't think you betrayed her confidence."

"Thank you. I don't want her to hate me—she's a great kid."

"One who inspires an equally powerful affection in her classmates." She winced. "I think I'm going to have some serious trouble when she turns sixteen."

"Lock her in a tower."

She laughed. "An option I hadn't considered." She cleared her throat, knowing she had to get to the point of their lunch.

"As for why I asked you to join me…"

He looked at her. "Yes?"

"I had a visit from Lillie's grandfather." She passed over the business card Steve had given her. "He wants to start seeing her regularly. Have a relationship with her, I guess."

"He hasn't been around before this?"

"No. He walked out on his family when Ned, Lillie's dad, was little. Ned was always so angry and bitter about his father. When we met, I took that as a good sign. We'd both had our fathers leave, so I figured we'd both be committed to staying for the long haul." She shook her head. "I was wrong."

"Have you met—" he glanced at the card "—Steve before?"

"Once. Before the wedding. He showed up, took us to dinner, made a lot of promises, then disappeared. I don't think he's dangerous, but I also don't trust him. Lillie doesn't need her grandfather showing up and then disappearing. I want to know what kind of man he is. I thought with all your training, you could help me figure that out."

"Sure. Easy enough." Justice tucked the business card into his shirt pocket. "What happened with Ned?"

Wilma reappeared with their drinks, then returned to the kitchen. Patience unwrapped her straw.

"Nothing very unusual. We dated. It was fun but not great. I wasn't in love with him or anything, but I thought maybe I could be. I don't know. I slept with him and I probably shouldn't have. It was a tough time for me. I was confused about what I wanted to do with my life. Young."

"Really young," Justice said, his gaze steady.

"You've done the math, huh?"

"Lillie's ten. You were a teenager when you got pregnant."

"I know. Out of high school, but barely. Anyway, I got pregnant. Ned wasn't happy but said he wanted to do the right thing. We got married. I worked part-time at Morgan's Books. A couple of months after Lillie was born, Ned told me he was leaving. He'd met someone else. She was a little older and very well-off."

She glanced out the window, willing herself not to show emotion. It wasn't that she was so crushed by what had happened. Not anymore. It was that she'd been so stupid and trusting.

"I thought he would be there because he promised he would be," she admitted. "Like I said, I assumed from the way he talked about his dad walking out on him that he would never do that to his kid. I was wrong.

I was shocked when he admitted he'd been having an affair and wanted out." She returned her attention to Justice. "He already had the paperwork ready. Her lawyer had prepared it. Ned walked away from me, and from Lillie. He made no claim on her."

She sipped her soda. "I thought about it for a long time and finally realized he wouldn't be there for her. He didn't want a child and, sure, I could have forced him to pay and have visitation, but to what end? So he could make her feel she wasn't important? On my good days, I tell myself he realized he was too much like his dad to commit to his daughter. On my bad days, I think he was a bastard. In the end, I signed everything. I moved back with my mom, went to beauty school and you know the rest of it."

He reached across the table and took her hand in his. His fingers were warm and comforting. "You never saw Steve through all this?"

"No. Never heard from him or anything. Yesterday I turned around and there he was, saying he wanted a relationship with Lillie."

"I'll find out everything I can before I go."

She pulled back her hand before she could stop herself. The temperature in the restaurant seemed to drop about fifteen degrees, and any hunger she'd had disappeared. She shouldn't be surprised, but she was.

"You're leaving?"

"For a couple of weeks. I still—" He leaned toward her. "Patience, no. I'm not leaving town. I'm still under assignment for the company I used to work for. I have one last job with them. I'll be gone about ten days. No longer."

"Oh." Relief washed through her. She cleared her throat and hoped she'd managed to maintain an expression somewhat close to normal. "Right. What kind of job is it?"

"Typical bodyguard assignment."

She smiled. "What does that mean? I'm not sure I know a single person who has ever needed to use a bodyguard." She held up a hand. "I take that back. My friend Charlie's mother has used them in the past, but she was a famous ballerina. You were here with her last year, right?" When he hadn't bothered to come see her.

Why couldn't she make sense of Justice? He was so supportive and friendly and sexy, but he'd stayed away. What did that mean? She really needed his help with Steve and she liked being around him, but was she paying too high a price for that?

Stay on topic, she reminded herself. "So, the bodyguard thing. You know, most of us manage to get through our day without protection. So, who's this guy?"

"I can't tell you."

She waited, but he didn't seem to be kidding. "Okay. Does that also mean you can't tell me where you're going?"

"Yes."

"Wow." She wasn't sure what to do with the information, although she knew she didn't like it. "Do they speak English in this mystery place?"

"No."

"So it's dangerous."

"Not every non-English-speaking place is dangerous."

"I know, but if you were going to a place where they spoke English, it probably wouldn't be dangerous. I can't see there being a lot of perilous moments on the Great Barrier Reef. Unless you count the sharks."

She did her best to keep her tone light, which was more for his benefit than hers.

"You don't have to worry about me," he told her.

"I'm not. Maybe a little. I don't want you to disappear like you did before."

"I won't. I promise."

Was that promise for this specific trip or did it include all of eternity? She had a feeling that asking that would change her from charming friend to scary, overintense nonfriend.

Wilma appeared then and placed their lunches in front of them. Patience thanked her and reached for a fry, all the while wondering if she could trust Justice to keep his word. She wanted to say she knew the man, but he was still a mystery to her. She knew who he *had* been, but that was a long time ago.

She knew she liked him and adored his kisses and would, perhaps foolishly, jump into bed with him, should he ask. But that wasn't the same as trusting him. Trust had to be earned. She just hoped she wasn't at risk of falling for a man who didn't deserve her heart.

JUSTICE WAITED ON the sidewalk outside the elementary school. Kids streamed past him, a few climbing into waiting cars, but the majority walking home with friends. It was that kind of place where children were safe walking around on their own.

He scanned the crowd, then spotted Lillie. She was talking to a couple of other girls. She looked up and saw him, then waved enthusiastically. She said something to her friends and hurried over.

"Hi! You're here."

"I wanted to talk to you about my research."

They walked together toward her house.

"Zack's been different lately," Lillie told him. "I knew you'd said something to him."

"We had a talk."

She gazed up at him expectantly.

"He's not stalking you or acting weird," Justice told her. "He likes you."

Two days before Justice had met with Ava, the school counselor, Zack's parents, the kids' teacher and Zack himself. What everyone had quickly discovered was that Zack liked Lillie. He wasn't trying to be stalker-guy. He was a kid with a crush.

His parents had been understanding and promised to teach him that staring at the object of his affection wasn't the best way to win her over, and Justice had agreed to share the results of the meeting with Lillie.

"I don't understand," Lillie said. "Why doesn't he just talk to me?"

"He likes you."

"But he's a boy. Boys are strange." She wrinkled her nose. "This isn't like TV, is it? With kissing?"

"There's no kissing."

"Good. Mom keeps saying that one day I'll look at boys different, but I don't think so." She looked up at him. "Thanks for helping me. I guess I just need to stay out of his way."

"He should be better now. Less intense."

"That's good." She smiled. "Are you going to send me a bill? I've never had a bill before."

"No. I did this one because I know your mom."

"That's nice. Thank you."

They had reached her house. He paused on the sidewalk.

Lillie was bright, friendly and sweet. A great kid. The kind of kid who made people who didn't want children second-guess their plans.

"I need to get going," he told her.

"Okay. Thanks, Justice."

"You're welcome."

He walked back the way he'd come. Maybe Ford was right. Maybe Fool's Gold wasn't the kind of place either of them should settle. But leaving—he couldn't. Not yet. The draw was too powerful, his need too extreme. He would have to remember to be careful and make sure he kept those who mattered to him safe.

PATIENCE SAT CROSS-legged on the sofa. She had a pad of paper and a pen. In front of her was a can of diet soda. She was walking that tightrope of needing the caffeine and slipping into jittery madness.

"The equipment is ordered," Ava said, holding up a folder. "I have all the receipts here. I've created a calendar with delivery dates. The plumber and electrician have to come in first, so we need to know where everything is going."

Patience drew in a breath. "Right. So we need to finalize placement. What do you think?"

"I think you should get another opinion," her mother told her. "Ask Justice what he thinks. He used to be military. He's used to slipping in and out of places. He should have a good idea about room flow and what can get in the way."

"Oh, I hadn't thought about that." Not that she minded a reason to see Justice. "You're right. He'll bring a fresh perspective. I'll call him later and set up a time."

"Perfect." Her mother flipped open her folder. "Between the construction and the equipment, we've used up most of our budget."

"I know. We knew that was going to happen."

Decent, professional equipment didn't come cheap. Then there were all the supplies that went with opening a coffee place. Cups, mugs, glasses, tables, chairs, napkins, cases, a dishwasher.

"We have the money to pay for staff," Patience said, "and our reserve fund. I won't be taking a salary for at least the first couple of months."

"Don't worry about the bills around here," her mother

told her. "I'll cover them. With the mortgage paid off, we have more than enough, plus a little extra to put into the store."

Patience nodded. None of this was new information. They'd been over their budget so many times before, playing out different scenarios. The difference was, this time it was real. They were doing this. The inheritance meant there wasn't a bank loan to worry about. Talk about a miracle.

"If nothing else, I have my fallback position," she said with a smile. "I can go back to doing hair."

"You won't have to," her mother told her. "We're going to take this town by storm."

"One cup at a time," Patience added.

"That's right." Her mother flipped through the paperwork. "We need to get together a work party. The contractor will install the built-ins and there's the plumber and electrician, but what about the general cleaning and painting? It's much cheaper to do it ourselves."

It would save a lot of money, Patience thought. "You're right. We're talking about what? Three weeks from now?"

"The remodeling starts Monday and it takes a week. The equipment comes in the week after that. So about three weeks seems right." Ava made a note. "I'll pull out the phone tree."

One of the advantages of living in a place like Fool's Gold was the community involvement. Neighbors stepped in to help each other. If the school needed classrooms painted, or a holiday production needed stage sets refurbished, people showed up and helped. Although Patience had been on the participating end of a lot of work parties, she'd never been one of the people doing the asking.

"Do you think we should bother people?" Even as she asked the question, she knew what her mother was going to say.

"Everyone who loves us will be delighted to help."

"I know. You're right." She drew in a breath. "Work now, freak out later."

"At least you have a plan."

They went over the rest of the details. In the next couple of days the local print shop would have the proofs of their logo ready. The logo would go on the signs, the aprons and eventually the mugs. She was even thinking of offering "Brew-haha" merchandise to sell.

"And we're done," Ava told her.

"Yay, us." Patience put down her pad of paper and her pen and straightened her legs. "Lillie should be getting home soon." Her daughter was at a friend's house for the afternoon.

"You heard the Zack issue was resolved."

Patience smiled. "Yes. Poor kid. He had to endure a whole meeting about his crush. That's going to leave a scar."

"Justice handled the situation extremely well. I know I have nothing to do with it, but I'm still proud of how he turned out."

Patience was impressed as well, but didn't think "proud" described her feelings. "He's a good guy."

A good guy who confused her. If only she didn't like him so much. She had thought to keep him far enough from Lillie that her daughter wouldn't start to bond, only to have Lillie take matters into her own hands. Now Justice was her daughter's hero. Kind of Patience's hero, too, for helping out Lillie.

He'd decided to start his business in Fool's Gold, which meant he was staying. But he still hadn't explained why he'd avoided her for years and years. Avoiding him until she figured it out seemed like the best option, only the town was small and in truth, she didn't want to. Maybe she needed an intervention.

At least being insanely busy with the store was going to help. She wouldn't have time to play the what-if game right now.

"It's interesting he chose to settle here," her mother said. "He could have gone anywhere."

"I think Ford had something to do with it. They're still friends." She laughed. "Or maybe it's all Fool's Gold. Once this town finds you, it doesn't let you go."

"That sounds a little scary."

"I didn't mean it that way." She looked at her mother. "I'm glad Justice is okay. Even though we were just kids, I thought about him a lot—what might have happened to him."

Ava nodded. "I remember the mayor trying to find out. Alice Barns used her contacts, as well."

Then Deputy Barns, now Police Chief Barns, Patience thought. "We were dealing with the witness protection program. There was no way we could have figured it out." Even now she had trouble believing someone had thought to keep a kid in danger safe in Fool's Gold. Nothing like that had ever happened here. Which was probably the point, she thought.

She reached for her pen, then straightened. A nagging thought reappeared and she knew she had to suck it up and tell her mother what was going on.

"Mom, Ned's father came by the other day."

Ava turned to her. "Steve?"

"Uh-huh. He says he wants to have a relationship with Lillie."

Patience braced herself for the rant. Ava had dealt with men abandoning her more than once in her life. First *her* father had cut and run on his family; then her husband had played the same disappearing game. She'd had to watch the same thing happen to her daughter.

No doubt Ava would have several not-very-nice things to say about Ned's father. After all, Steve had also left his family. There was an epidemic of men who weren't in it for the long haul.

"How was he?" her mother asked instead.

Patience shrugged. "He was quiet. Pleasant. He apologized for what he'd done to Ned and for how Ned had treated Lillie and me. He says he's a changed man and wants a second chance with his granddaughter."

"Do you believe him?"

"I don't know. I'd only met him once before. Ned never had anything good to say about him, but he's hardly someone I'd trust as far as judging character goes. I asked Justice to check him out."

Her mother's expression was unreadable. "That's a sensible solution. Justice will find out if he has any issues we need to be concerned about."

Patience waited. "That's it? You're not going to call him an SOB or tell me to grab Lillie and run?"

"People change."

"You think Steve has changed?"

Ava shifted in her seat. "I'm not sure. I'm just saying he might mean what he says. Time has a way of making things more clear. For some people, that means dealing with regrets. If Steve is genuine, then you might want to take him seriously."

Patience was less sure. "I don't want Lillie to get hurt. She never talks about her dad, but I know she thinks about him. Her friends have fathers. Even the ones with divorced parents still see their dads. She never has. He's just gone and he's not coming back. It would be different if he'd died—then his absence wouldn't be a choice. What if Steve hasn't changed? What if he sees her a few times and then disappears?"

"Maybe he wouldn't."

"You're taking his side."

"I'm saying you need more information."

Patience didn't understand. It almost felt as if there was something her mother wasn't telling her.

"I'm going to wait to hear what Justice has to say,"

she told her mother. "If he clears Steve, then I'll consider letting him meet Lillie. Otherwise, there's no way he's getting close to my daughter."

CHAPTER SEVEN

Jo's Bar was one of those places unique to Fool's Gold. Decorated in female-friendly colors, with TVs turned to shopping networks and fun reality TV, the place catered to the women in town. There were plenty of low-calorie choices on the menu, a play area for toddlers during lunch and a complete lack of single guys on the prowl. While men were welcome, they tended to avoid Jo's Bar. If they did show up, they migrated to the back room where they could find a pool table and smaller TVs with professional sports playing.

Patience walked in and saw her friends at the table by the back wall. Usually they settled in one of the large booths, but with Annabelle due to give birth at any second, and Heidi about seven months along, sliding into a booth had become complicated.

"How are you?" she asked as she approached.

"Huge," Annabelle said.

The petite redhead did look uncomfortably large, Patience thought as she hugged her. Heidi was a little taller and carrying a bit less baby.

"I'm good," Heidi said with a smile.

"She's serene," Charlie announced. "It's kind of annoying."

"I'm in the Zen part of my pregnancy." Heidi laughed. "Very one with the universe."

Heidi was a pretty blonde who lived on the Castle Ranch just outside town. Charlie was a local firefighter. Strong, tall and possibly the least girlie woman Patience had met. She was attractive, but had an air of competence that scared off most men.

Last year the three friends had fallen in love with the Stryker brothers. As their friend, Patience had had a front-row seat to all the excitement, heartache and ultimately the happy endings.

Now she took one of the remaining chairs and hung her purse on the back. "I invited a friend of mine to join us. I hope that's okay."

Charlie leaned toward her. "You know that's perfectly fine. We like a big crowd. It keeps the conversation lively. Who is she?"

"Her name is Isabel Beebe. Her family has owned Paper Moon forever. She's been living in New York for the past few years, but is back for a while. Her parents want to sell the store. Isabel is going to run it and get it ready for sale."

Annabelle's eyes filled with tears. "She's selling Paper Moon? But I was going to get my dress there. It's a Fool's Gold institution. I want to be part of an institution."

"More like you need to be locked away in one," Charlie muttered, rubbing Annabelle's back. "Come on. Take a few breaths. You're very emotional. It's the hormones. Nothing is really wrong."

Annabelle sniffed a couple of times. "I can't help it. I cry at everything."

Heidi patted her hand. "Charlie's right. Try breathing."

"I need to pull it together," Annabelle said with a tiny sob. "I don't want to scare Isabel away. Even if she is closing the store."

Patience glanced at Charlie, who rolled her eyes. "You've never even been in the store," Charlie told her. "How can you be this upset?"

"I had p-plans."

"I really hope the baby comes soon," Charlie muttered. "I can't take much more of this."

Patience held in a smile. She didn't remember her pregnancy being so emotional, but everyone was different.

Annabelle raised her head and sniffed. "Oh, look. That's her. She's very pretty. Isabel is a nice name. Maybe we should put it on the list."

"Kill me now," Charlie said with a sigh. "I'm never getting pregnant. It's not worth it."

"Oh, it's wonderful," Annabelle told her earnestly. "You'll be a great mother."

"And the tears are gone."

Patience waved Isabel over, then made the introductions. Isabel settled in the seat next to her. She eyed the two pregnant women.

"I think I'm going to drink my water out of a bottle while I'm at this table."

Heidi laughed. "It's not contagious."

"I'm not taking any chances." She turned to Charlie. "How have you escaped their fate?"

"Careful planning."

Heidi leaned close. "Clay, her fiancé, is more worried about getting her married than anything else right now."

"We're getting married," Charlie said. "Just as soon as I knock some sense into him."

Patience glanced at Isabel. "Clay wants a big wedding. Charlie doesn't."

"It's stupid to have a bunch of people over for a big ceremony. We should elope."

Annabelle's eyes filled again. "You hate weddings?"

Jo, the owner, walked over. "Nice to see all of you for lunch." She looked at Isabel. "I'm Jo."

"Isabel Beebe."

"Paper Moon," Jo said. "Great store. I know your sister, Maeve. Now, there's a woman committed to having children." She pointed to the chalkboard by the bar. "We have two specials today. One of them is a salad. Plenty of lean protein and lots of greens for my pregnant customers. I've also been working on a new smoothie. Lots of dairy. I can do chocolate or blueberry."

Heidi took a deep breath, as if finding her Zen center. "Yes to both, please. Chocolate."

"I'm still in emotional distress," Annabelle admitted.

"We'll need a few minutes," Charlie told Jo. "Bring the weepy one some herbal tea. Iced and with extra lemon."

"Diet soda," Patience said.

"I'll have the same," Isabel said.

"A double shot of tequila," Charlie told Jo, then held up her hand. "I'm kidding. But I will take a mint chocolate milkshake."

Jo nodded. "If it's too early for alcohol, then go for the sugar." She wrote down the orders. "I'll let you look over the menus."

When Jo had left, Annabelle sniffed, then glanced at Isabel. "You grew up here, too, then."

"Uh-huh. I couldn't wait to escape." She wrinkled her nose. "So let me be clear. My return is temporary."

"You're talking to Fool's Gold converts," Patience told her. "They won't get that."

"Too many people know too much about each other here," Isabel said. "When I was a kid, I felt like I had fifteen mothers and fathers."

Patience smiled. "She's right. It was like that, but I didn't mind it as much. Isabel had big dreams."

"Where have you been living?" Charlie asked.

"New York. I was in advertising." Isabel's blue eyes flashed with emotion.

Patience had a feeling she was thinking about the divorce and all the changes that went with it. "Charlie was proposed to in Times Square."

Charlie leaned back in her chair. “Do we have to talk about that?”

“It was wonderful,” Heidi said. “Charlie’s fiancé is very inventive and totally crazy about her.”

“That’s nice.” Isabel sounded wistful.

“You should give him the big wedding he wants,” Annabelle said.

“I’m not the big-wedding type.”

Patience wondered if her reluctance was because she really didn’t like big weddings or if she was uncomfortable with the whole idea of it: the feminine dress, being the center of attention. Charlie was the most capable person Patience knew, but like everyone else, she had her demons.

“It’s the dress thing,” Heidi announced, confirming what Patience thought.

Isabel studied her. “I have a great selection of gowns that would look pretty fabulous on you.”

Charlie glared at her. “I find the word *gown* off-putting. We’ve just met. Why aren’t I intimidating you? Most people are frightened by me when they meet me.”

“Oh, sorry.” Isabel’s grin was impish. “I’ll tremble next time.”

Charlie glanced at Patience. “Okay, I like her.”

“We have a new friend.” Annabelle looked at both of them, and her eyes filled with tears. “That’s so nice.”

Charlie covered her face with her hands. “Kill me now.”

Jo returned with the drinks, and talk turned to what was going on in town.

"Are you really selling Paper Moon?" Annabelle asked.

"Yes, but not for a while. I promised my parents I would spruce it up and we want to wait until after the wedding-season rush."

"When's that?" Heidi asked.

"Late fall through early March. There are a lot of engagements followed by plans for June weddings. Brides tend to order their dresses several months in advance."

Charlie nudged Annabelle. "See? They'll still be there for you."

"That's a relief."

Heidi looked at Patience. "Do you have an opening date yet? We're all so excited about Brew-haha."

"A month, give or take," Patience said, and pressed a hand to her belly. "I'm excited, too, and nervous."

"You're going to do great," Charlie told her. "The location is excellent and I've personally inspected the building. It's completely safe."

Heidi leaned toward Isabel. "Charlie has this thing about fire. It's related to her job."

"I can hear you," Charlie told her.

"Yes, and you love me anyway."

"Yeah, yeah. Maybe."

Heidi giggled.

Charlie returned her attention to Patience. "You

know we're all here for you. Whatever you need. Are you planning a work party?"

"Yes. We have to get the remodeling finished first."

"Let me know when it is and I'll make sure I'm available. I can trade a shift if I have to."

Heidi and Annabelle shared a glance.

"We're useless," Annabelle said.

"Not useless, but less than helpful," Heidi added.

"Don't sweat it," Patience told them. "You can't be around paint or cleaning supplies. You can help next time."

"Are you sure?" Annabelle asked.

"I swear," Patience told her. She turned to Isabel. "I'll expect you to show up early, though."

"A work party? You mean like when we were kids and all the neighbors would arrive to help with a move or something like that. Still? Really?"

"We're big on tradition," Patience told her.

"There's a rumor about another store opening," Charlie said. "A Christmas place. Mayor Marsha was mentioning it."

"I'd love that," Heidi said. "Is there a location yet?"

"I heard across from the park and next to the sporting-goods store," Isabel said. "Around the corner from Brew-haha."

"All of us starting businesses at the same time," Patience said. "That's only good news."

Heidi batted her eyes. "Let us not forget the bodyguard school your handsome friend is opening."

Patience sipped her soda and did her best to look innocent. "I've heard about it."

"Uh-huh." Annabelle rested her hands on her belly. "He's very hot. All strong and protective. Excellent qualities in a man."

"We're friends. I barely know him."

"That's not what your blush says," Charlie told her.

Isabel's eyes widened. "You're dating Justice?"

"No. I've seen him around town. He came over for dinner. With my daughter and my mother," she added, refusing to even *think* about the kisses they'd shared. "He's nice."

"Nice, huh?" Heidi didn't look convinced. "I think there's more to the story."

Jo appeared. "You five ready to order?"

"I am," Patience said quickly, eager to change the subject.

Isabel leaned close and lowered her voice. "Saved by Jo. Don't think I'm not going to want details later."

Patience shrugged, as if she had no idea what her friend was talking about. As for sharing details, there really weren't very many. Justice was appealing, but potentially dangerous. Better that she avoid him. Okay, maybe not better, but smarter.

So much for being smart, Patience thought the next afternoon as she stood in what would soon be her store and waited while Justice walked through the place. She had the tape down on the floor, marking off the various locations. The main counter, the cold case, the bakery display, tables and chairs.

He moved between the two-dimensional representation of what would be real objects, then circled back. Finally he looked up at her.

"You have a well-thought-out plan," he said. "There's good flow here."

"Does that mean it's a good layout to hold a South American dictator or a bad place to do that?"

He smiled at her. "I could arrange a kidnapping here. Or prevent one. Flexibility's important."

She did her best to ignore the way his smile made her toes get all curly in her athletic shoes. Right now her business had to be her prime focus. Not the handsome man prowling around. Although he did look good prowling. Competent and determined. As a quick "Oh God, what am I thinking?" shudder washed through her, she thought longingly of strong arms to hold her close. She supposed it was good to know that in a battle of strength, hormones beat common sense. Knowledge was power and all that.

He turned to her and raised his eyebrows. "Cold?"

"Terrified."

"New business jitters?"

"Mostly. I've been telling myself that I don't get to be scared. I mean, in the grand scheme of life, what's opening a business? Look at what my mom has to deal with every day with her MS. I should be able to handle this with grace and dignity, right?"

He moved toward her. "It's okay to be scared. It's natural, considering what you're doing."

His dark blue eyes seemed to suck her in. She felt herself losing all her will, not to mention her sense of self-preservation. Asking his opinion was one thing, but longing for some serious naughty time was just plain stupid.

"This is a big change," she admitted, knowing that confession was much safer than telling him about the voice in her head. The one screaming, "Take me now!"

She cleared her throat. "I've read the articles. I know what percentage of new businesses fail."

"You're not going to be one of them. You have a great product in an excellent location. You'll be local and get the support that goes with it." He put his hands on her upper arms. "You're going to be fine."

"That's what I keep telling myself." She found herself wanting to lean into him, which wasn't a good thing. Distraction, she thought. She needed a distraction.

"Hey, you'll be doing all this and killing people," she said, her voice perky. "That's some stress, too."

He gave her that damned slow, sexy smile. "We don't plan to kill people in class."

"Just after. If they're late or mouthy?"

"It's one way to deal with problems." He dropped his hands to his sides. "So, what's the next step?"

"Plumber, electrician and the contractor all fight for space." She led the way to the main counter. "See the big squares? Those are the espresso machines. They have to be plumbed for water and hardwired into the electrical system. The cold and display cases are already on their way. The espresso machines will arrive on Monday."

The details were both a distraction from being so close to Justice and a direct route to a twirly tummy. She pressed her hand against her midsection.

"All the professional work will be done within two weeks. Then comes the fun stuff. Painting, cleaning, setting up. We'll do a work party for that. Then another week to pull it all together, train whatever staff we hire, and then we open."

He faced her. "A work party?"

"Sure. We put out the word that we need help and people will show up and do whatever needs doing." Patience tilted her head. "I've been to tons of them but have never asked for help. It feels weird, but I can't take care of everything myself, and paying the contractor for the simple stuff chews up too much of the budget."

"Another small-town benefit?" he asked.

She smiled. "We could come help you, if you'd like. Stock the shelves with lethal darts and pens that use invisible ink."

"I think we'll be fine."

"If you're sure."

"I am." He studied her. "You never wanted to live anywhere else?"

"This is home. Do you think there's somewhere better?"

"Not for you. You belong here."

She wasn't sure if his words were a good thing or a bad thing. Maybe they just were and she should go with it.

She opened her mouth to say something else, then happened to catch sight of his watch. "Is that the time?"

He held out his arm so she could see more clearly. "It's accurate."

"I have highlights in ten minutes."

He pushed her toward the door. "Go. I'll lock up and drop off the key."

"Really? Thanks."

She bolted out the door.

She almost wished he wouldn't be so nice, she thought as she hurried toward the salon. Justice was enough of a temptation without being thoughtful and sweet, too. With everything going on, she found herself feeling more vulnerable than usual.

Yes or no, she thought. Yes to Justice and possible disaster, but such a thrill ride. Or no. Which really meant yes to being sensible.

She wanted it all, she realized. The man who made her tingle and laugh, who was also dangerous and mysterious. She wanted uncertainty *and* a sure thing. An impossible combination.

JUSTICE DID AS he promised. He locked up the store, then returned the key to Patience. She was busy painting some mixture onto thin strips of hair, then wrapping them in what looked a lot like aluminum foil.

The mysteries of being a woman, he thought as he

ducked out of the salon before he was noticed. But he was happy to help her. Being around Patience relaxed him. He felt better when she was in the room. The sexual attraction was a problem he hadn't solved. Giving in was the easiest solution, but then what? How did that help her? Excluding all the ways he planned to please her, of course.

He'd never been the kind of man who settled into relationships. Between his work and his past, he knew he wasn't a good bet. So far, resisting the call of settling down had been easy, but lately…

He shook off the thought and headed down the street. As he reached the corner, he saw a man walking in front of him. The guy was tall, with dark hair. There was something familiar about him. Something that put Justice on alert. He knew the other man wouldn't start the fight, but he would end it.

By the time Justice had closed the gap, the information was in place. So when the guy turned, Justice was able to put the name with the face and know there wasn't any danger. Not yet, at least.

"Gideon Boylan," he said.

The dark-haired man didn't look surprised. "Garrett."

Gideon looked like a dozen other guys Justice knew. Scarred, tattooed and dangerous. He had a scar by his eyebrow, but Justice was sure there were others. In their line of work, it wasn't a matter of *if* you were injured but rather *when*.

"Funny seeing you here," Justice said.

"I heard you were in town. It was just a matter of time until we ran into each other."

"You live here?"

Gideon nodded. "Moved here last year." He glanced around at the quiet street and tidy storefronts. "Hell of a place." He returned his attention back to Justice. "Ford told me about it. One day I had nowhere else to go, so I thought I'd swing by. Decided to stay."

Justice knew there was a whole lot more to the story. Gideon had worked black ops. The kind that took a man so deep he often couldn't find his way back. From what Justice had been told, Gideon had been captured. The nature of his mission meant he wasn't sanctioned and therefore couldn't be missing. And if you weren't missing, no one came looking.

From what Justice had pieced together, nearly two years had passed before Ford Hendrix and Angel Whittaker had found Gideon. After that much torture and captivity, he'd been more dead than alive.

Obviously he'd recovered. At least on the outside. There was no way to know about the internal scars. People thought the real danger of what soldiers did was physical. The truth was the worst damage was often in the heart and in the mind. How you were changed by everything you saw during war. That's what couldn't always be fixed.

"What do you do here?" Justice asked.

"I bought a couple of radio stations. I'm the night DJ. Oldies mostly. Some talk. Hell, I don't know if anyone's listening, but so far I haven't been run out of town." He offered a brief smile that didn't reach his eyes.

The smile faded. "I wouldn't have thought Fool's Gold was your kind of place."

"I spent a year or so here when I was a kid," Justice said. "Ford kept reminding me about it, and one day I decided to come back." He pulled a business card out of his shirt pocket and passed it over.

Gideon took it. "CDS. Cerberus Defense Sector." The smile returned. "The three-headed dog that guards hell? Talk about delusions of grandeur."

Justice chuckled. "It seemed appropriate. It's me, Ford and Angel."

"Angel's moving here, too? Seriously? Do you think he'll fit in?"

"I think Fool's Gold can handle him."

"We'll see." Gideon started to return the card.

"Keep it," Justice told him. "Maybe you want to join us."

"I have my gig."

"You could teach a couple of classes. Keep your hand in, so to speak."

Gideon shoved the card into his jeans pocket. "I don't think so. Keep my hand in for what? Have you seen this place? We're all pretty safe here."

That might be true, but Justice knew the danger never went away. That for the rest of his life, Gideon would be on guard against the dark, if nothing else.

"You might change your mind," Justice said. "If you do, call me. We could use a guy like you."

Gideon held up both hands. "I'm a civilian now. Just doing my thing."

"Married?" Justice asked.

Gideon dropped his arms to his sides. "No. I haven't settled in that much."

Which might be a problem, Justice thought.

Gideon's gaze sharpened. "I saw that," he said. "Why do you care if I'm—" He swore. "No way. She's coming here?"

They both knew who the "she" was. Felicia.

"She is and you'll stay away from her."

Gideon's posture tensed. "You're going to make me?"

"She's important to me. Like a sister."

Gideon winced. "That makes it worse."

"Yes, it does. It means I'll always care about her. She's family, Gideon, and if you hurt her, I'll kill you."

They both knew Justice meant what he said. They also both knew that Gideon wouldn't go easily. Which left them at an impasse.

"I'm sure she's forgotten about me," Gideon said. "It was a long time ago."

"I'm sure, too."

But as the two men walked away from each other, Justice found himself wondering if both of them were lying or only him. Because Felicia *was* family to him, which meant he knew she'd never forgotten anything. Not about Gideon or their night together. And when she found out he was in town, there was no telling what was going to happen.

CHAPTER EIGHT

PATIENCE SAT ON the sofa in her living room and ignored the folder Justice had set in front of her. "Are you sure?"

"You sound disappointed."

"I was hoping you'd tell me that Lillie's grandfather is a known felon, wanted in fifteen states. That would make my decision easier."

"Sorry. He has no criminal record. A couple of traffic tickets over the years. He doesn't seem to be very successful with his personal relationships, but other than that, he's paid his taxes on time and runs a fairly successful business. He sold that a year ago, put the proceeds into safe investments and moved here about four months ago."

Patience grimaced. "He's really close?"

"Renting a house on the outskirts of town." Justice sat on the sofa and faced her. "I can't speak for his character, but for the rest of it, he's a regular guy."

"Which means I have no real reason to keep him from Lillie."

"Not the answer you wanted."

She shrugged. "I know that makes me sound like a

terrible person, but I'm willing to live with the judgment."

"You're trying to keep your daughter safe."

Patience wished she could accept the compliment, but she wasn't being completely truthful. "I might have other motives. I'll admit there's a part of me that doesn't want my relationship with my daughter to change. I don't want to share her with Steve. I'm also scared that if he gets involved, Ned might find out and have a spiritual awakening or something."

Justice shifted a little closer and took her hand in his.

She let him, liking the physical contact and sign of support. He had big hands, she thought idly, then had to clear her throat when the slutty part of her mind whispered that old wives' tale about men and the size of their hands.

Foolishness, she told herself. And not the point.

"I checked out Ned, too," he told her. "He's a jerk. For what it's worth, I don't think you have to worry about him suddenly having a guilty conscience. From what I can tell, he doesn't have much of a conscience to begin with."

"Which makes me really stupid for getting involved with him." She held up her free hand. "I'm being scattered. The point is Steve isn't a bad guy and I should probably give him a chance."

"What does your mom say about him?"

"She's on his side, which surprises me. I would have thought she would be more concerned about him. But she's all in favor of Lillie getting to know her grandfather." Patience bit her lower lip. "That worries me, too. Her agreeing. She's been odd lately. Getting calls and taking them in private. Not saying what they're about. I don't expect her to share every detail of her life, but there's something going on."

Justice's gaze was steady. "Do you think it's about her health?"

He'd voiced her greatest fear. "I hope not, but I do worry. What if she's sicker than she's letting on? She could be eager for Lillie to have more family because she's not going to be around as long as she would like."

Pressure built up in the back of her throat and her eyes began to burn. Patience blinked and swallowed, not wanting to break into hysterical sobs just now.

Justice grabbed her other hand. "Hey, look at me."

She did as he requested.

"Your mom isn't dying. You've seen her around here. She's moving great. She's doing as much as she used to and she's completely involved with Brew-haha. Right?"

"Yes."

"So whatever she has going on, it's unlikely to be her health. But if you're still concerned, ask her."

"That's so sensible."

"Not your thing?"

"Not on purpose."

He laced his fingers with hers. "Ask her."

"I will. After the opening. I don't want her to feel I'm spying on her, and we're both stressed right now."

Plus, his observations about how Ava was dealing with her activities were right. There hadn't been any changes, except for the mysterious phone calls. Ava was still going out with her friends and working regular hours.

She drew in a breath. "I guess I have to call Steve and let him know he can see Lillie."

"Want me to be there for the first visit?"

She leaned toward him. "You wouldn't mind? It would help so much." She managed a smile. "I know you can step in if things get difficult."

Justice would also be a nice distraction for her daughter. And hey, if the professional bodyguard made Steve a little nervous, all the better. Patience acknowledged that her plan of keeping Justice and her daughter apart had just gone down the toilet. But right now Steve was the bigger threat.

"I wouldn't have offered if I hadn't meant it," he told her. "Lillie's a great kid. I'm happy to make sure nothing bad happens."

"Thank you. You have your secret bodyguard trip coming up. I'll schedule the visit before that." She laughed. "It's some rock star, right? Like a band, and you're embarrassed, so that's why you're pretending it's dangerous."

His blue eyes flashed with an emotion she couldn't read. "You've caught me."

"I knew it."

"You're pretty smart...for a girl."

She straightened. "Seriously? You did not say that to me."

"I like that you're a girl."

"Don't try to be all nice now. I'm insulted."

She started to stand, but he grabbed her around the waist and pulled her against him. She wasn't really trying to stop him, but even if she had been, she was suddenly not in control of the situation. He shifted and twisted and there she was, sitting on his lap, his face inches from hers.

His thighs were rock hard beneath her butt. His arms came around her and both supported her and held her captive. She could inhale the scent of him—clean soap and something slightly more sensuous and masculine.

"Are you taking control of this situation?" she asked softly.

"I am."

She knew there were concerns. That who he was and who he had been weren't the same. She was assuming the boy she'd known had grown into the same kind of man. Her gut said to trust him, but it wasn't her gut she was worried about. It wasn't even her body. It was her heart.

Justice was a blue-eyed knight riding to her rescue. After years of taking care of herself, that was tough to resist. But she had her questions. At the risk of sounding like a father in an eighteenth-century novel, what were his intentions? This was not a good time to get her heart broken.

But when he leaned in and kissed her, she couldn't find it in herself to resist. The man was hot, and she had been without any hotness for what felt like a lifetime.

She welcomed the heat and pressure of his mouth on hers and parted her lips instantly. He slipped his tongue inside and she got lost in the erotic dance as shivers rippled through her. Her arms settled around his neck and she leaned in to feel his body against hers.

Closer, she thought, tilting her head and kissing him deeply. She needed to get closer.

Fortunately mind reading seemed to be one of his skills. He shifted his hands, then shifted all of her so she was straddling him. They were close enough to do a lot of intriguing things.

She opened her eyes and stared at his face. Slowly, not wanting to rush the moment, she touched his cheek, then traced the line of his jaw.

"Tough guy," she murmured.

One corner of his mouth turned up. "That's me. Tough."

She supposed *lethal* was a better word, but not for her purposes. She rested her fingertips on his broad shoulders and let herself get lost in his gaze.

"You sure about this?" she asked.

"About moving back to Fool's Gold, opening the business or being here with you?"

"All of them, I guess."

"You think I'm better than I am."

Talk about not answering the question. "Shouldn't that make you happy?"

He put his hands on her waist. "I don't want to disappoint you."

"Is that possible?"

"In life if not in bed."

"Oh, please. That is so like a guy."

"Guilty. And I still want you," he said quietly. "Kiss me, Patience."

She leaned in to comply with his request. As her mouth touched his, she felt his hands settle on her breasts. He cupped her curves in his palms. Long fingers brushed against her nipples and sent jolts of desire all through her. She sank into him, wanting that and more.

She pushed her tongue against his. They circled and stroked even as he rubbed her nipples a little harder and a little faster. She found it more and more difficult to breathe. When his hands dropped to her hips, she nearly whimpered, then realized he was pulling her closer. Settling her on his erection.

He was hard and thick and she pulsed against him, wishing there weren't layers of clothing between them. She was starving for what he offered, desperate with need.

His hands slipped under her T-shirt with the dancing rhinos. With an easy flick of two fingers her bra was undone; then he was touching her breasts, skin on skin, and she straightened to give him more room.

She rubbed herself against him, even as he pulled

up her shirt, removed her bra and settled his mouth on her breast.

The soft, wet contact made her gasp. He licked her nipple before closing his lips around her and sucking gently. She slipped her hands through his hair and strained toward him, wanting all he had to offer.

He moved to her other breast and repeated his action. When he drew back, his eyes were dark, his pupils dilated, and they were both breathing hard.

"We should—"

Go upstairs. Do it now. Get naked. Patience wasn't sure what she was going to say next, although she had an idea of the context. But instead of finishing her sentence, she heard a familiar laugh from outside.

Lillie.

"Crap," she shrieked, scrambling off Justice's lap and reaching for her bra. "We're in my living room in the middle of the afternoon. We can't do this here."

He glanced toward the door, then stood and walked over to the wing chair by the couch. It took her a second to realize he was positioning himself behind it so his *condition* wouldn't be obvious.

"You're right," he said. "This isn't the place." His mouth twitched. "I can apologize if you'd like, although technically I'm not sorry."

She hooked her bra back together and pulled down her shirt. After making sure everything was in place, she glanced at him and smiled.

"I'm not sorry, either. But the last time I made out on the sofa, I was still in high school."

His gaze locked with hers. He didn't speak, but she would swear she heard the words. *It should have been me.*

In that second, she agreed. It should have been him. Her first kiss, her first time. Because whatever she'd felt for Justice before had stayed with her all this time. It wasn't love and it probably wasn't smart, but it was still there. A sense of connection. Which meant walking away was impossible to imagine.

JUSTICE HADN'T BEEN sure what to expect from the work party at Brew-haha. Even so the crush of forty or so volunteers was still a surprise. Over the past two weeks Patience had put together a list of what needed to be done and collected supplies. He'd seen her a few times, but never alone or in a setting where he could take advantage of them being alone.

He couldn't remember the last time he'd spent so much time wanting what he couldn't have. Even as a teenager, he'd been more focused on dealing with the situation with his father than getting the girl. He'd had feelings for Patience, but she'd been so young and he'd known he didn't have the right.

Over the years, he'd learned to lose himself in his work. When he wanted or needed a woman, there were always plenty to be found. But wanting and not having was new to him.

On this bright, warm, spring morning, he stood on the fringes of the crowd and listened to Patience explain her plan.

"There's a master list posted by the door," she said, pointing to the brightly colored paper with a long list of projects. "Supplies are in the center of the room, on the tarp. Once a project is finished, please cross it out so everyone else will know it's finished."

She'd pulled her long, wavy hair back into a ponytail. Her T-shirt was red with a cartoon cat on the front. She looked about seventeen. All fresh-scrubbed and pretty.

He knew that Lillie was spending the day with friends and that Ava had been having trouble lately. She would be using a wheelchair. He knew the color of paint in the cans and what was on the list, but he was still separate from what was going on. Watching rather than participating.

It was how he preferred things. Only with Patience he was in deeper than was comfortable for him. Still, pulling back didn't seem to be an option.

"Ethan and Nevada have brought tools," Patience continued. "She's in charge of construction. If you're feeling the need to pound a hammer, go see her."

A man groaned. Justice would guess he was Ethan. A tall blond guy punched him in the arm.

"Your sister is in charge, dude. Talk about humiliating."

Ethan turned to his friend. "You notice she didn't mention you having tools, Josh. You want to think about what that means?"

Josh laughed.

"Thank you again for coming," Patience said. "I really appreciate it."

"We're all here for you," someone called.

There were murmurs of agreement; then the crowd broke up and people started to go to work.

A tall, lithe blonde walked over to Justice and stared at him.

"Okay," she said with a sigh. "I give up. I can't remember your name. I'm Evie Stryker. I moved here last year and I'm still figuring out who is who." She held out her hand. "I teach dance, if you have any daughters."

They shook hands.

"No daughters," he said. "I know Patience's daughter, Lillie."

"She's in one of my classes. Sweet girl." Evie looked around the room. "So, that's Dante over there. My fiancé. And those three guys wrestling over who has the biggest paintbrush are my brothers." She shook her head. "Okay, never mind. It's too much. This town. The people are too friendly and they know every little thing about everyone's life. It's crazy. Seriously, you should get out now while you can."

"I don't see you leaving."

"They caught me at a weak moment and now I can't imagine living anywhere else. They suck you in."

"I spent some time here as a kid."

"And you came back, thus proving my point."

"There you are!"

Justice turned and found himself face-to-face with Denise Hendrix. She hugged him, then smiled broadly.

"I'm still so excited you're here, Justice. And that Ford is coming back. Did I invite you over to dinner yet? You have to come as soon as Ford is home. We'll have the whole family over."

"I remember those dinners," he said, thinking those were good memories. "It was loud."

With six kids plus any friends they'd brought home sitting around the table, there had been plenty of conversation. The Hendrix house had been one of the few places he'd been cleared to visit. Patience's house had been on the list, as well. He'd wanted to go as often as possible. Being around other families had allowed him to forget why he was on the run. Around them he could pretend he was just like everyone else.

"We still have a wonderful time," Denise told him. "It's a little more crowded with spouses and grandchildren, but that only makes our times together more wonderful."

He bent down and kissed her cheek. "I can't wait."

"Good."

Denise excused herself.

Justice was about to go join a work group when he saw Ava roll into the busy space. Her wheelchair moved easily over the hardwood floors. He saw her glance around as if unsure what she was supposed to do. He quickly moved toward her.

"Taking charge?" he asked as he approached.

She gave him a grateful smile. "I think Patience is doing a good job already. I just wanted to stop by and see the town coming through for my girl."

"There are plenty of people here."

Patience hurried over. "Hey, Mom. Doing okay?"

"I'm fine."

Patience didn't look convinced. Justice nodded toward Ava. "I'm happy to stay here," he said. "It gets me out of the real work."

Her gaze lingered for a second. "Thank you," she mouthed silently. "Okay," she said aloud. "I'm not even surprised. Typical guy enjoying the act of watching other people work."

He pulled up a chair and settled next to Ava. The older woman's gaze was speculative.

"You want to keep an eye on what's going on and you're using me to do it."

"Maybe," he said easily.

"Not maybe. You're different, Justice. Time has passed, so of course you've grown up, but that's not the only change, is it?"

He automatically stayed outwardly calm, even as he glanced at Ava. "Are you asking or stating an opinion?"

"Both." She studied him. "You went into the military after your father was taken into custody."

He nodded.

"Whatever you did was dangerous. Patience and I have speculated, but I'm sure we won't be able to guess."

"Probably not."

"You've seen things."

More than she could ever know.

"Now you're going to open your school here."

He chuckled. “It’s not a school.”

“You know what I mean.” She leaned toward him. “Can you do it? Settle in a small town?”

“I don’t know,” he admitted. “I want to be here.”

It was an honest answer, he thought. As much as the town drew him, he was concerned about fitting in. He could fake his way through any situation for a period of time. But in the end, who he was would come out.

He’d done things no man should be able to live with. Yet, as Ava had said, here he was. There were questions he couldn’t answer. Like how much of his father lived in him? Could he escape Bart’s cruel influence? Would he end up hurting the people he cared about? He’d never taken the risk. It hadn’t been worth it. He’d always been content to move on. But now he was starting to think he wanted to stay.

“Where does Patience fit in your decision?” Ava asked.

“She’s a draw. I never forgot her.”

“You’re both different people now.”

“She’s not so different.” She was older, more beautiful. But the essence of her remained. The sweetness, the humor, the unique worldview that, in her case, came out through her wardrobe of cute T-shirts.

“What are you afraid of?” Ava asked.

He turned to her. “That I’ll hurt her.”

“Then don’t.”

“It’s not that simple.”

“Sometimes it is.”

PATIENCE STUDIED THE to-do list and felt the last of her stress fade away. Everything was getting done and more quickly than she could have imagined. The cleaning was done and all the plates, mugs and glasses had been unpacked. In the back room, a team worked on her shelves. Nevada kept a tight control on her team, ordering the guys around easily.

Charlie walked over. "The trim is painted. Finn, Simon and Tucker are putting up the curtain rods. Tucker has the professional experience, but Simon brings his surgeon's precision to the experience, so imagine how that's going. Finn's egging them both on because it's fun. I won't bother telling you the trouble the Stryker brothers are getting into, but know that later, they will be punished."

Patience laughed. "I'm not worried. Everyone is working really hard and my list is nearly complete." She hugged Charlie. "I love this town."

"The town loves you back." Charlie turned her head and groaned. "Old ladies at ten o'clock."

Patience followed her gaze and saw that Eddie and Gladys had shown up. No doubt the near octogenarians were hoping to catch sight of good-looking guys in tight jeans. The two were completely shameless. Last year Clay had arranged for some male-model friends to pose for a charity calendar. When Eddie and Gladys had found out, they'd shown up with folding chairs and stayed to watch the show.

Some of the shots had required the guys to get naked, which had delighted the friends. They'd taken pictures with their cell phones. Charlie had been forced to edit out the "frontal" nudity pictures, much to the dismay of Eddie and Gladys.

"I'll go make sure they behave themselves," Patience said.

Charlie put her hand on Patience's arm. "I'll do it. You need to stay focused on the projects. Plus, you're too nice. They at least pretend to be scared of me."

"Thanks."

"What can I say? I'm an amazing friend and you're lucky to have me in your life."

Patience laughed.

She watched Charlie head for the old ladies and saw the two trying to duck away. But Charlie was faster and soon they were corralled. Patience made the rounds, stopping to check on the various projects.

Simon and Tucker were glaring at each other. "It's a thirty-second of an inch off," the surgeon said. "Do you know what that means?"

"Nothing," Tucker told him. "Because it's not off. It's even. Look at the level."

"I'm measuring and that's more accurate than a bubble."

Finn leaned back against the wall, enjoying the show.

"The curtains look great," Patience said. "I love them."

"See?" Tucker said.

"You have to be on a ladder to see the difference," Simon informed him.

"I'm thinking not many of my customers are going

to do that," Patience said; then she smiled and kept moving.

As she circled around the room, she passed by Kent Hendrix and his mother. Denise was staring up at her son.

"Are you sure?" she asked, her voice hopeful.

"It's been long enough," Kent told her. "I want to move on. Lorraine is gone and not coming back. I need to get going with my life. I've wasted enough time on her."

Denise reached for him.

Patience inched away, not wanting to intrude on such a private, family moment.

She knew the basic facts. Kent had been married. He and Lorraine had a son, Reese. Several years ago Lorraine had decided she didn't want to be married, or a mother, so she'd taken off, leaving her husband and her son. Sort of like Ned, Patience thought.

Josh and Ethan came by with two-by-fours over their shoulders, trapping her in place.

"I'm so glad," Denise told her son. "You need to start the next chapter of your life. Are you dating?"

"Mom, let it go. I'll find my own girl."

"But I want to help."

Patience looked around frantically, still pinned in by moving wood. Any second now Denise was going to start searching for a suitable future Mrs. Kent Hendrix, and she didn't want to be the one the other woman saw first. Kent was a great guy, but they'd only ever been friends.

She finally managed to duck under the wood and make her way to the back room. She would hide out until the danger passed, she thought humorously.

Now that she was safe, she could almost pity Kent. Denise was a formidable woman. If she decided she was going to get Kent involved with someone, he was going to find himself with a parade of women moving past his house.

She looked into the main room and saw Justice with her mother. They were speaking intently, heads bent together.

Although she wondered what they were discussing, her real attention was on how much she wanted to walk over and stand next to Justice. To be close and have him smile at her. She knew she was getting too involved, too quickly, and didn't know how to slow things down.

With the business only a week or two from opening, she was frantically busy, yet still found time to dwell on Justice. Maybe it was good that he was going to be gone a few days on an assignment. She could try to forget about him. Or if that wasn't possible, maybe gain a little perspective.

Mayor Marsha walked up to her. "Everything is turning out so beautifully," the mayor said. "Congratulations."

"Thank you." Patience took in the skirted suit the older woman always wore. "No pants, huh? I was hoping." Mayor Marsha had worn pants to a work party over the holidays. It had made quite the impression on everyone.

The mayor smiled. "It was very cold out. I made an exception." Her head tilted. "Hmm, I wonder what that means."

"What?"

The mayor pointed.

Patience turned and saw Charlie pulling her cell phone out of her pocket. She pressed it to her ear, then shook her head.

"Everyone, be quiet for a second, please," Charlie yelled. "This might be important."

The room went silent.

Charlie listened. Everyone around her watched, waiting to hear. Was the news good? Was there a problem?

Charlie grinned. "Okay. I'll spread the word." She lowered her phone. "It's Annabelle. She's in labor!"

CHAPTER NINE

JUSTICE TURNED DOWN the road leading to the ranch. If there was a hot spot in the world, a dangerous place, he'd probably been there. He knew how to get in, get the job done and get out. He'd faced soldiers, assassins and dictators. He knew how to take care of himself. None of which explained why he was going to a ranch to visit a woman he didn't know, who had just given birth to a baby he had no interest in, with a casserole he hadn't made.

"You okay?" Patience asked. She sat in the passenger seat and watched him curiously. "You have a scrunchy face."

"No, I don't."

"I'm the one who can see your face, so I get to say."

Justice surrendered to the inevitable. "I'm trying to figure out how I got here."

"On earth at all, or here with me at this particular moment?"

"The latter."

She flashed him a smile. "You offered to drive me."

"What was I thinking?"

"Oh, come on. It'll be fun. Annabelle had her baby. Now we have to be a part of the celebration."

"Why?"

"It's what we do. We visit the new mother, take over food so she doesn't have to cook. Coo over the baby."

Just one more version of hell, he thought. "I'm not cooing."

"I'll coo for both of us. Besides, the whole town will be there."

"When do you people get work done?"

She laughed. "We do have a lot of community obligations, but it's fun. If you want, I can ask Shane if he'll let you ride one of the horses."

"No, thanks."

He'd returned to Fool's Gold thinking he could find his past. And maybe a piece of who he had been years ago. Instead he'd discovered that this town was possibly the best and the worst place to be. There were good memories here, but also the constant pressure to connect and belong. He was happier on the outside, looking in. But no one was going to allow that. Not for long. They wanted to pull him in and make him a part of things.

He couldn't risk it. Not until he knew if he was safe enough to be around ordinary people. He glanced out the side window and wished he could shake the feeling that his father was out there, watching.

The old man was dead, he reminded himself. Had been for more than a decade—burned alive in a prison fire that had taken several lives. Justice had mostly believed it—only over the past couple of years, he'd had a growing sense Bart was around. Hiding, but close.

More proof that he couldn't escape his DNA, he thought. However much he might want to.

They drove onto the ranch. There was a sign offering goat cheese and milk for sale, along with goat manure. Beyond the main house were stables and corrals. In the distance he saw a couple of sheep, a llama and—

He brought the car to a halt and stared. "Is that—"

Patience followed his gaze. "An elephant? Yes. Her name is Priscilla."

"A real elephant?"

"She's not fake, if that's what you're asking. It's a long story, but she lives here now and everyone likes her. She's a part of the community."

He returned his attention to the drive through the property. "Of course she is."

"We love Priscilla. She was in the nativity last Christmas."

"An elephant?"

"Everyone should get to participate."

He wanted to point out that Priscilla was an elephant, not a person, but knew that Patience would probably object. In her world, elephants could be family and townspeople showed up to work on soon-to-be-opened businesses. No doubt small woodland creatures did the housecleaning, whistling all the while.

He shook his head. "I need a break."

"From what?"

He pulled up in front of a large house. There were

several cars parked in front already. People stood on the porch, chatting.

Patience touched his arm. "Justice, are you okay?"

He turned to her. The sight of her face calmed him. He could stare into her eyes and find equilibrium again. With Patience around, he could handle the eccentricities that were Fool's Gold.

"I'm good."

"If you're sure."

She waited, but he didn't say anything. She turned to the people on the porch.

"Okay, the pregnant woman is Heidi. She's married to Rafe, who's the brother of Shane, who's the father of the baby. Annabelle and Shane aren't married yet. She didn't want to walk down the aisle pregnant. It's kind of funny because Annabelle is sort of traditional, so for her to do this all backward isn't like her. But they're blissfully happy together."

She studied the crowd. "You met everyone else at the work party. Don't worry about remembering names."

"I remember their names."

"You can't. You've only been in town for a few weeks."

He allowed himself a slight smile, then started on the left. "The two blondes are Dakota and Montana. Next to them are Finn and Simon. The older woman is their mother, Denise, and the white-haired lady talking is Mayor Marsha."

"Wow."

He shrugged. "It's part of what I do, but remember, I was friends with Ford way back when."

"If I hadn't been born here, I doubt I would have remembered everyone's name."

"It's a parlor trick."

"A good one."

He wanted to impress her and knew the danger of making her believe in him. He reminded himself he had to make up his mind. Was he willing to risk getting involved with Patience? Did he trust himself that much? Or was it too late to have the conversation? Because he was starting to think he was already in too deep to find his way out.

PATIENCE HELD THE tiny baby in her arms. "Aren't you handsome?" she whispered to the sleeping little boy. "So precious."

Annabelle sat on the padded rocking chair in the baby's room and smiled. "I feel useless. Everyone is helping out so much there's nothing for me to do."

"Oh, you should hold him," Patience said, walking toward her.

Annabelle shook her head. "I wasn't complaining. I was very stressed about having him. I wasn't sure I would know what to do. But it turns out I don't have to worry at all. We're never alone, and I mean that in a good way."

"How's Shane handling fatherhood?"

"He's excited and freaked. It's a fun combination. He kept saying having a child was no big deal. Nature takes care of the details. But he's discovered it's not exactly like having one of his mares drop a foal."

"The power of being smug," Patience said, returning little Wyatt to his mother's arms. She settled in the chair next to Annabelle's and leaned close. "He's adorable."

"I think so." Annabelle grinned. "So, tell me. How many casseroles are there in my freezer?"

"At last count there were thirty-two, but more are coming. Oh, and there's a beautiful fruit arrangement in your refrigerator. Very upscale. There are cookies and brownies and I'm not sure what else."

Annabelle leaned back in the rocker. "I love this town. I'm never leaving."

"No one wants you to." Patience gave her a quick hug, then stood. "I need to head back. I'll call you in a couple of days to see how it's going. By then you should be less busy here."

"Thanks for coming by."

"I wouldn't have missed it."

She returned to the front part of the house and found Justice talking to Clay Stryker. When Justice saw her, he excused himself and joined her.

"You ready to go?"

She smiled. "Are you done pretending to be excited about the baby? Did you want to hold him?"

He flinched. "No."

"Not a kid person."

"I like kids. Babies make me nervous."

"So you're ready to go?" she asked, amused by his infant phobia.

"Say the word."

They walked out of the house and made their way to his car.

"What about you?" he asked as he held open the passenger door. "Did you hold the baby?"

"Of course. He's wonderful. So tiny. I remember when Lillie was first born. I was so scared."

He closed the door and walked around to the driver's side.

"You had your mom," he said as he slid onto the seat.

"And Ned," she added. "Although by then, things were already falling apart. He left shortly after. But even with half the town in my living room, I was still terrified. I was too young to be a mother. I had no idea what I was doing. But from the first second I saw her, I loved her so much."

She glanced at him. "Do you remember your mom?"

"Some. She was always hugging me." His mouth twisted. "As I started getting older, I would squirm away. Now I wish I hadn't resisted so much."

"It's part of growing up," she said quietly. "She didn't blame you."

"You can't know that."

"Sure I can. I have a daughter. Kids grow and separate. One day Lillie will roll her eyes at me. It doesn't mean we aren't close."

"I think my father killed her."

Patience stared at him. "What? How?"

"She died in a car accident. The brake line was cut. They said in the report it was inconclusive, but when I was a little older I went to the junkyard, found the car and saw the line myself. He did it."

She saw his hands tighten on the steering wheel as they drove toward town.

"Justice, I'm so sorry."

She tried to think of something else to say, but couldn't. Was it possible he was right? That Justice's father murdered his wife? Her worldview made the concept inconceivable, but the truth was hard to deny. Justice had been in the witness protection program because his father had broken out of prison and come after his own son. The U.S. Marshals didn't take care of someone on a whim. There was a real reason. Bart had been put away for killing a man. Sadly, that made the concept of him murdering his own wife much more real.

"Once she was gone, I was biding my time until I could leave," he continued. "Trying to stay out of the old man's way. I was big enough that he didn't try to beat me very often, but that didn't make him any less dangerous."

"Then you came here."

He nodded. "It was like an alternative universe."

"I must have seemed really foolish to you."

"No. Never that. You were an anchor. You showed me what was possible. I knew I didn't want to be like him and that I'd have to always be on guard."

"You're nothing like him."

He glanced at her. "You don't know me. You don't know what I've done."

"I might not know the details, but there are plenty of clues. Look at you. You just came with me to deliver a casserole to a formerly pregnant woman you've never met. Tomorrow you're going with me while Lillie has her first meeting with her grandfather. You've worked in the store. You care about my mother. How can you worry you're anything like your father?" She knew she had to lighten the mood.

"Is this a *Star Wars* thing? Do all boys pretend to be Luke Skywalker?"

He chuckled. "No, and my father isn't Darth Vader."

"It kind of sounds like he is."

"There was no good in him."

"There's good in you."

"I hope you're right."

PATIENCE FELT HER stomach turning over and over. "I brought a Q-tip," she whispered to Justice as they walked toward the park. "In case, you know, Steve gets out of hand."

Justice put his arm around her shoulders. "I can subdue him without a weapon," he assured her. "Keep the Q-tip for your own protection."

"But I don't know how to use one that way."

Lillie looked at her. "Mom, are you really talking about Q-tips?"

"Yes, and it's weird. I accept that."

"Is it because you don't know what to say to my grandfather?"

"Mostly." Patience stopped and dropped to one knee. She faced her daughter. "Are you okay with this?"

She and Lillie had talked several times about Steve wanting to meet her. Lillie had been accepting from the beginning and hadn't asked many questions. That worried Patience. Had Lillie disconnected from the thought of more family? Or was she simply a normal kid who took things as they came?

"I'm fine," Lillie said. "Mom, it's okay to have more family."

"I know." Patience had continued to tell herself that Steve was simply some old guy who wanted to get to know his granddaughter. That was hardly newsworthy. But she couldn't shake the sense of impending disaster.

Patience stood. Lillie took her hand. "Don't be scared, Mom. Justice and I will be right here with you."

"Aren't *I* supposed to be comforting *you?*" Patience asked.

Lillie grinned. "I'm very mature for my age."

"Yes, you are."

Lillie took Justice's hand as well and walked between them.

The park was close and they reached it a few minutes later. Steve was waiting where they'd arranged, on a bench by the duck pond. Lillie's grip tightened as they approached, and when they were within speaking range, Steve rose and the three of them came to a halt.

Patience saw that he was exactly what she'd been telling herself for days. A man in his sixties who looked nervous and tentative. Not a monster. Just an ordinary man who had made awful choices and was now paying for them.

"Hello, Lillie," Steve said quietly. "Thank you for agreeing to meet me today."

Lillie studied him. "I've seen you before. In town."

Steve's eyes widened. "I've been living around here for a while."

"Okay." Lillie pulled her hands free and walked toward Steve. "You know my dad, don't you?"

"Yes."

"Do you ever see him?"

"I don't. We haven't spoken in many years."

"I don't see him, either." Lillie looked at the lake. "We usually feed the ducks."

"Your mom mentioned that. I brought bread."

They collected the bag from the bench and walked down to the water. Patience followed, close enough to hear what was going on, but far enough away to give them the illusion of privacy. Justice stayed with her.

"Thoughts?" she asked. "Is it going okay? Is your Spidey sense tingling?"

"I'm tingle free."

She sighed. "You must think I'm a freakish worrier."

"No. I think you're a concerned mom who doesn't want to trust her kid with a man she barely knows. You're right to be wary. Steve checked out, but he's also the man who left his family. Sure, people change, but he has to prove that to you."

He had a point, she thought, still worried, but now less so. Of course, she had planned to keep her daughter safe from Justice, and that hadn't happened. He'd been so supportive and kind that she'd just plain forgotten.

The fact that he was buying a warehouse and starting a business in town implied he was sticking around. So it wasn't as if he would simply disappear from her daughter's life. She sighed. Was that her being rational or rationalizing? She wished she knew.

She continued to watch her daughter. Lillie was talking about her teacher and her friends at school. Steve listened with what looked like genuine interest.

Patience stepped closer to Justice. "You've been great. I'm sorry if I've been claiming too much of your time. You moved here to start a business and ended up getting sucked into my crazy world. I have to say, usually my life is really calm. Even boring. But the last few weeks have been wild."

"I like your crazy world. It's delightfully normal."

She laughed. "You're not the kind of guy who says *delightfully*."

"I do now. Fool's Gold is changing me."

She wondered if that was true. "In your bodyguard job, do you hang out with other military types?"

"Mostly."

"So being here means you don't know quite what to do with us civilians."

“You’re not as different as you think. Besides, most of my clients are civilians.”

“How disappointing. I was picturing you with ousted dictators who have a price on their heads.”

“Not this week. It’s mostly successful men with a price on their heads.”

She wasn’t sure if he was teasing or telling the truth. She had a feeling it was the latter, which wasn’t the least bit comforting.

“You have that assignment coming up,” she said. “You promise you’ll be safe?”

“Yes.” His dark blue gaze locked with hers. “I will be safe and I will be here for the opening. You have my word.”

“You’re very sexy when you make promises.”

She spoke without thinking, then wanted to call the words back. A quick glance at Lillie and Steve showed her they were deep in their own conversation, which was a relief, but Justice had still heard.

“Sexy?”

She cleared her throat. “You know. Um, well…” She waved her hand. “Oh, look. Ducks. We should feed them.”

She started to walk toward the water, but Justice grabbed her hand and held her in place.

Tension spiraled between them, making her want to step closer. He got to her, and she couldn’t figure out a way to mind.

“Don’t act all surprised,” she told him, her voice

low. "You know what you are. Dangerous. Powerful. Plus, the kissing was nice."

One eyebrow rose. "Just nice. Not great? Not spectacular?"

"I've had better," she said with a sniff.

He drew her close. "Now you're lying," he said with a growl.

She smiled. "Maybe a little."

She glanced at her daughter and saw both Lillie and Steve watching them. She took a quick step back.

"So. Ducks. How are they doing?" she asked.

Lillie gave her a "sometimes you're really strange" look. "They're fine, Mom. They like the bread."

"Then it's good your grandfather brought some."

Justice stepped behind her. "That's the best you can do?" he asked in a whisper. "You'd never make it undercover."

"Fine. Be critical, but I'd like to see you try to cut hair, mister."

CHAPTER TEN

PATIENCE WANDERED AROUND the main showroom of Paper Moon Wedding Gowns. Big windows opened up onto the small square of "exclusive shops" in the center of Fool's Gold. Across the courtyard were the brightly colored windows for da bump Maternity. A humorous connection for those who weren't getting married or pregnant.

Inside the shop, several wedding dresses were on display, with more racks of them available for browsing. There was a second, smaller room devoted to bridesmaids' dresses and gowns for the mother of the bride.

"I swear, this place hasn't changed at all," Patience said, touching the sleeve of a beautiful, traditional white gown.

Isabel wrinkled her nose. "That would be part of the problem. We're well into a new century. The store should reflect that. The stock is current. My mom paid attention to trends, but the rest of the place is very 1999."

"You're going to change that?"

"As much as possible. I have a budget and some

ideas. If we're going to sell, we might as well get as much as we can for the place. That means making it fresh."

Paper Moon had always been a part of the community. Patience remembered friends with older sisters coming in to be fitted for junior bridesmaids' dresses. Before the samples went on sale, the teenaged girls were allowed to come in and play "bride for a day," trying on different dresses and wondering what it would be like on that far-off special day.

"I bought my wedding dress here," Patience admitted. "From the sale rack, which turned out to be a good thing. It wasn't like the marriage lasted."

"I'm sorry," Isabel said. "That must have been difficult. And you had Lillie, too."

"She was who got me through. Her and my mom. They were both what kept me going." Patience looked at her friend. "How are you doing with all the changes?"

Isabel shrugged. "I don't know. Some days are easy, some are hard. Come on back to the office. I'll buy you a soda."

They walked through the dressing-room area. There were two fitting rooms large enough to accommodate the fullest of skirts. Each had several chairs for the various family members who might be in on the decision. Smaller fitting rooms, still huge by normal standards, lined the back wall. In the middle of the space were a five-way mirror and a low platform where the bride-to-be could show off.

Isabel walked past all of it and entered a door

marked Private. Behind that was an office with several desks, a table and chairs, computers, stacks of fabric samples and a small refrigerator.

"Diet okay?" she asked as she pulled open the door.

"My favorite."

She removed two cans, then motioned to the chairs by the table.

"This is the store that time forgot," Isabel said as she popped the top on her drink and took a sip. "When I first saw it, I felt like I'd been whipped back in time ten years. I knew my parents had lost their enthusiasm for the place, but the lack of changes was surprising."

"You're not tempted to just take it over and fix it up how you'd like it?"

Isabel shook her head. "No, thanks. I have plans and they don't include sticking around here. I know you love it, but I would go crazy here."

"In the store or in town?"

"The store for sure. I couldn't deal with the brides for the rest of my life. I want to do something more. It's not the retail I mind. As I mentioned before, I have plans with a friend to open a store in New York. High-fashion designs. Very upscale."

"That's still retail, my friend."

Isabel smiled. "New York retail."

"So you're really going back?"

"Uh-huh."

Patience wondered what it would be like to live somewhere else. She'd never not known her neighbors or the people in her town. She understood the rhythms of life—with seasons marked by festivals as well as the changes in weather.

"I suppose New York is exciting," she said slowly.

Isabel laughed. "You're are such a country mouse, and I say that with love. I can't see you living anywhere else."

"Me, either. Isn't it hard to make friends and figure out where everything is?"

"Yes, but that's what makes it exciting. The city is big and loud and crazy and I enjoy that." She took another sip of her soda. "But I'll admit, it's nice to be here, even for a few months."

"Getting away from what happened?"

Isabel's blue eyes darkened with a flash of pain. "Eric and I are still friends, but I don't care how friendly a divorce is. It's not something easy to go through."

"Have you talked to him much?"

"A few times. I'm not sure what to say." She looked at Patience. "I'm actually not surprised we split up, and yet I'm completely shocked. I don't know if that makes sense."

Patience suspected in her heart she'd known something was wrong. But living a divorce was completely different from guessing there was a problem in the relationship.

"You're still healing," Patience said. "The cliché about time happens to be true. After Ned left, I didn't think I would ever recover. But I did. Now I can't imagine what it was I saw in him."

"I'll get there, too," Isabel said. "At least I hope so. It's just some days I feel so pathetic. When some excited, bright-eyed bride-to-be walks in the store, I can't help wondering if she'll still be married to the guy in twenty years or if she'll be a statistic, too." She sighed. "Okay, I've officially become the depressing friend. I don't want that."

"You're still healing. Give yourself a break."

Isabel managed a smile. "What? You're saying beating myself up isn't the quickest way to a happier tomorrow?"

"Not even close. You've temporarily left New York. Take advantage of that. Lose yourself in the quaint, small-town gooeyness that is Fool's Gold. Go to a festival. Gain five pounds from eating locally made goat cheese. Seduce a handsome tourist."

"Not sure I'm up to that last suggestion, but the others sound fun."

Patience drank some of her soda. "You're not ready for transition guy?"

"Not even close." Isabel studied her. "I can't see you having one, either. Not with a child to worry about."

Patience was too embarrassed to admit there hadn't been a man in her life since Ned left. "No transitional man for me, either. I was busy with Lillie, and now it's been too long. But I do like the theory." She grinned. "Ford is coming home any day now. What about him? You had a huge crush on him years ago. Maybe he's still gorgeous and sexy."

Isabel's expression brightened. "If only that were

true. You promised he wouldn't be." She sighed, obviously remembering. "I was so insanely in love with him."

"The love of a fourteen-year-old girl is very special."

Isabel laughed. "I hope he saw it that way rather than as something he had to escape." Her smile turned rueful. "Of course, my sister had just dumped him, so I doubt he had much time to think about my feelings. He was too busy wrestling with his own."

Patience had been only a couple of years older than Isabel, but even she remembered the scandal. Ford had been engaged to Maeve, Isabel's older and very beautiful sister. Only a few weeks before the wedding, he'd caught Maeve in bed with his best friend, Leonard. Words and possibly blows had been exchanged. Maeve had been apologetic, but refused to give up Leonard. The engagement had been broken and Ford had left town. He'd joined the navy, had become a SEAL and until recently had pretty much never returned.

There had been the one or two weekends when he'd been spotted around town, but mostly he'd seen his family in other places. Patience wasn't sure if that was a logistical choice or if he'd been avoiding Maeve. Either way, after close to fourteen years, he was coming home now.

"Maybe he kept all your letters," Patience said, her voice teasing. "Read them when things were tough."

Isabel laughed. "Sure he did. Because hearing about my life was so special. I just hope I edited myself and didn't dump on him, emotionally. High school is never pretty, and I don't think telling him about my experiences would have been very entertaining."

Patience leaned toward her and lowered her voice. "Or they could have been *extremely* entertaining."

Isabel winced. "Oh God. You're right. I remember going to a prom with a guy named Warren. There was no happy ending." She picked up her soda. "I'm sure I didn't mention that."

"You could get on the welcome committee," Patience told her. "Be one of the first to greet him."

"There's a welcome committee?"

"Not that I've heard of, but who knows what this town will do? Ford is a returning hero."

"He's going to hate hearing that over and over again."

"You could comfort him."

Isabel sighed. "Stop trying to throw us together. The man isn't even home yet."

"I'm a romantic. I can't help it. One of us has to have a summer romance."

"I'm fresh off a divorce. Any romance is up to you. What about that guy? Justice?"

Patience cleared her throat. "I have no idea what you're talking about."

Isabel raised her eyebrows. "Uh-huh. You're blushing."

Patience ducked her head. "I am not." But she was. She could feel the heat on her cheeks. "I like him," she admitted. "But it's confusing. Exciting, but confusing."

"Good luck with that. I'm the last person you should come to for advice. I still have a tan line from my wedding ring."

Patience sighed. "I really am sorry about that."

"Me, too. But I'll move on."

"OKAY, so here's the counter, obviously. And this is where the magic will happen." Patience ran her hands over the large espresso machine. It was big and shiny and the most perfect thing she'd ever seen. At least in the mechanical world. Lillie was the most perfect in the life-form department.

"I know all the specs by heart," she continued. "Want me to tell you how many cups per hour and the amount of milk we'll go through making lattes?"

Justice leaned against the counter and smiled at her. "If it's important to you."

"It is but I won't torture you. Not when you've said you'll help me."

There were the last, most recent boxes of mugs and plates to be unpacked. As the dishwasher wasn't coming in until next week, they would also have to be stacked neatly next to the others in preparation for their professional sanitizing.

She turned toward the space that would be filled by a very large dishwasher and sighed. "Held up by a shipping glitch," she said. "Mom and I decided that since we hadn't picked an actual date for the opening, we're going to delay it three days. That way the dishwasher will be installed and we'll have more time to train the staff."

She drew in a breath and pressed her hands together. "There's going to be staff. Actual employees. And we have our food on order and the coffee is here. We'll have intermittent times when we're open for about a week, then the real thing."

She turned to him. "You said you could make it. Is that still true?"

"Yes. My trip's been cut back—I'll only be gone a couple of days."

"To the dangerous place you can't name."

His blue eyes brightened with amusement. "That's the one."

"You could give me a hint. Is it an island or a continent?"

"There's a big size difference there. It's a continent."

"But not this one."

"No."

She tilted her head. "You're really not going to tell me, are you?"

"I'm not."

"Fine. Be that way. I still owe you. You've helped so much. So when you're ready to unpack your bullets or whatever for CDS, I'll be there for you."

"No bullets."

"I thought you were going to have a shooting range."

"Okay, some bullets."

She beamed. "See. I can be helpful."

It was a beautiful spring afternoon, with sunlight

spilling in through the freshly washed windows. Crisp curtains fluttered in the breeze or would if the windows were open. Right now they were closed and the front door was locked. Patience had learned if she didn't keep the place locked, people tended to wander in and ask when she would open. While she appreciated the interest, every conversation took time, which meant she was always running behind on her work schedule.

She looked at the tables and chairs, the humming cold case and the shiny floor. There was coffee for sale on the shelves, along with various coffee supplies. The last delivery of mugs, glasses and plates had come in. She'd hired some help, been instructed on using all the equipment and once the dishwasher made its debut, she would be ready to open the doors to her new business.

"I can't believe it," she admitted. "This is really happening. Did you see the sign?"

"I saw the sign."

She clasped her hands together in front of her waist. "I love it so much."

The logo she and her mother had chosen was a yellow oval with a red coffee cup in the middle. Adorable hearts graced the cup. "We're going to have T-shirts and aprons with the design," she added.

"You mentioned that."

She looked at him. "Is that your polite way of saying I'm getting boring?"

"You could never be boring."

She frowned. There was something about the way

he was looking at her. An intensity. She couldn't figure out what he was thinking, but something was wrong.

She crossed to him. "Justice, what is it?"

"Nothing. We should start unpacking your mugs."

She put her hand on his chest, as much to feel the rock-hard muscles as to hold him in place. "Am I keeping you from something?"

He took a step back and shoved his hands in his pockets. "No. But you're on a schedule."

He wasn't making sense. "I don't understand. What's going on?"

His expression sharpened. He looked away, then back at her. He muttered something under his breath, then moved so quickly he was a blur. One second he was putting distance between them; the next he was hauling her against him and pressing his mouth to hers.

The kiss shocked her, but only for a second. Then she leaned into him, wanting to take all he offered. He moved his tongue against hers, igniting sparks and inspiring need. His hands moved from her waist to her back, then lower, cupping her rear. She grabbed hold of his shoulders, feeling the power in his arms. From there it was an easy journey to his chiseled chest.

"Patience," he breathed against her mouth before kissing his way along her jawline to that sensitive spot below her ear. He nipped on the lobe before drifting lower.

His tongue teased even as he grated lightly with his teeth. Shivers rippled through her. He went down and down, across her collarbone to the neckline of her T-shirt. After dipping his tongue into the valley between her breasts, he made the return journey up the other side.

With each brush, each nibble, she found it difficult to breathe. Her skin was sensitized, her body exquisitely poised for the next erotic assault. Her breasts ached and she knew her nipples had tightened into anxious points. Between her thighs she was already wet.

Her head dropped back, giving him more access. When he shifted his hands to her breasts, she closed her eyes to avoid the distraction of looking instead of feeling.

As his thumbs and forefingers closed over her nipples, his mouth settled on hers. He pushed his tongue inside and stroked her in rhythm with the magic he worked on her breasts. The combination had her straining toward him. Liquid heat pooled in her center and she knew she was seconds away from begging him to never stop.

He dropped his hands to her waist and drew her against him. She went willingly, needing the contact. His erection was hard against her belly and she pressed into him, happy to know she wasn't the only one enjoying their game.

Only Justice wasn't playing. He cupped her face in his hands and stared into her eyes.

"I want you," he breathed.

Words designed to thrill, she thought, as a shiver raced through her.

"I want you, too," she murmured before she could

think if that was wise or not. And then more truth tumbled out. "But I'm not on any birth control, and it's not like I came prepared."

She hated to be practical. In a perfect world they would both suddenly be naked, maybe on a private beach somewhere or on a bed in the forest. They would make love with no awkward bits or consequences. Only life wasn't that tidy.

He held her gaze for a handful of heartbeats, then reached into his pocket and pulled out a condom.

"Oh." She blinked. "Either you're a careful planner or we have to talk about your lifestyle." Because being with a man who always hoped to get lucky wasn't her idea of a good time.

"I've been a careful planner since my second week in town. And only around you," he added. "It wasn't an assumption. It was wishful thinking." He touched her cheek. "About you, Patience. No one else."

She felt any stern resolve melt away. "You mean you don't have a thing for Mayor Marsha?"

"Sorry, no."

"I'm not sure that's something you need to apologize for," she said, leaning into him.

He pulled her against him and lowered his head. Their mouths brushed once, twice, before he settled in for a good long kiss. She wrapped her arms around him and gave herself over to the sensation of being seduced by him.

His mouth was gentle yet determined. He claimed her with an intensity that left her breathless. Just when she was wishing he would start touching her in other places, he began easing her backward, toward the storeroom.

Not a bad idea, she thought, realizing the main part of the store had windows that faced one of Fool's Gold's primary streets. Perhaps getting naked in front of traffic and pedestrians wasn't the best plan.

She pulled back as she realized doing "it" surrounded by boxes and packing crates wasn't, either.

"There's no real place," she began as she stepped away from him and moved toward the doorway. "It's not like I keep a pile of blankets around or a cot. We don't even have stairs. I've seen people have sex on stairs in the movies. It looks really uncomfortable. Besides, I'm not very bendy and I haven't done it in a while…"

Her voice trailed off as she realized he was simply watching her.

She swallowed. "I'm just saying it's been a long time and I might not be very good."

The last confession was delivered in a whisper.

"About done?" he asked.

She nodded.

"Have you changed your mind or are you nervous?"

She licked her lips. "You know. That second one."

Something flashed in his blue eyes; then he crossed to her and pulled off her T-shirt. Just like that. Without asking. There they were in a small back room with shelves and boxes and a big hole where the dishwasher was going to go, and he was taking off her clothes.

"I remember the first time I met you," he said, turning her so that she stood with her back to him. He picked up her hair and shifted it over one shoulder, then lightly kissed the back of her neck.

"You were fourteen and I was eighteen and scared as hell. But then you walked into history, sat next to me, smiled and introduced yourself. That was it. One smile and I was hooked."

The warm heat of his mouth made her break out in goose bumps. "You were?"

"Uh-huh. Being around you made me feel I wasn't on the run. I could pretend I was just like everyone else."

She started to turn to face him, but he wouldn't let her. Instead he held her in place, her back to his front, her butt nestling against his erection. He settled his hands on her belly, his fingers splayed. She watched as he moved them around in a slow circle.

"I wanted to kiss you," he admitted, doing just that on her neck. "I wanted to hold you and touch you." He hesitated. "Let's just say there was more to the fantasy."

"I'm scandalized," she murmured, a smile in her voice.

"I knew I was too old for you and the wrong guy, but I couldn't help myself."

He slid his hands up to her breasts and cupped them, as he had before. The difference was now she could see what he was doing. She could watch him move his fingers against her bra, focusing on her tight nipples, and at the same time, she could feel the electric jolt that surged through her.

"Even after I left, I thought about you," he continued. "All the time. I never forgot you."

His hands moved against her breasts, exploring them, his fingers returning again and again to her nipples. With each stroke, she found it more difficult to breathe. Maybe it was her, but the room seemed to be getting a little warmer. And wouldn't this all be better if there weren't so many layers of clothing between her and what he was doing?

"I want to just..." She reached between them and unfastened her bra.

He pushed it away and paused for a moment. She knew he was looking over her shoulder, staring at her. She wasn't huge, but figured he'd guessed that already. If he was expecting big boobs, he wouldn't have started this in the first place.

He returned his hands to her breasts, his tan skin a contrast to her pale flesh. He inched his thumbs closer to her nipples. As she watched, she saw the puckered flesh almost strain toward him, as if seeking his—

He swore and spun her, then bent down to capture her nipple in his mouth. He sucked hard, pulling her in deep. She hung on to him, as wanting surged through her, making her knees weak.

He shifted to the other breast and repeated his actions, this time adding his tongue to the mix. She let her head fall back as she grew more aroused by the second.

Back and forth, back and forth. She touched his head, wanting to feel his cool, soft hair. Wanting to hold him in place.

As he continued to minister to her breasts, he reached for her waistband. As he undid the button, she shifted so she could put her toe to her heel and slide out of her athletic shoes. She took care of her other foot just as he slid down the zipper. Then Justice pushed her jeans down to just past her hips. Her tiny panties went along for the ride and she seemed to be helping and before she knew what was happening, she was stepping out of the last of her clothes.

She had just enough time to register the fact that she was standing there, naked in her storeroom, when he slid a hand between her legs. Even as one finger slipped inside her wet, swollen body, his thumb found her core and circled it.

She gasped as her world reduced itself to the man holding her and the sensations he could produce. She was all hunger and need, desperate to have more of what he offered. She couldn't think, could barely breathe. She parted her legs and surrendered to the pleasure pouring through her.

Another circle, another tease. He moved his finger in and out, making her push toward the contact and wish there was more. The soles of her feet burned. Her body trembled. If he hadn't kept an arm around her waist, she would have fallen.

She was sure he planned some long, fancy seduction, but she had been without for what felt like six lifetimes. Or maybe it was just being with Justice, knowing she trusted him with the very heart of her. Either way, she couldn't hold back. Couldn't do anything but feel the steady strokes over and over, the growing tension.

She whispered his name even as she moved her hips in time with his hand. Tension grew as she pushed toward her release. Pushed and strained and then she was coming and shuddering and hanging on as if she would never stop.

He stayed with her, holding her steady, touching her, plunging in and out. She cried out as the pleasure filled her, then overflowed.

But it wasn't enough, she thought frantically. Even as the shudders faded, she still wanted more. She turned to him and fumbled with his belt. Fortunately, the man wasn't an idiot. He pulled out the condom, then helped her with his jeans. After shoving them down, he put on the condom and reached for her.

"How are we going to do this?" she asked, looking around for a table or a—

He wrapped his arms around her waist and raised her off the floor. She barely had time to scream before he lowered her onto him, filling her until she knew she was going to die from the wonder of it. He eased them both against the wall, bracing her, then withdrew and filled her again.

Instinctively, she wrapped her legs around his hips. The movement brought her core right against him so that every stroke, every push, aroused her even more.

Later she would figure out how strong he had to be to support her like that. Later she would think about mechanics and physics, but right now all she cared about was him thrusting into her. Hard and fast, as if he could do it forever.

She wanted to watch him, to sense him getting closer. Only what he was doing felt too good. He was hitting something deep inside, some place filled with sensation and pleasure. She worked with him, pushing down as he pushed up, straining to get closer, wanting, wanting…

"Patience."

Her name came out with a guttural cry. She felt the tension in him and knew he was close. His gaze locked with hers as he struggled to hold back.

She was close, too, on the edge of her release. But not yet there. Not yet ready. She needed…

"Come for me."

Apparently she needed for him to ask, she thought as she arched against him and shuddered. Her orgasm ripped through her, making her hang on as she flexed and writhed and pulled his release from him. They drove toward each other, calling out, their contractions matching and growing before easing into complete satisfaction.

When she was conscious again, she felt the trembling in his arms and suspected it had nothing to do with sex and everything to do with exhaustion.

"Put me down," she told him.

"I'm not going to drop you."

She smiled. "Let's not test that theory."

He lowered her to the floor, but didn't release her. Instead he held her close. She felt his heart pounding in his chest. They were both sweaty and breathing hard and she never wanted to let go.

"Amazing," she breathed, then wondered if she should have been slightly more restrained.

He chuckled. "I agree. If this is you with no practice, I'm going to have to be careful. In another couple of weeks, you'll be so good you'll kill me."

"I promise not to let things get that far."

He straightened and kissed her. "I'm willing to risk it."

When they parted, she had a moment to realize that while she was completely naked, he was nearly fully dressed. But while the clothes-gathering could have been awkward, it wasn't. Justice steadied her while she slipped into her panties and insisted on doing up her bra himself. That led to him making sure it fit right and checking out whether or not he could squeeze his hand between her breast and the cup, which led to more kissing, so it was a while until she was clothed again.

When they finally returned to the main room, she was feeling relaxed and smug. She wanted to think she'd just forgotten how good sex could be but had a feeling making love with Justice was in a special category. Which meant she was unlikely to duplicate the experience with anyone else.

Nerves surfaced, but before she could squash them, someone knocked on the locked front door of the store.

Patience crossed to open it. She didn't recognize the woman standing there and wondered if she was a lost tourist.

"Can I help you?" she asked, taking in the other woman's long, wavy hair and warm smile. Her irises were cat's-eye green. She was tall and lean, but with a hint of perfect curves under her tailored black pantsuit.

She looked so happy to be there, Patience couldn't help smiling back. Only to realize the happiness wasn't aimed at her.

"Justice!"

The tall, elegant woman brushed past Patience and launched herself at Justice. Just as horrible, he caught her in his arms and swung her around.

"You made it," he exclaimed.

"Of course. I couldn't let you be here all by yourself."

"Why doesn't that surprise me?"

All the pleasure Patience had just experienced bled away, leaving her with the sense of having been played for a fool.

CHAPTER ELEVEN

PATIENCE STOOD THERE, watching the happy couple. Shock didn't describe the combination of dismay and mortification burning through her. Not three minutes ago, she had been naked and making love with Justice. Now he was hanging on to some other woman? The chasm of the years he'd been gone had never stretched so far between them. She wanted to run but couldn't make herself move. Then she remembered this was her store and her town. Even if Justice wasn't her man.

Justice and the woman hugged again, laughing happily. Patience glanced around, idly wondering if there was anything she could throw at them. China. A bucket of water. She wasn't feeling particularly picky.

Justice finally looked up and saw her. Amazingly, there wasn't any guilt in his expression. Just contentment.

Sure, she thought bitterly. Why not? Talk about having his cake and all that.

"Patience, let me introduce my business associate Felicia Swift. Felicia, this is Patience. The girl I knew when I lived here."

The tall, elegant beauty moved toward Patience,

her intentions obvious. They were going to greet each other politely. Because that's what civilized people did.

"I'm so happy to finally meet you," Felicia said with a brilliant smile. "Justice told me a little about your past together." She gave him a wry look. "Not that he talks about his personal life very much at all, right?"

"Right," Patience said. "He's very secretive. Not necessarily a good quality in a man. In fact, it can be annoying."

Justice looked at her, his brows pulling together.

She wanted to stomp her foot. Seriously? He was going to pretend to be confused?

Felicia laughed. It was a low, throaty, sexy sound that made Patience hate her instantly. Not that she'd especially liked her before.

The other woman patted Justice's arm. "And for the record, I'm not your associate. Not anymore."

Justice kept his gaze on Patience. "That's right. Felicia is going to help us set up the business, but then we're on our own."

"How sad," Patience murmured.

"It is. She's a logistical expert." He turned back to the stunning redhead. "You've saved my ass more than once."

"Just doing my job." She smiled at Patience. "As I'm sure he's already told you, I worked with Justice when he was in the military. Then we both went to work for the private security company. Now we're here."

"How very special."

Patience pressed her hand against her stomach. It

was writhing again, but this time for very different reasons. She'd never experienced jealousy before. Not like this. When Ned had announced he was leaving, she'd been stunned and upset, but not jealous. Her pain had mostly been for her daughter—losing her father before she'd even gotten to know him.

It was her ability to let go that had convinced her she hadn't loved Ned at all. Theirs had been a marriage of convenience, brought on by her pregnancy.

This time was different. This time the jealousy burned hot and bright. The need to throw or possibly destroy was still there. Reminding herself this was her store and any damage would be hers to fix helped keep her in check. As did her basic grasp of normal behavior. But she was furious and devastated. Crying and screaming seemed equally likely outcomes.

She felt her control slipping and knew she had to get away from the happy couple. Or at the very least, get them to leave so she could throw up in private.

"You two probably want to catch up," she said with what she hoped was a smile. "Don't let me keep you."

Not her most subtle moment, she thought. But she wasn't in a position to be picky.

"Are you all right?" Justice asked.

"Peachy."

His frown deepened.

Not knowing what else to do, she walked over to the front door and held it open. "You should show Felicia around town. Fool's Gold is really lovely this time of year."

"I've seen some of the town," Felicia said happily. "It's charming."

"Isn't it?" Patience motioned to the exit. "And it's waiting for you to go explore. Bye-bye."

Justice hesitated for a second, then walked out. Felicia paused to smile at Patience.

"It was wonderful to meet you. I look forward to spending more time together."

"I can't wait," Patience lied, then slammed the door shut behind them.

Silence was everywhere. Silence and pain and the sense of having been a complete idiot.

The facts were really simple. Justice had lied when he'd moved to Fool's Gold all those years ago, and he was lying now. Okay, *withholding* was more accurate, but so what? In the end, he hadn't told her the truth. Not about who he was or why he was around.

A case could be made that while he was in the witness protection program, he couldn't be honest. But since then? He'd never called, never come to see her. That was a really big clue about his character.

She drew in a breath and paced the length of the store. Okay, she could figure this out. She'd had sex. She'd been smart and insisted on protection, so she wasn't pregnant. Basically a man she found attractive had given her fantastic orgasms. Yes, he was also a complete dirtbag, cheater, liar, skunk-dog. So based on this new clarification of his character, her choices were really simple. Keep pining for said skunk-dog or find a functioning brain cell and move on.

Which would be easier said than done, she thought grimly. But she was tough. Or if she wasn't, she would be by the time she was over him. And over him she would get. She'd already been to this dance with Ned, and there was no way she was going back.

JUSTICE STOOD ON the sidewalk with Felicia. "Where do you want to start? A tour of the town? Or would you rather go to your hotel?"

"I've already been to the hotel," she told him. "I went there first."

"You found it."

She rolled her eyes at him. "Yes, I was able to manage the drive here all by myself and then locate a hotel. My ability to navigate public roads has never been called into question before."

He laughed, then pulled her in for a hug. "It's really good to see you."

She sighed. "It's nice to be missed."

He released her and they started walking down the sidewalk. "Knowing you, it would be silly of me to tell you anything about the town's history."

"Of course. While scholars disagree on the original settlers, the first documented residents were the Máa-zib tribe, a matriarchal society. In the 1300s, the women migrated north, seeking a life away from their Mayan roots."

Felicia kept talking, but Justice tuned her out easily. A habit born of practice, he thought contentedly. Felicia was one of the smartest people in the world. But with brilliance came a need to share what she knew, and that could get old.

On the bright side, she had one of the best minds for logistics he'd ever seen. She'd joined his special forces unit as a support member. Give her a time and place and Felicia could get anything, anywhere in the world. She would anticipate delays and plan for the unexpected. She was so good that when they had joint task force operations with other branches of the military, she was the one who ran the logistics.

She was also socially awkward and a little bossy, but he could put up with that. If Patience was the girl he left behind, Felicia was his family. They'd been close nearly from the first day they'd met. His favorite sister, he thought. They knew and understood each other.

They walked past City Hall and turned left.

"Where are you taking me?" she asked, breaking off her lecture on the history of the town.

"To Starbucks. You need a mocha. You're always in a better mood after you've had chocolate."

"I'm in a good mood now."

Some guy walking in the other direction glanced at her and did a double take. Justice sighed. "Why'd you have to go and have that surgery? You were fine before."

She looked at him. "Fine. Words to incite excitement in every woman's heart. You know what it was like for me. No man would look at me. I didn't enjoy not having a social life. I want to be like everyone else." Her voice turned wistful. "At least as much as I can be."

"There was nothing wrong with you."

"You don't like the idea of me having a social life."

"I worry about you. Look what happened in Thailand."

Felicia glared at him. "Not as much happened as I would have liked. You broke down the hotel door. What were you thinking? People knock."

"I didn't know what he was doing to you."

"You had a good idea. I'm all grown up, Justice. You have to accept that."

"Not really," he said cheerfully.

Felicia had only been nineteen when they'd started working together. She'd grown up in the sheltered world of academia, always around kids older than herself. Because of that she'd never had many friends, hadn't been on a date. Justice had been open to being one of the former, if not the latter. He'd taken her under his wing, had made sure the other guys stayed in line.

Five years later she'd come to him, begging him to consider getting drunk and sleeping with her. It wasn't that she'd been madly in love with him; it was that she was tired of, as she put it, not being like everyone else. He'd refused as gently as he could. They'd been in Thailand at the time. Two days later she'd picked up a guy in a bar and gone back to his room.

Justice had rescued her, but it had been a little too late. When he'd tried to yell at her, she'd told him to stay out of her sex life. As it wasn't a place he wanted to be, he'd agreed. The only problem was, the guy from the hotel was currently living in Fool's Gold.

Justice knew he had to tell her. The question was when and how. Oh, and could he walk away without any life-threatening injuries? While Felicia didn't have half his skills, she fought dirty and he couldn't bring himself to put up much of a fight with her.

They passed Morgan's Books, then turned right at the corner.

"Don't get used to coming here," he said. "Patience is opening a coffee place. You'll want to go there and support a local business."

"I'm not sure that's a good idea."

"Why not?"

"I don't think Patience liked me."

"She barely met you."

Felicia studied him. "Are you sure she knows we're just friends?"

"Of course. I told her."

"Well, then, I'm sure everything is fine."

He thought maybe Felicia was mocking him, but it was hard to tell. She was pretty much always mocking him.

They walked into the Starbucks and approached the counter. "How long do I have?" he asked. "When are you going to abandon me for your selfish plans?"

"I don't know. I want to figure out what I'm going to do with myself by the end of summer."

"That's not very long."

"Justice, you're opening a business, not launching a new government. I can have everything organized in two weeks. Maybe less."

He chuckled and motioned for her to place her order. Now that Felicia was in town, he could get serious about CDS. Once all the plans were in place, he would let Ford and Angel know and his partners could move to town. He wondered what the residents of Fool's Gold were going to say about having men like them hanging around.

SHE WAS JUST so stupid!

Patience threw packing material onto the floor and shoved the mugs onto the counter, then resisted the urge to stomp her foot. It had been nearly twenty-four hours. What was the military term? Radio silence? Whatever it was, she hadn't heard from Justice at all. No visit, no phone call, not even a text. The man had vanished completely. No doubt making himself happy with his beautiful friend.

Patience told herself she'd been right to decide to end things. Unfortunately, she also wanted to see him. To tell him in person. Or maybe just because she liked being around him.

"No!" she said aloud. "I don't want to see him." At least not very much. But he was busy with Felicia.

Felicia. Talk about a stupid name. And she was stupidly tall. Who was that tall? And seriously, were her eyes really that color of green?

Patience kicked the empty box, sending it sliding across the room, then sank onto the floor and covered her face with her hands. The real problem here was her, and she knew it. She'd made love with Justice impulsively and now she was suffering the consequences.

Sure, he'd been good to her since moving back to town. Attentive, even. Nice to her mother and her daughter. But they hadn't talked much about his personal life. He'd claimed to have never been married, but what else did she know about him? For all she knew, he was currently having his way with the overly tall, too-beautiful byotch who had shown up the previous day.

That image made her stomach hurt, so she tried not to think about it. She had to get herself together. The dishwasher was going in soon. Once that was done, she would be training staff, then opening her business. That's what mattered. Moving forward. Living the dream. Possibly running over Felicia if she had the opportunity.

"Hey."

A hand touched her shoulder at the same time she heard the voice. She screamed and tried to scramble away, only to find herself staring into Justice's amused gaze.

"How did you get in here?" she demanded, her heart pounding in her chest.

"Through the door."

"I locked it."

"I knocked, but I guess you didn't hear me." He shrugged, then sat down in front of her. "I wanted to see you."

"So you picked the lock on my door?"

"Uh-huh."

A man with a variety of skills wasn't always a good thing.

She pushed her hair out of her face and wished she'd put on something more classy than old jeans and a T-shirt with a glittery surfboard on the front. Plus, she wasn't wearing makeup. Not that any of that would make her look like Felicia, whom she hated a lot.

"How are you?" he asked.

"Fine." A lie, but she was okay with that.

"Seriously?"

"Sure. I'm great." She tried to smile, but wasn't sure she succeeded.

He reached for her hand. "About yesterday."

That was supposed to be her line. "About yesterday. It's over, skunk-dog."

Only before she could speak, he brought her fingers to his mouth and kissed her knuckles. Then he gave her his best slow, sexy smile. "Impressive."

Tinges zigzagged down her arm to her chest and belly. She ignored them and the need to swoon. "Okay," she said cautiously. Maybe she would wait to hear what he had to say. *Then* she would end things.

"Just okay?" He studied her, then nodded, as if he'd figured out what was wrong.

She wasn't sure that was a good thing. "I wasn't sure what to think. Everything happened so fast." She glanced around, hoping to find something on fire, or see an alien landing. Anything to distract him from her confused emotional state.

"I'm sorry about the timing of Felicia's arrival," Justice told her, his blue gaze steady.

"Me, too."

He continued to study her. "You know she and I are friends, right? She's like a sister to me. Always has been. Just friends. There's never been anything between us."

Patience felt herself start to lean toward him, then forced herself to pull back. "You mentioned something about it," she admitted. A long time ago, when the information hadn't seemed very important. It was much more significant now.

"We worked together and we're family. I'll always be there for her—like you're always there for your mom."

If he was trying to make her feel better, he was doing a fine job. She gave him a real smile. "Thanks for telling me that."

"I didn't want you worrying." He kissed her hand again. "I'm not very good at this."

"At what? Sitting on the floor? Because you seem to be a natural."

He chuckled, then leaned in and kissed her mouth. "Being with someone like you. Someone regular."

"You usually sleep with superheroes?"

"I usually don't stick around until morning."

"You didn't. Technically you left with a very tall, very beautiful woman." She sniffed. "I'm just saying."

He grabbed her and pulled her into his arms, twisting her so she found herself draped across his lap, looking up at him.

"I missed you," he said, staring into her eyes. "After I left. I thought about you and wondered what you were doing. Part of me wanted you to find some guy and be happy, and part of me…"

Didn't.

"You never called. You never got in touch," she said. "If you like me, you should have done something."

He nodded. "I know." He looked away, then back at her. "Patience, I've been places and seen things. More than seen. You're light and good and gentle. I worry that by simply being close to you, I'm corrupting your soul." He gave her a lopsided smile. "Maybe that's too dramatic, but it's how I feel. I don't want to hurt you."

"I don't want that, either."

He touched her cheek. "The smartest thing would be for me to stay away from you. Only I don't think I can. You'll have to be strong for both of us."

She wasn't sure she agreed with that plan. Especially when he lowered his head and kissed her. The pressure of his mouth on hers was soft and caring. There was passion, but it was restrained. If she had to guess, she would say this was more about connecting.

She wrapped her arms around him, hanging on, aware that the man knew how to get to her. Yesterday with how he touched her body and today with how he touched her heart.

Everything was happening so quickly, she thought. She had to step back and think. Make sure she knew what she was doing. And she would…just as soon as he stopped kissing her.

Justice raised his head. “Your mom will be here in a few seconds.”

She blinked. “How do you know?”

“I just saw her car pull up.”

Patience scrambled out of his lap and staggered to her feet. “We have a meeting. Store talk.”

“Then I should leave you to it.”

Justice rose. He lightly kissed her cheek, then walked to the door. She watched him go, thinking she wanted to call after him. But to say what? The man confused her, that was for sure.

She was going to have to spend some serious time figuring out what was going on. Or she could simply try to get him alone so they could make love again. It wouldn’t provide any answers, but she would enjoy it more than thinking or being sensible.

Before she could pick a course of action, her mother walked in. Today Ava was using a cane. Sometimes her MS acted up and she needed her wheelchair, but since the work party, she’d been having a lot of good days. Always a blessing.

“Did I see Justice leaving?” Ava asked.

“He stopped by to say hi.”

“He’s such a nice boy.”

Patience laughed. “Mom, he’s in his thirties.”

“I knew him when he was a teenager, so he’ll always be a boy to me.” She looked around the store. “Look at what you’ve done. You should be so proud of yourself.”

"We're in this together."

"With you getting stuck with all the hard work. Still, I'll be able to do more when the store is open. I'm excited to learn how to use the espresso machine." Ava smiled. "My friends and I are talking about some after-hours parties here."

"I don't want to hear about spiked coffee."

"Then I won't tell you."

They crossed to one of the tables where Patience had already set up their piles of paperwork. After they were seated, Patience opened the first folder. Although they'd made a few hires, they were going to need more staff.

"We have plenty of applications, which is great. We have the college kids who want to work in the evenings and a few moms with school-age kids interested in morning shifts."

Her mother closed the folder. "I'd like for us to talk about something else, first."

Patience fought against a rush of cold. "Mom, are you okay? Are you sick?"

Because with MS, danger always lurked. Even with the good days, there was the fear that something bad was going to happen.

"I'm fine. This isn't about my health, but it is about something I've been keeping from you." Ava glanced down at the table, then back at her daughter. "I haven't been completely honest with you. About Steve."

It took Patience a second to put the name with the

face. "Lillie's grandfather? What about him? Oh no. You found out something horrible about him."

"No, it's not that."

Ava pressed her lips together. If Patience didn't know better, she would swear her mother was blushing.

"Mom?"

Ava drew in a breath and looked at her. "Steve got in touch with me about five months ago. He'd just sold his business and was thinking about what to do with the rest of his life. He'd tried to make contact with Ned several times, but his son didn't want anything to do with him. He wanted to reach out to Lillie, so he came to see me and ask my opinion."

Patience stared at her mother. "You knew about him?"

"Yes. We talked and he seemed nice, so I agreed to meet with him. It started out innocently enough. I wanted to make sure he was the kind of man who deserved to be in Lillie's life, and I knew you were busy. I thought I was helping."

Which all sounded reasonable and generous, even. So why was her mother acting so strange?

Ava's brown eyes darkened with emotion. "I've been seeing him regularly."

"Okay. I get that. To make sure he wouldn't hurt Lillie and…" Patience felt her mouth drop open as she figured out what her mother was *really* saying. "You're dating Steve?"

"I have been for a while."

"That's what the secret calls have been about? The disappearances? You have a boyfriend?"

"Are you mad? I know I should have told you, but I was nervous. I felt strange, going out at my age. Plus, he's Ned's father. He walked out on his family the way Ned walked out on you. I thought you might see him as the enemy. I was afraid you'd disapprove. And the more I saw him the more I liked him. I guess I acted like a coward and I'm sorry."

Her mother was dating Lillie's grandfather? Patience turned the information over in her mind. It was a little strange and would take getting used to. But it wasn't bad.

"Mom, I want you to be happy. If you're having a good time with Steve, that's great. I just wish you would have told me. I asked Justice to run a background check on him."

"I wanted you to make your own decision about him. I didn't want to influence you." Ava shrugged. "I think a part of me wanted you to come to your own conclusions because I was afraid I was seeing what I wanted to see, rather than what was there. I don't exactly have a good track record when it comes to men. It's one thing for me to make a mistake. It's another for me to drag you and Lillie through the mess."

"Oh, Mom." Patience stood and moved around the table. She bent low and hugged her mother.

Ava held on tight. "I love you so much."

"I love you, too." She crouched in front of her mom. "So you're doing the wild thing with this guy?"

"Maybe."

"You're practicing safe sex, right? There are issues that don't involve pregnancy."

Ava laughed. "Yes. We're very safe."

"Then I'm happy for you. I wish you would have told me, but I understand why you wanted me to make my own decision about Steve." She stood and smiled. "Admit it. You were secretly thrilled when Justice's report came back clean."

"I was very pleased to hear the man I was dating didn't have a criminal record."

Patience returned to her chair. "Anything else I should know?"

"That's it." Ava's humor faded. "I hope you understand. After I was diagnosed with MS, I couldn't seem to pull myself together. Then your dad left and it was just the two of us. I was so scared. Since then, I haven't met a man who could see past the disease. Until Steve."

"You handled your diagnosis with grace, Mom. I mean that. You were a rock. I'm glad you're happy with Steve. I still want to take things slow with Lillie. I don't want her to get confused or hurt. Having her grandfather show up after a decade is a lot for her to take in."

"I understand and I agree. No matter what, even if things don't work out with me and Steve, he still wants to be a part of her life. But I agree with being cautious."

They smiled at each other. Patience opened the folder. "Okay, then. Now on to company business."

They started to talk about the store. Patience thought briefly about her mother's decision to keep her relationship with Steve a secret. Two days ago she would have been a little more outraged. But she and Justice had recently taken things to the next level, and she had no intention of mentioning that to her mother. She supposed it wasn't unreasonable to expect them both to have secrets. Even if it meant that she would have to keep an extra-close eye on Steve.

CHAPTER TWELVE

PATIENCE SCOOPED SOME guacamole onto her chip and listened to her friends. It was nearly six and she was pleasantly tired after a day spent in her soon-to-be coffee shop.

The dishwasher was installed and happily doing its cleaning and sanitizing thing with the new mugs and plates. She'd hired staff, and training sessions would start in the morning.

Heidi sipped her virgin margarita. "I'm just waiting for Annabelle to tell me to leave her alone. I swear, I'm at her house every fifteen minutes."

"She doesn't mind," Isabel said. "How could she? She's a new mom, getting up four or five times a night to take care of a newborn. She's grateful to have a little downtime."

"I hope so." Heidi touched her growing belly. "I promise to be happy to see any of you as much as you want when I have my baby." She sniffed. "Don't you love the circle of life?"

Charlie groaned. "Sweet Mother of God. What is going on with you? Is the crying thing contagious? I swear, I can't take another crier." She glared at Heidi. "You'd better snap out of it."

"You're not really mad at me, are you?"

"Of course not." Charlie picked up her beer. "I am never getting pregnant."

"Or married," Isabel said cheerfully. She grinned. "No matter how many times I've invited Charlie over to my store, she won't come in and try on the latest styles."

Charlie glared. "I could so kill you and hide the body. You know that, right?"

Patience leaned back in the booth and sighed with contentment. Isabel had only been in town a few weeks, but she was already fitting in. Patience liked that all her friends got along.

"I have a new dress with French lace," Isabel said, her voice teasing.

Charlie glared.

Heidi giggled and turned to Patience. "We should change the subject. How are you doing? Are you having sex with Justice yet?"

Patience nearly choked on her chip. "Excuse me? What kind of question is that?"

"A nosy one."

"She's not today," Charlie said. "He's gone." She shrugged. "He worked out next to me at the gym yesterday." She turned to Patience. "The guy's strong. Seriously strong. If he offers to carry you anywhere, let him."

Patience reached for her margarita and took a hasty

sip. She hoped the girl-flattering lighting in the bar would hide her blush as she thought about how easily Justice had supported her when they'd had their wild encounter.

"How did you working out next to him lead you to this information?" Heidi asked.

"He and I walked out of the locker rooms at the same time. He had a suitcase with him. Said he was heading out of town." Charlie reached for a chip. "So, do you like him?"

Isabel leaned toward her. "Yes, please tell us. My personal life is still in recovery. I need a distraction."

"I like him," Patience admitted. "He's been great with the store and my mom and Lillie."

"I respect a man who runs a good background check," Charlie said.

Patience had already told them about Steve.

"It's an intriguing quality," Patience said, then glanced toward the door as it opened. A tall, beautiful redhead stepped inside. Despite Justice explaining his relationship with Felicia, Patience felt her good mood fade away.

"The only flaw seems to be his business partner. I'm not a fan. She's so beautiful and apparently smart. I'm sure tiny forest animals come and dress her every morning while singing about how glorious she is."

Heidi grinned. "You're not kidding about not being a fan."

"I hate her. Okay, maybe not hate her, but I don't like her much and I wish she hadn't moved to town."

Charlie groaned. "I wish you'd mentioned this sooner," she said, holding up an arm and waving. "I met her earlier and invited her to join us."

Felicia spotted Charlie and waved back.

Patience sank back in the booth. "You didn't."

"I try to be friendly from time to time. I figure I need to balance out my karma."

Isabel scooted over to make room for Felicia. "This is going to be so great. Like a flash mob or something."

"You need more than four or five people for a flash mob," Heidi said helpfully.

"Good point."

Patience shifted. "No one say anything," she said in a low whisper.

Heidi gave her a quick hug. "I swear we'll always like you best."

"You'd better."

Felicia reached the table and gave them all a warm smile. "Hi. I'm Felicia Swift. It's nice to meet all of you."

"You know me," Charlie said. "This is Heidi Stryker, Patience McGraw and Isabel Beebe."

Felicia's gaze settled on Patience. "Oh, hi. We've met. I'm Justice's friend."

"Uh-huh," Patience murmured. "Nice to see you again."

Felicia slid in next to Isabel. Her long red hair was still perfectly layered and curled. She had on a bit of makeup, but with her features, she didn't need the help. Her pale yellow sweater clung to perfect curves. Patience thought about the rips in her jeans and how her hands were a wreck from all the work she'd done at the store and the fact that her T-shirt featured a grinning possum. Not exactly sophisticated.

"How do you like Fool's Gold?" Charlie asked.

"It's wonderful." Felicia's large green eyes sparkled with excitement. "I've never lived in a small town before. I've lived on a university campus, which has some similarities in size and sense of community but the demographics are totally different."

Jo hurried by. "What'll you have?" she asked, barely slowing.

"A margarita," Felicia called after her.

Heidi turned to Felicia. "Your parents were professors?"

Felicia hesitated. She reached for a chip, then pulled back her hands and rested them on her lap. She seemed to be making a decision. "I was raised by several professors and scientists, but they weren't my parents."

Charlie leaned toward her. "What? Why is that?"

"I'm very intelligent. I was doing complex math equations when I was three, and by the time I was four I'd become more than my parents could handle. When a professor approached them about admitting me into a special program through the university, they agreed." She gave a brief smile. "It was for the best. I would have been impossible in a regular school."

Patience stared at her, trying to process the matter-of-factly delivered information. "You didn't live with your parents?"

"No. They moved away and had other children. Oh, they also adopted several special-needs kids. That was easier for them to handle. I stayed at the university until I was sixteen. Then I joined the army."

She shrugged. "I admit I forged my identification so that it said I was eighteen. I handled logistics and got moved to Special Forces, which is where I met Justice."

She relaxed as she said his name. "He's been my family all these years. When I was in my car accident, he was the one who took care of me."

Patience felt as if her head was spinning and she was on her first margarita. "Car accident?"

"I was hit by a car. I had several broken bones, mostly in my face, but everything turned out great." Felicia glanced around and lowered her voice. "I was really unattractive before the accident. But when my face got smashed up, the plastic surgeon who fixed it made a few tweaks. Actually we collaborated. I made a few sketches of how the bones could be adjusted and the muscles placed, and he agreed."

Felicia reached for a chip. "Our standards of beauty can be reduced to a mathematical formula. It's all about symmetry. When I saw what he'd done, I was thrilled. It's really tough being the smartest person in the room, let me tell you. Add in some mismatched features and it's nearly impossible to fit in."

Heidi looked at Patience and raised her eyebrows. Patience knew what her friend was thinking. Felicia was a little bit strange but not unlikable.

"How smart?" Charlie asked.

Felicia sighed. "You don't want to know. People get scared when I tell them."

"How many degrees do you have?"

"Five. Oh, I assume you meant advanced. Like PhD level. If you want me to count up all of them—"

Charlie nearly choked on her beer. "Pretend I didn't ask."

Heidi smiled at Felicia. "Are you married?"

"No. I don't date much. Men are afraid of me. Some of it is I'm not very good with the details of mating rituals. Growing up the way I did, I missed normal socialization. I'm trying to figure it out, but it's not going well. Getting a guy to sleep with me the first time was so complicated."

She paused. "I shouldn't have said that, right? It's too soon. I'm not used to having girlfriends, either. My assignments in the military put me around men, and with the traveling..." She pressed her lips together. "Not that I'm implying we're friends. We've just met and—"

Patience had been prepared to really hate Felicia. She was too beautiful not to. But after five minutes, she realized that despite the incredible good looks and perfect body and apparently the genius mind, Felicia was just like anyone else. She wanted to fit in and wasn't sure she would be accepted for who she was.

Patience leaned toward her. "Felicia, we're friends. Now relax. We're all crazy here. You get to be crazy, too."

Felicia nodded. "Actually the health profession

doesn't use the word *crazy* as a definition for mental illness." She paused. "That's not what you meant, is it?"

"No."

Felicia nodded. "Sometimes I have that problem. I know nearly everything you can learn in a book and very little that you learn in life. Like my fear of spiders. It's silly, really. I've studied arachnids in an effort to get over my ridiculous overreaction, but still, every time I see one…" She shuddered. "It's not pretty. I simply can't control myself. A flaw—one of many."

"If you're not perfect, then you came to the right place," Charlie told her. "Fool's Gold is a lively town with plenty of characters. You'll get a crash course in how the little people live."

"I hope I can fit in."

Patience saw the concern in Felicia's eyes and touched her arm. "You're going to do just fine."

FORTY-EIGHT hours and counting, Patience thought as she put mugs into the dishwasher.

Melissa Sutton walked into the back room with a tray in her hands. "This is the last of the dishes," she said. "I wiped down the tables and the chairs."

Patience took the tray and set it on the stainless-steel counter. "Thanks, Melissa. You're great. I appreciate all you're doing."

The statement had the advantage of not only being true, but sounding so rational. It sure beat "I'm going to throw up from nerves" or "Never, ever open your own business."

She'd reached the place of panic, which was a little scary. With two days left before the opening, where did that leave her to go? Extreme panic? Extreme, extreme, icky panic?

Either Patience was doing a good job of pretending to be normal or Melissa was really polite, because the eighteen-year-old only smiled.

"I'm happy to be working here," she said. "It's a cool job that's going to be lots of fun."

"Saving money for college?" Patience asked. Melissa was working through the summer.

"I am. I go in late August. UC San Diego. My mom is a little nervous about me going out on my own. I keep telling her I'll be living in a dorm and not to worry, but you know how she gets."

Patience wasn't close friends with Liz Sutton-Hendrix, but they'd known each other most of their lives. Liz was a few years older. Technically Melissa and Melissa's younger sister, Abby, were Liz's nieces. A few years ago Liz had moved back to Fool's Gold to raise them when their dad went to prison and their stepmom skipped out on them.

Complicating everything was Liz's relationship with Ethan Hendrix and the fact that he had a son Liz had never told him about. They'd worked through their issues and were happily married. Patience understood Liz's worry about her oldest going away to school. She didn't think she would ever be emotionally prepared to let Lillie move out.

"You might want to go talk to Isabel at Paper Moon," Patience told the teen. "She had an unexpected experience at UCLA. You need to avoid what she did."

Melissa laughed. "It didn't go well?"

"She had beautiful highlights and a fabulous surfer boyfriend, but didn't do so well with the going-to-class part."

"That's never good."

"It's not."

Melissa shook her head. "You don't have to worry about me. I'm big on being responsible. I would never blow off class for a guy."

"Good for you. Picked a major yet?"

"I'm looking at a couple of different options. What I do know is that I'm going to law school. I'm thinking Harvard."

"Ambitious. You don't want to be a writer like your mom?"

"I think I have just enough of her skill to write a good brief." Melissa untied her apron. "I'll be here at four opening morning."

"Me, too," Patience said. "You sure you can get up that early, then go to class?"

Until high school was over in June, Melissa would work mostly on weekends and a couple of evenings. But she had wanted to work on opening morning.

"You're going to be super busy. You know how the town loves a grand opening," Melissa said. "I can be sleepy for one day."

"Thanks."

The teen waved, then left.

Patience watched her go, thinking Liz and Ethan must be so proud. They had three great kids.

She finished loading the mugs and plates, then turned on the dishwasher. Their last practice run had gone well. She'd kept the numbers small and by invitation only, and they'd worked out a few kinks with the espresso machine. The rest of her coffee would be delivered tomorrow morning, along with most of the food.

Patience pressed a hand to her stomach and wondered how she was going to get through it. Talk about being on edge.

But despite her nerves, she knew she'd made the right decision. Great-Aunt Becky had given her a wonderful opportunity. The store had been her dream for a long time. She wanted to be a part of the fabric of Fool's Gold. To be one of the small businesses in town. To have a place in people's memories.

Because that's what this place was about—making memories. Mrs. Elder, the head librarian, had been the one to hand Patience her first Judy Blume book. Years later, Patience had been in Morgan's Books when she'd realized her feelings for Justice weren't just friendship. She'd been fourteen, it had been a Tuesday and they'd been browsing. He'd turned to tell her something. She remembered how blue his eyes had been and how his hand had accidentally brushed against hers. She'd felt the tingles clear to her heart.

Later, in high school, she'd had her first kiss in Pyrite Park, after the Fourth of July fireworks show. A couple of years later, when she'd realized she and Ned would have to get married, she'd gone window-shopping at Jenel's Gems. Not that they'd bought her ring there. Ned had claimed it was too expensive and why did she need an engagement ring? He'd purchased a plain gold band somewhere in Sacramento and she'd convinced herself it was enough.

Good and bad memories, she thought. But all in this town, and she wanted future generations to remember being at Brew-haha. Which meant she was going to have to pull herself together and survive the terror of opening in the first place.

She walked into the main part of the store only to find someone stepping through the unlocked front door. Patience recognized the tall, beautiful redhead at once.

"Felicia. Hi."

Felicia gave her a tentative smile. "I know you're not officially open, so don't worry. I won't try to buy anything. I just wanted to talk to you. Or check with you. Check in would be more accurate, of course." Long, slender fingers twisted together. "It's about the dinner the other night when I shared far too much information. When I get nervous, I talk too much. Over-explaining and babbling are a way to show a person isn't dangerous or trying to obtain higher social status. Animals do that all the time, in their own ways." She pressed her lips together. "And I'm doing it right now."

Patience pointed to one of the chairs. "Have a seat."

"Thank you."

Felicia sat down gracefully. Patience settled across from her.

"You're unique," Patience said. "I'm now picturing you as a very elegant dog, maybe a poodle, showing your belly to us."

"That's a good description. Not the poodle part. I like to think I'm more like a pit bull."

"Sorry, no. You're all poodle. Besides, they're considered very intelligent."

Felicia nodded, her expression resigned. "Yes, there is that. But I would like to be intimidating and tough."

"If it helps, you're intimidating."

"But only because I'm freakishly smart, right?"

"Isn't that enough? I'm not intimidating at all." Patience wasn't sure how they'd gotten into this line of conversation, but she found herself having a good time. Apparently she really did like Felicia.

"You're very warm and welcoming," Felicia told her. "I can see why Justice likes you so much."

"He does?"

"Yes. I can see it in the way he looks at you." She leaned forward. "He never looked at me that way at all. He sees me as his baby sister. I like it. He's my family. But back when I was younger, I desperately wanted to belong in a more romantic way. I thought my virginity was the problem. I was twenty-four years old and I'd never even been kissed. So one night I begged Justice to get drunk enough that we could have sex and…"

Her voice trailed off and her eyes widened. "I'm doing it again, aren't I?"

"Yes, you are," Patience said, not sure if she was more stunned or amused. She supposed that because they were discussing Felicia trying to sleep with Justice, stunned won. "And you're going to tell me what happened."

Felicia seemed to crumble in her seat. "Nothing. Nothing happened. He wouldn't even consider it. He put his arm around me and told me one day I would find a man who would appreciate all of me. Then he walked away. I was crushed."

"I'm sorry," Patience said, and found she actually was. She wouldn't have liked knowing Justice and Felicia had been intimate, but she could understand the other woman's pain. No one liked being rejected, no matter the circumstances.

"I got over it." Felicia shrugged. "I went to the local bar where the security guys hung out and got one to buy me a drink. He took me back to his room and…"

This time when she paused, it was to smile. "Let me say I discovered I was very fond of orgasms."

"Virginity cured."

"It was."

"And the guy?"

"That was an unhappy ending. Justice and one of his friends broke down the hotel room door the next morning. Justice thought he was saving me, but he wasn't. I never saw the man again." She hesitated, as if she was going to say more.

When she didn't, Patience spoke. "Justice really broke down the door?"

"Yes. He's quite strong. All the Special Forces guys are. If we were in a pack, Justice would be the alpha male. There's both status and safety in belonging to him, you know."

"And here I thought all the good news was about the orgasms."

Felicia laughed. "That, too." Her smile faded. "I want to ask you a question and I'd appreciate you being honest with me."

"Sure."

"Do you think it's possible for me to fit in here? In Fool's Gold? I'm going to help Justice and Ford get their business started, but after that's done, I want to get out of the security business. I want normal."

"Normal can be boring."

"That's okay. I'm so tired of not belonging."

Patience leaned toward her. "I hope you decide to stay here, Felicia. Fool's Gold would be lucky to have you."

Felicia flashed her a dazzling smile. "Thank you. I was thinking I could be a teacher. Maybe kindergarten."

"An interesting idea." Patience had a feeling Felicia would bring her unique brand of brilliance to whatever it was she decided to do.

"You don't think I'd frighten the children?"

"No, but you'd terrify their parents, and that's not a bad thing."

Felicia drew in a breath. “Thanks for talking to me today. I feel better. I know I’m a little awkward and you’ve made me think I can do all right here.”

“You’ll be fine. You’ve already started making friends.”

“I have. Justice said I’d do well here. He said everyone was very welcoming when he was here before. When he was a teenager.”

“Right. That was the strangest thing.” She still couldn’t believe she’d known someone who had been a protected witness. “One day Justice was here and the next he was gone.”

“You know his father had been sighted in the area?”

“Uh-huh. Now. But back then all I knew was that I’d lost a close friend.” And the first boy she’d ever liked. “I guess his dad was really scary.”

“Bart Hanson was a sociopath,” Felicia said flatly. “Justice worries he has too much of his father in him. I’ve told him that pathologically, they’re nothing alike, but he won’t listen. His concerns aren’t rooted in fact.”

“That doesn’t make them any less real.”

“I know. The human mind is a constant surprise. All the logic and facts available can be meaningless when put up against a visceral emotion. Like my fear of spiders. I try to stay focused on reality rather than feelings, but I’m not always successful.”

“Welcome to my world,” Patience told her. She hesitated, then asked, “Do you think Justice will stay?”

“He’s said he will.” Felicia nodded. “You’re attracted to him.”

"Very much so. But I don't want to get my heart broken."

Felicia tucked her long, wavy hair behind her ears. "You know the heart doesn't really break."

Patience laughed. "Yes, I know."

"Although there have been studies that show the sadness of losing a loved one can physically damage..." She cleared her throat. "Never mind. No one finds that sort of thing noteworthy except me. Justice keeps a lot of his emotions to himself. He doesn't trust easily. He would die for someone he cares about, but I'm not sure he's ever admitted to loving anyone. He wants to settle here. He's never wanted to put down roots before. I realize these are disjointed facts, but I believe they point to a logical conclusion."

"That while Justice might be staying, he's also a risky man to fall for."

Felicia sighed. "Yes. I need to learn to be more succinct and colloquial."

"I like you just as you are."

"You're very kind."

"Not really. Ask anyone."

Felicia laughed. Patience joined in and knew that whatever happened with Justice, she'd just made a friend. And that meant today was a very good day.

THE TOWN OF Fool's Gold relied on tourists for a steady stream of income. There was skiing in the winter, the wineries and lakes in the summer. Hiking, biking and all the adorable shops in town. But what drew the really big crowds were the festivals. They were well-known and much loved.

The town didn't just celebrate traditional events like the Fourth of July or Christmas. There was the Great Casserole Cook-off and the Sierra Nevada Balloon Festival.

Patience knew that being a part of the town's festivals would mean more tourists in her store. To make sure that happened, she'd set up an appointment with Pia Moreno, who was in charge of all things festival.

She climbed the stairs to Pia's office two minutes before the time of their appointment and knocked on the half-open door.

"Hi," she said as she entered.

Pia, a pretty woman in her early thirties, looked up. Her curly hair was mussed and her hazel eyes seemed slightly glazed.

"Hi, Patience. Did we have a meeting today?"

"Yes. My store opens tomorrow and I wanted to talk about how I could support the festivals. You know, advertise in my windows and be a part of things. Tulip-shaped cookies for the Tulip Festival and a special Fourth of July iced coffee drink. That sort of thing."

Pia stared at her. "That's great. Clever. Sure. It would help us and your business. We're very supportive of new businesses in town. I hope you know that. How much we're going to support you."

Without warning, tears filled her eyes. "Oh God, I just can't do this."

Patience froze in the center of the small room, not

sure what to do. "Pia? What's wrong? Are you not feeling well? Has there been some bad news?"

Pia shook her head and dug a tissue out of a drawer. "I'm fine. Seriously, it's okay." She drew in a breath and let out another little sob. "I'm sorry. I don't know what's wrong with me. I'm just so tired all the time."

Patience inched closer. "Can I get you something? Water?"

"No." Pia waved her hand toward the chair on the other side of her desk. "I'm running in circles. The twins are two and Peter is thirteen. Raoul is so great and supportive, but he's busy with his work and I'm tired all the time. Do you know the festivals are every month? I used to love that, but lately I'm constantly scrambling. I feel like I'm failing everyone and if I could just sleep more I'd be fine." Tears trickled down her face. "I'm so sorry. I'm frightening you."

"No. I want to help. Just tell me what to do."

Pia blew her nose. "I'm a disaster. Let's reschedule this for when I'm sane, okay? I'll make sure Brew-haha gets added to the list of stores taking posters. And I'll add you to our business email loop. I'm in charge of that, too. I swear, I need to tell Mayor Marsha we need a new business-development person. And we're out of milk. I knew I forgot something at the grocery store."

She scribbled a note, then glanced up at Patience, her expression perfectly blank. As if she'd completely forgotten she was there.

"We'll reschedule," Patience said, coming to her feet. "When things calm down."

"Thank you. I'm sorry for the meltdown."

"No problem. I'm opening my business tomorrow. Come see me at three. I'm sure I'll be hysterical."

Pia offered a slight smile. "Right. We can bond."

Patience let herself out, then walked down the stairs to the street. Whatever was going on with Pia, Patience hoped it got straightened out and soon. The poor woman sounded as if she couldn't take on one more thing.

Patience walked back to her store and then paused in front of the big front window. The logo was beautiful in reds and yellows. The tables were in place, as were the hooks for the opening-day banner.

She'd done it, she thought happily. Tomorrow she would open her business. There was no going back now—just moving forward. As she unlocked the front door, she crossed the fingers of her free hand. For luck.

CHAPTER THIRTEEN

AT SEVEN THAT night, Patience stopped in front of her business and looked toward the dark windows. She didn't see anything wrong. But Police Chief Barns had phoned a few minutes before to say there was a problem. Ava had said she would watch Lillie while Patience hurried over to check the business.

"Nothing bad," she whispered, reaching for the front door. "Please, nothing bad."

She used her key and opened the door, then flipped on the lights.

"Surprise!"

She jumped back and shrieked as over a dozen women gathered around. All her friends were there holding bottles of champagne and presents. Charlie; Heidi; Julia, Patience's former boss; Dakota, Montana and Nevada; Annabelle; Isabel and even Felicia.

Charlie hugged her first. "Sorry to scare you, but we wanted this to be a surprise."

Patience had trouble taking it all in. "You mean there's no emergency?"

"Nope. I called Alice and she was happy to be part of the surprise. Your mom was in on it, too."

Patience pressed a hand to her still-pounding heart. "She and I are going to have a talk about this when I get home."

"Come on," Isabel said, taking her arm and leading her forward. "We're going to get you drunk."

"I have to be up at three-thirty to be here at four in the morning. I don't want a hangover."

Isabel grinned. "Sure you do. The headache will distract you from any nerves you might have."

Charlie and Nevada opened the bottles of champagne and poured. On the coffee bar were platters of appetizers along with a pitcher of what looked like herbal iced tea. No doubt for the recent moms and the mother-to-be. The tables had been dragged together with chairs pulled around.

When Annabelle came over to hug her, she smiled. "I can't stay all that long because I'm between feedings, but I didn't want to miss this."

"I'm glad you came."

"You're going to do great. You'll see. The whole town will support you."

"I'm counting on that."

"I swear, the second I'm done breast-feeding, I'm coming right here for coffee. I miss lattes and double shots and caffeine in general. I also miss wine. I'll have to go somewhere else for that."

Isabel and Charlie led Patience to one of the chairs. Glasses of champagne were handed out and the food passed around. Everyone settled in for a good gossip session.

Montana looked at Felicia. “Wow, you’re really gorgeous.”

“Thank you,” Felicia said. “I wasn’t born this way.”

Charlie chuckled. “It’s her way of saying not to hate her.”

“I’m more likely to make people uncomfortable than generate hatred,” Felicia said. “I am hoping you’ll like me, though.”

“Honesty,” Heidi said. “Impressive.”

“You’re not the only new girl in town,” Charity Golden said. “I heard a rumor that a woman was looking at retail space right next to the sporting-goods store.”

Charity would know, Patience thought. She was the city planner.

“Do you know what kind of store she’s opening?” Isabel asked.

“Afraid you’ll have gown competition?” Heidi sipped her herbal tea.

“No. Just curious.”

“I don’t think she said,” Charity admitted. “I didn’t see the paperwork for her business license.”

Charlie looked at Charity. “Tell your husband he needs to name his damn store.”

“It’s the sporting-goods store.”

“That’s what it is, not what it’s called.”

Charity laughed. “It’s what the sign says.”

“Right. Like there’s a big sign that says *library* in town, too, but it has a name.”

“I’ll tell him you’re concerned.”

Isabel got up and walked over to the sound-system controls tucked into the bookcase. She turned it on and quickly dialed in one of the local radio stations. An oldies song started to play.

"Tell us about the hunky bodyguards coming to Fool's Gold," Dakota said to Felicia. "With my brother being one of them, you'd think we'd know something, but he's barely been in touch."

Nevada nodded at her triplet. "I sent him an email the other day. I swear, his reply was the written equivalent of a grunt."

"He's okay, isn't he?" Montana asked.

Felicia looked at the three sisters. "Last time I saw Ford, he was fine. I'm sure he's busy wrapping up his time in the army. There's a lot of paperwork and a process for soldiers to acclimate to civilian life."

"He's not emailing you, either, then," Dakota said.

"Not very much. Justice corresponds with him regularly."

"Did you want to go out with him?" Montana asked. "I'm only mentioning it because our mom is determined to get him married to someone local. So he'll stay. We think it's a good idea."

"*We* do not," Nevada said. She glared at her sisters. "*You* think it's a good idea. I think we should leave the man alone. He's plenty capable of getting his own girl. If you get in his face, he might just leave."

Felicia stared at them with undisguised interest. "You disagree about what to do about Ford."

Dakota nodded. "We disagree a lot. I've explained

their lives would be better if they would simply listen to me, but what can I say? They only look smart."

Montana rolled her eyes. "Oh, please." She turned to Felicia. "She thinks she's all that because she has a psychology degree."

"Yet you're genetically identical."

Dakota shifted toward her. "I know. It's fascinating, isn't it? That when the cell divided in utero we were identical in every way possible. But over time, through random events, experiences, even minute biological differences, we've become completely different people."

Nevada groaned. "Oh, please. We're not that interesting."

"Has anyone ever studied the three of you?" Felicia asked.

"No," Montana said loudly. "And we're not going to be studied now." She softened her words with a quick pat on Felicia's hand. "Maybe you should get some mice or something. You know, to keep you busy."

Felicia nodded. "I had thought of getting a dog."

Patience leaned back in her chair and sipped her champagne. This moment was exactly what she loved about her hometown. She was surrounded by her friends, having a great time, feeling supported and listening to some very bizarre conversation. Whatever people might say about small towns, life in Fool's Gold was never boring.

Annabelle picked up her tea. "You never told us if there were any other guys coming."

"Interested?" Heidi asked with a grin.

"You know my heart will always belong to Shane. And our baby. But now I'm curious."

"There is a third partner," Felicia said. "Angel."

"Ooh," the triplets said together.

"Angel, huh?" Charlie sniffed. "That means he's nothing but trouble."

"He's a former sniper who went to work for a private company. I've known him for a while, but we're not especially close." Felicia paused. "There's something about his eyes. With Justice and Ford, you know they've seen things. That they're strong and capable. But with Angel…" She shrugged. "I don't want to be fanciful."

"Be fanciful," Isabel said.

Felicia looked uncomfortable. "It's like he's been to the depths of hell. He's very nice," she added quickly.

"Right," Charlie said. "In a 'hey, I can kill you without blinking' kind of way."

Patience thought about the mysterious Angel. The men who served went places and did things the rest of them couldn't begin to imagine. Justice must have dark memories in his past. Not just with his father, but while in the military. But when he was with her, he was tender and funny. He was perfect with her mother and with Lillie. Was it difficult for men like him to be back in the regular world?

She wanted to ask. Just as much, she wanted to see him. She hadn't heard from him since he'd left and wasn't willing to ask Felicia if she'd gotten a call or a text. Still, he'd promised to come to the opening and she was going to trust him to be there.

On the radio, there was a second of silence, followed by a sexy voice.

"To a very special lady tonight, Patience McGraw, whose new business, Brew-haha, opens tomorrow. This one's for you."

The party went quiet as everyone paused to listen. The opening sounds of "Good Vibrations" spilled into the room. Patience laughed.

"I hope he's right," she said. "I need all the help I can get." She glanced at Charlie. "Did you tell him about the party?"

"I might have mentioned it."

Felicia leaned toward Patience. "That man on the radio. Who is he?"

"Gideon? Have you met him? He moved here last year and bought a couple of radio stations."

"Gideon Boylan?"

"Yes."

Felicia went pale. "Excuse me," she said as she stood.

Patience half rose. "Are you okay?"

"Yes. My stomach's been bothering me a little lately. I shouldn't have had the champagne."

"The bathrooms are back there," Patience said as she pointed.

Felicia hurried off.

Patience wondered if she should go after her. She decided that some events should occur in private and that if Felicia wasn't back in a few minutes, she would check on her.

Unless the problem wasn't her stomach at all. Did Felicia have a past with Gideon?

The tall, dark-haired man was plenty appealing, she thought absently. He had the same dangerous aura about him as Justice, but with a couple of tattoos and an attitude that was far more Wolverine than James Bond. Patience would say that Justice fell into the James Bond category. She would bet he looked spectacular in a tux. Or without one.

She sipped her champagne and sighed. If he kept his word and returned for the opening, she would see him sometime in the next twenty-four hours. The thought of that got her nerves dancing nearly as much as the thought of opening her business.

"I WOULD die without you," Patience told Melissa. "Seriously. I owe you."

The teenager grinned. "You owe my mom. She said I could take the day off school. She thinks that being a part of a business from the first day is a good experience. You know how she gets."

"As far as I'm concerned, Liz gets an award of some kind." Patience took the latte Melissa had finished making and slid the mug across the counter. She smiled at the waiting customer. "Thanks so much for coming in today."

Coach Green smiled back at her. "We're all excited about your new store," he told her. "Good luck."

"Thank you."

The coach turned away and joined the huge crowd filling her store. Her business had officially been open five hours and had been busy from 6:01 until right this second.

A steady stream of customers had flowed in, and many of them didn't seem to want to leave. Her plan had been to offer samples as a way to entice people, but so far everyone was insisting on buying their drinks. She'd run out of pastries by eight, and they were working their way through a cookie supply she thought would last three days.

The official ribbon-cutting ceremony was at noon. If the people already hanging out didn't leave, they would have to hold the speeches outside.

A great problem to have, Patience thought as she worked her way through the crowd, greeting friends and keeping an eye out for tourists who might not understand why there was such a crush to get coffee.

She spotted a pretty blonde standing by the window. At first Patience thought she was staring out at the park, but as she got closer, she realized the woman was studying the window casings.

"Hi," she said as she approached. "I'm Patience."

"Noelle," the blonde said with a warm smile. She was on the thin side, but tall, with delicate features and blue eyes. "Your store is beautiful. I love the old building, how you've retained some of the original features of construction while updating the look."

"You sound like you know what you're talking about."

Noelle smiled. "I wish I did. I'm faking it."

"You're doing an excellent job." Patience paused. "I haven't seen you around town before. Are you visiting friends or family?"

"No. I don't know a soul in the area. But I'm moving here." Noelle squared her shoulders. "That sounded convincing, didn't it? Hi, I'm Noelle, and I'm moving to a strange town where I don't know anyone and opening a store when I've never worked in retail." She flashed another smile. "Crazy, huh?"

"Maybe a little. But it also sounds exciting."

"I'm ready for exciting," Noelle told her. "Adventure. Grabbing at life with both hands. I'm looking at renting that store over there." She pointed through the window to the space next to the sporting-goods store.

"For what it's worth, I'm jumping in the deep end, too," Patience said. "Last week I was doing hair at a salon. Now I'm opening this."

"Good for you," Noelle said. "You're brave."

"Right now I feel stressed rather than brave, but I appreciate the compliment."

Before Patience could ask what kind of business Noelle was going to open, the front door opened and at least ten more people pressed into the space. She and Noelle were separated by the growing throng. She felt like that scene from *Titanic* where the sinking ship had created a vortex and the swirling waters had pushed Jack and Rose apart.

She supposed an alternative explanation for that visual was that she hadn't gotten much sleep in the past couple of days and she was a little punchy.

"Okay, okay, that's enough." Charlie pushed her way into the store. "Everybody out on the sidewalk. I have a whistle, people. It's not a sound you're going to enjoy. Don't make me use it."

Charlie, in uniform and looking more crabby than usual, turned to Patience. "You've officially violated fire codes with your success."

Patience beamed. "Really?"

"Don't look so happy about it. They're going to have to stand outside and take turns coming in."

Because there were too many people buying coffee, she thought. Too many people coming to her store. She impulsively hugged her friend.

"Thank you," she whispered.

"I wish everyone took bad news as well as you did." But her eyes were bright with humor as she spoke.

Patience helped usher everyone outside. Cones had already been set up, blocking off part of the street. Ava said she would take care of letting people in and out to place their orders while the party spilled over the sidewalk.

Patience paused to smile at her mother. "We're a hazard."

"I know. Isn't it wonderful?"

The official ribbon cutting was in a half hour or so. Patience knew the mayor would be there, along with most of the city council. All her friends, her teachers from her twelve years of public education and pretty much everyone she'd ever met in town. But even as she accepted congratulations, she couldn't help scanning the crowd and wishing for the one person who wasn't there.

Justice had probably gotten held up, she told herself. A delayed flight. He'd been working and maybe the job had gone on longer than he'd expected. All reasonable explanations, but she didn't want any of them to be true. He'd told her he would be here and she'd believed him. So where was he?

She told herself that if there was a problem he would have called. Or at the very least, gotten in touch with Felicia, who could have passed on the message. But although the beautiful redhead had been by earlier that morning to buy a latte, she hadn't said a word about Justice.

Lillie arrived with a couple of her friends.

"Mom, this is great! Look at everyone who came."

"I know."

"Are we rich now?"

"I wish we were, but not really."

"Maybe next week?"

Patience laughed and kissed the top of her head. "I'll put it on my to-do list."

Lillie returned to be with her friends. It was closer to noon and the ribbon cutting. She should probably—

"Patience."

She stood in place for a single heartbeat, then turned toward the low, familiar voice and saw Justice standing beside her. Relief eased the last of the tension in her stomach, and she flung herself at him. His tailored suit was smooth and cool to the touch.

"You're back."

He wrapped one arm around her and held on tight. "I am."

"I was afraid you wouldn't make it."

"Here I am."

She drew back and looked at him. He was pale, she thought. His eyes less focused than usual.

"Are you okay?"

"Fine. It was a long trip."

She could understand a normal person being tired, but not Justice. It didn't seem the sort of thing he would allow to happen.

He gave her a weary smile. "I wanted to be here for you, Patience." He looked up. "The mayor is on her way. The ceremony is starting."

"Okay." She hesitated, studying him. "I feel like something's wrong."

"You're imagining things."

Before she could argue, her mother hurried over. "It's time. Oh, hi, Justice."

"Ava."

"Did you try the cookies? You should get one before they're gone. Everything is going so well."

Patience watched her mother lead Justice inside the store. She wanted to follow, but there wasn't time. Not with the official opening about to begin.

She glanced back at him, then turned toward the

small podium that had been set up by the curb. But before she could get there, Pia touched her arm.

"Hey, hi. I wanted to apologize for my meltdown the other day."

"Don't worry about it," Patience told her.

"I feel like an idiot. I was sick to my stomach the next couple of days, so I guess I was coming down with something. I just feel horrible for how I acted."

"Don't. You've got a lot going on."

Pia nodded. "You're sweet. I'm never like that."

Patience faced her. "Pia, stop. You had a bad day. It happens. I'm fine, really."

"Good." The other woman smiled. "I'm glad you want to be a part of the festivals and everything else going on in town. I've added you to our email list. There's a chat group for local businesses. I've put you on that. We're not that active. More information sharing than social."

"I appreciate that. I'll do my best not to share any emotional ups and downs and stick with town business."

Pia laughed, then hugged her. "Perfect. Thank you so much for understanding. And congratulations. Oh, look. It's time."

Mayor Marsha had arrived. She walked to the podium and stepped up so she was facing the crowd. Patience hovered, not sure what to do, then walked toward her when the mayor beckoned.

As the chimes from a nearby church clock struck the hour, the crowd grew quiet. Mayor Marsha stepped up to the microphone and smiled at the throng of waiting people.

"Welcome to the grand opening of Brew-haha," the mayor said. "There are many satisfying elements of being mayor of Fool's Gold. In addition to my traditional civic duties, I have the pleasure of welcoming every baby born in town and being at the start of grand adventures like this one."

She paused while people applauded. Ava came up and stood next to Patience. The two women linked arms.

"I'm so excited," her mother whispered. "And so proud of you."

"I'm proud of both of us."

Mayor Marsha glanced toward them. "I remember when Patience was born," she went on. "I was there to greet her." She paused. "Not at the exact moment of birth. Ava needed her privacy."

Everyone laughed.

"As a child, Patience was a sweet girl who was very much a part of our community. Ava was always there for her daughter. She worked hard, gave back to the town and now the two of them are opening this business together. Patience and Ava, you are both an integral part of this community."

Patience had to blink against the sudden burning in her eyes.

"Now you've gone and done something grand," the mayor continued. "Taken your dream and made it into a reality. I am delighted to have Brew-haha as one of the premier businesses in Fool's Gold. Congratulations to Patience and Ava."

Two city council members stretched out a wide length of ribbon. Charity Golden, the city planner, handed the mayor a large pair of scissors. The mayor stepped down from the podium and cut the ribbon. Everyone applauded.

"Speech! Speech!"

Patience looked at her mother. Ava nudged her toward the podium. "You've done all the hard work, kid. It's up to you."

Patience couldn't remember ever addressing a group formally before and didn't like the sudden leapfrogging in her stomach. But she stepped up to the microphone and looked at all her friends and neighbors.

"Thanks for coming," she said, her voice shaking a little. She drew in a breath. "I love living here and I'm so excited to be able to open this store with my mom. We couldn't have done it without you and without Great-Aunt Becky, who basically funded this."

"That's my mom!"

Patience saw Lillie pointing at her and laughed. Her gaze was drawn to the doorway to the store. Justice stepped out. He looked at her and offered a smile, as well. Only there was something wrong with his expression. Or maybe it was his eyes.

He was even paler than he had been, she realized. He was holding his arm against his side.

She knew she had to finish her minispeech, but couldn't rip her gaze away from him to focus. Not when he seemed to stagger slightly. His arm dropped and she saw blood seeping through his white shirt. A lot of blood.

He started to speak, then went down like a rock.

CHAPTER FOURTEEN

THERE WAS SOMETHING about the smell of a hospital, Justice thought as he lay on the bed and watched the IV bag drip slowly as fluids were replaced. No, he thought with a grimace, the color coming into focus. Blood. He would guess two pints. He'd lost a lot when he'd been shot and even more at the grand opening. Which had been when, exactly? Earlier today? Yesterday? He wasn't sure how long he'd been out of it.

He knew he was in Fool's Gold. He'd made it just in time for the grand opening. He also knew that checking himself out of the hospital in D.C. had been a calculated risk. One that hadn't worked out.

The last thing he remembered before he collapsed was seeing a man in the crowd. A man who looked exactly like his father. One second he'd been there and the next second he'd been gone. Justice didn't need a doctor to tell him that too much exertion, not to mention blood loss, had played tricks on his mind.

"You're awake."

He turned toward the voice and saw Patience had walked into his room. She looked tired and worried—both of which were his fault.

"Hey," he said. "Sorry to screw up the party."

She walked over to the bed and took his hand. "I so want to yell at you."

"Go ahead."

"It's difficult to scream really loud at a guy with a gunshot wound."

"I'm weak," he told her. "I can't fight back."

"I know. That's part of the problem."

There were shadows under her brown eyes and she'd pulled her hair back in a ponytail. Her T-shirt was one from the store, with the Brew-haha logo on the front. He wondered if she would wear only those shirts now. He understood the need to advertise, but he liked the dancing hippos and martini-drinking flamingos.

She continued to hold on to his hand, her fingers worrying his. "You were *shot.*" Her voice accused.

"I tried to duck."

She pressed her lips together. "Don't be funny. You could have died."

"I didn't."

"That's not the point. Dammit, Justice, what were you thinking? What do you really do at your job that you come home with a bullet in your side?"

Her worry wrapped itself around him like a blanket. Warm and comforting. No one had ever worried before. His team wanted him alive because it made their lives easier. He had friends who would miss him if he died, but no one worried.

"They took out the bullet in D.C.," he told her.

"You know what I mean." She shook his arm. "You scared me."

"I'm sorry for that."

"Stop apologizing. I can't decide if I should kiss you or hit you."

"Do I get to pick?"

She leaned in and touched her mouth to his. The light pressure did more for his battered body than any IV.

"I assume that's the one you wanted," she said, staring into his eyes.

"Good guess."

She sighed. "You should have stayed put. You could have called. I would have understood."

"I promised I'd be there."

"You said you'd be at the grand opening. Not that you would risk life and limb flying the red-eye across country after checking yourself out of the hospital against doctor's orders."

He winced. "Felicia told you that?"

"I haven't seen her, but she told my mom, who told me."

He knew Felicia would have shared the basics, but nothing else. Not the details of his assignment.

"I needed to be there for you, Patience."

He hadn't meant to say the words, but now that he had, he wouldn't call them back. She deserved him keeping his promises.

"That's the drugs talking," she muttered, straightening.

He knew it wasn't, but decided it was better to pretend. After all, who was he to offer her anything?

"How long was I out?" he asked.

"Nearly twenty-four hours."

"The opening was yesterday?"

"Uh-huh. You caused quite the scene. You're on the front page of the paper."

"Lucky me." He frowned. "You need to get back to the store."

"I will. Felicia's coming to look in on you, and when she gets here, I'll head back."

"I don't need you to babysit me. I'm in a hospital."

"I'm clear on the where, mister. But I'm not leaving you on your own. You can't be trusted."

He'd been injured before. Dozens of times. In the army his C.O. checked on him. Once he'd gone to work for a private company, his boss had followed up with him. A few friends stopped by, but otherwise, he was expected to get better on his own.

"Thank you," he told her.

They were still holding hands. Or rather she was hanging on to his with both of hers.

"The doctor is going to check your blood count. If it's where it's supposed to be, you'll be released later today."

"Okay."

"Into my care."

She made the statement defiantly, as if she expected him to argue.

"Is that so?"

"It is. The doctor wants a responsible adult around. You're going to be tired and weak and drugged for a few days. So I'm taking you home. You can have Lillie's room."

Bummer, he thought hazily. Because he liked the idea of settling into Patience's bed. "Where will she sleep?"

"Downstairs. She's very excited. Right now she's deciding which of her stuffed animals will make you feel better fastest."

"That sounds like a lot of work. You don't need to worry about me. I'll be fine."

"Sure you will. And go where? A hotel?"

She made it sound as if he would be bleeding to death on the street.

"A hotel works."

"I don't think so. You need someone looking after you."

She was still holding on to his hand and looking so damned earnest. As if she meant what she said. What Patience couldn't know was that no one took care of him. Not for longer than he could remember.

"I mean it, Justice," she added. "This isn't your decision. It's done. The doctor is releasing you to me."

"Okay. Then I guess I'm your responsibility."

She blinked. "You're not going to fight me?"

"No."

"Oh."

In truth, he liked the idea of Patience fussing. He knew it was dangerous, but he couldn't seem to help himself. A sign that he really was in bad shape, he thought.

"Then I guess I'll be back later to take you home. I want to go check on the store." She glanced at her watch. "Felicia can't stay long, so Charlie will be here in an hour after her to sit with you."

"Charlie?"

While he knew and liked the firefighter, he wasn't looking for a babysitter.

"Don't try to get rid of her. She could so take you."

"Especially today," he murmured. "You don't need your friends wasting their time while I'm in the hospital. What could happen here?"

"You could leave. Face it, Justice. I'm not budging on this. I flat-out don't trust you to stay put."

She released his hand and then pressed her palm against his forehead.

He smiled. "I think the nurses would notice if I had a fever."

"Maybe. I'm not taking any chances." She kissed him. "I'll be back this afternoon to take you home."

With that she turned and left.

Justice felt his eyes drift closed as exhaustion swept over him. Home, he thought. Home with Patience would be a very good thing.

PATIENCE WONDERED HOW long it would take her to get used to a 4:00 a.m. alarm. She'd changed her shower schedule to evenings. Once the alarm went off, all she had to do was wash her face, get dressed and braid her hair. She applied a little mascara and lip gloss and called it a win. She could be out the door in less than twenty minutes.

But this morning, she went extra fast so she could have a couple of minutes to check on Justice. He was sleeping in Lillie's room at the end of the hall.

The previous afternoon, Charlie had stayed until Patience had returned and Justice had been released from the hospital. The two women had gotten him upstairs where he'd fallen asleep almost instantly. He'd awakened long enough to eat a light dinner, take his meds and then he was out.

She'd checked on him several times during the night, but he'd been sleeping. Now she walked quietly down the hall and pushed open the door.

"Morning," he said, his eyes open, his voice a little groggy.

"Morning, yourself. It's early. You shouldn't be up."

"I'm not up. I'm lying down."

The night-light in the base of the lamp provided a soft glow in the room. He was a big, tough guy who barely fit in her daughter's small bed. His broad shoulders practically spanned the mattresses. He needed a shave—which contrasted nicely with the princess sheets. An assortment of stuffed animals crowded between him and the wall, no doubt a gift from Lillie.

He should have looked foolish. Instead, she found his vulnerability sexy and appealing. Maybe because she knew that in just a few days, he would be his powerful self again. But for this moment in time, he needed her.

"Sorry you have to share your bed," she said, pointing to the array next to him.

He raised one bare shoulder. "The frog is my favorite."

"Lillie's, too. When she was little, she kept waiting for him to turn into a prince. She was hoping he would agree to be her baby brother." She moved toward the bed. "Do you need to get up and use the restroom?"

She wasn't sure how she was going to maneuver him there and back, but she would make the effort.

"Already went about an hour ago."

"You got up?"

"It beats making a mess in the bed."

"You're not supposed to get up."

"I'm supposed to take it easy for the next few days," he corrected. "I was there, Patience. I know what the doctor said."

"Were you also there when he yelled at you for leaving the hospital in D.C. too early and for nearly bleeding out in my store?"

"I remember a little of that conversation, yes."

She crossed to the bed and pulled the desk chair close, then sat down. "How are you feeling?"

"Like crap, but better than I did."

"You lost a lot of blood."

She started to reach for his hand, then pulled back, not sure if she should. It had been different in the hospital. She wasn't sure how, but it had been.

He solved the problem by grabbing her hand in his.

"I'm sorry I spoiled the grand opening," he said.

"You didn't. You made it memorable."

One corner of his mouth twitched. "How they'll be talking."

"Exactly. It makes my place part of the story, so they'll be lining up to see where handsome Justice Garrett was shot."

"I wasn't shot there."

"They won't worry about details like that." She studied his strong hands, then looked into his eyes. "Can I ask where in the world you *were* shot?"

"I can't tell you. I'm sorry."

"The civilian equivalent of classified?"

He nodded.

She knew so little about him, she thought. She could find him in the dark by scent or touch, but she knew almost nothing about what he did with his day. Where he went, who he worked for. He was a man who disappeared for several days and then came home with a gunshot wound.

"It scares me," she murmured.

She thought he might ask for clarification, but instead he squeezed her hand.

"I'm nearly done with them. I'm going to be here, opening the academy."

"Is that going to be enough? You won't crave the excitement?"

"I'm ready for a change."

"This is a small town. Are you sure it's what you want? Maybe you'd be happier in the big city."

He smiled. “Do you really call other places ‘the big city’?”

She grinned. “Of course, but we always use a condescending tone when we say it.” Her humor faded as she realized he hadn’t answered the question. “You’re not a kid anymore. You can’t be anonymous in a place like this. Everyone knows everything about you. You’ll be expected to get involved. To show up at events and not almost bleed to death.”

“Trying to scare me away?”

“I want you to be sure before you get in any deeper… with the town.”

She didn’t want him to make promises he couldn’t or wouldn’t keep. Because sometime between Felicia showing up and the second he’d collapsed in front of her store, she’d accepted that she was in love with Justice. It wasn’t smart and she wasn’t sure it was going to end well, but she’d given away her heart.

“I came back, Patience.”

“What if that’s not enough? Where did you go and why did you get shot? Who is in your past? What have you done and is it going to be okay now?”

“All good questions,” he told her. “This probably isn’t the time to get into them.”

She glanced at the cat-shaped clock on the nightstand. “You’re right. I’m going to be late.”

He squeezed her fingers, then released her. “We’ll talk,” he said. “I’ll answer all your questions.”

“Okay.” She rose and put the chair back by the desk,

then crossed to the bed and kissed him. "Go back to sleep."

"I will."

For a second she stared into his dark blue eyes and told herself everything was going to be fine. They would talk and she would find out everything she needed to know. But would the answers make things better, or make things worse? Because finding out the truth wasn't always happy news.

ABOUT SEVEN-thirty that morning, Justice woke to the sound of running footsteps on the stairs. He'd barely had time to remember where he was when Lillie burst into his room.

"It's okay," she yelled back down the stairs. "He's awake." She smiled at him. "Grandma said not to bother you, but I said you wouldn't mind. Are you still hurt?"

"A little, but it's better than it was."

She studied him from the door, as if not sure if she should come in or not. He waved her closer.

She stepped into the room. "Do you like my stuffed animals? I'm getting too old for them, but sometimes they're nice company."

"I'm enjoying them. Thanks for sharing."

"You're welcome."

She was so like her mother, he thought. There were the odd bits that had to have come from her father, but mostly she was Patience's daughter.

Lillie moved to the side of the bed and lowered her

voice. “I’m not supposed to know you were shot, but I heard at my friend’s last night. Her mom was talking. Were there bad guys? Like on TV?”

In her world there were still good guys and bad guys, he thought. Where he had gone, there were only shades of gray. The rich oilman who had traveled to a part of Africa where the rules didn’t apply. There’d been an ambush and a shoot-out. He knew who had won, but in the scenario he’d just survived, he couldn’t say who was good and who was bad.

“We were attacked,” he said instead.

“Were you scared?”

“Not when it happened. I didn’t have time. But later, my heart was beating fast.”

She tilted her head. “It hurts, huh? Getting shot?”

“It hurts.”

Ava called for her granddaughter.

“I’m sorry, I have to go eat breakfast,” Lillie said. “I’ll see you after school.”

“Sounds good.”

She clattered down the stairs as quickly as she’d run up. About a half hour later, he heard her leaving the house. A few minutes later, someone else started up toward his room. Felicia walked in, a tray in her hands.

“Morning,” she said as she approached. “How are you feeling?”

“Like I was shot.”

“That’s not good.” She set his breakfast on the dresser, then walked to the bed. “Can you sit up?”

“Yes, and don’t help me.”

She ignored his instructions and held out her arm so he could use it to pull himself upright. When he was leaning forward, she shoved all the pillows behind his back.

"I'd forgotten how crabby you get when you don't feel well," she said cheerfully.

"Sorry. I don't mean to be."

"You don't enjoy any physical manifestation of what you would view as weakness," she said, placing the tray in front of him. "Nor do you like the reminder that you're not in charge of every aspect of your life."

"Remind me not to invite you to my next party," he grumbled, studying the scrambled eggs and bacon next to buttered toast. While he wasn't hungry, he knew the value of eating. The nutrition was necessary to heal.

"You don't have parties. Besides, you wouldn't invite me. You'd want me to plan it. I would attend by default."

He paused, the fork halfway to his mouth. "Felicia?"

She dragged over the chair Patience had sat in earlier, then settled herself on the seat and sighed.

"I'm emotionally unsettled and therefore prone to outbursts," she told him. "Ignore me."

"Hard to do when you're the only other person in the room." He stared at her. "Look at me."

She turned her green eyes in his direction.

"I'm sorry," he told her.

"You haven't done anything wrong."

"I'm sorry I made you feel as if I don't value your company. I would want you at my party."

"You're saying that because you think I'm upset and you don't want to have to manage my feelings and because you feel guilty."

He chuckled. "Never give a guy a break."

"I'm just telling the truth."

"Fine. If I were to have a party, I would ask you to help, but I would still want you there. You're all I have, kid."

She smiled. "That's not true, either, but it's nice that you said it."

"Thanks for bringing me breakfast."

"You're welcome."

He took a bite and chewed. "Don't take this wrong, but why are you here?"

"Patience called and asked for my help. She's at work, Ava can't climb the stairs and there was some concern that Lillie couldn't manage a heavy tray."

"I'm a problem," he said, knowing he had to leave as soon as possible.

"You're not a problem. They like you. They want to take care of you. I suggest you not try leaving. Patience was very angry with you yesterday. She was also upset about you bleeding. You should stay here while you can."

She spoke in her usual matter-of-fact tone. In his experience most women were ruled by their hearts more than their heads, but Felicia couldn't ignore something as powerful as her brain. It wasn't that she was especially logical; it was that she knew everything, in every situation.

Which made her comment all the more curious. "While I can?"

Felicia sighed. "They're not like us. Patience, her family. This town. They're so…"

"Ordinary?"

"Yes. This is exactly what I wanted. I said I wanted to live with regular people. To belong. But now that I'm here, I'm confused."

"I'm confused, too."

"You are?"

He nodded. "It's easier when the bullets are flying."

"Right. Because there's no planning. You react and either live or die. But this place is all about ritual and nuance." She opened, then closed her hands. "I want to fall in love."

He continued eating his breakfast.

"You're not reacting," she said.

"I know you don't mean with me."

"I don't. While you're very physically attractive, I don't have an internal, chemical reaction when you're around. There are several possible explanations, if you want to hear them."

"No, thanks."

She nodded. "Do you remember Gideon?"

He'd just taken a bite of toast. He forced himself to keep chewing. "Uh-huh."

"He's here, isn't he?"

Justice swallowed. No point in avoiding the inevitable. "You've seen him?"

"I heard him on the radio. I haven't seen him. You know he's the one I—"

Justice wanted to put his hands on his ears and hum. "Yes, I know," he said quickly, interrupting her, then swore. "You're like a sister to me, Felicia. I don't want to hear about you having sex with some guy."

"Despite being my first time, it was a very satisfying encounter."

He glared at her. "What part of 'I don't want to hear' was unclear?"

"I need to talk to someone about it."

"That's what girlfriends are for."

She winced.

He swore again. "I'm sorry."

"Don't apologize. You're stating the obvious. That *is* what girlfriends are for."

But she didn't have any here. At least not yet. It wasn't ever easy for Felicia to make friends.

"Consuelo will be here soon," he said, knowing it wasn't enough.

Consuelo was going to be one of the instructors. She was small but a great fighter. He never wanted her to know, but he was pretty sure Consuelo could seriously kick his ass.

"We can talk," he said, trying not to grit his teeth. "Until she gets here. You know, about Gideon."

"And my feelings?" she asked, her eyes bright with amusement.

"Sure. Feelings are good."

She touched the back of his hand. "You're very sweet to me."

"I want you to be okay. Happy."

"I am happy. Or I will be." She drew back and shrugged. "Life is complicated."

She didn't mean life; she meant relationships. "Do you, uh, want to be with Gideon? You know, date him or something?"

"I don't know. There was an attraction before. I would like to find out if that still exists and if it's a precursor for other feelings or if we simply have a sexual connection."

Justice winced. "Okay, so you'll talk to him and find out, right? That's easy."

She smiled. "Right. Easy. You're a lousy girlfriend."

"Because this is where we talk endlessly about the same thing over and over again?"

"It helps. I understand that logically it shouldn't. That repeating the same information without new input doesn't resolve any issues, but I find the process comforting." She shrugged. "It's a girl thing. Something you're going to have to get used to if you want to make your relationship with Patience a success." She paused. "You do want that, don't you?"

"Yes," he said slowly. He pushed away his breakfast. "I want to, but I don't know if I can."

There were obstacles. Dangers. Some he couldn't explain. He ached for her, and not simply in his bed. But could he risk being with her?

"Like you said, they're so damned normal here," he muttered.

"You're normal, too."

He glanced at her and raised his eyebrows.

"You *are,*" she insisted.

"All evidence to the contrary?"

"You're not what you do for a living. I understand the male psyche likes to define itself through tasks, but you have to believe you are more than what you've accomplished."

"I'm not talking about accomplishments. I'm talking about killing people, Felicia. I'm talking about being a danger to everyone around me."

"You're not Bart."

She knew about his father—knew what he'd been through and what his father had done to him.

"You've left that behind you," she added.

"I left the job, but I can't change what's inside." That's what he feared the most. The darkness. "Every now and then I get the feeling he's still here."

"He's dead."

"So they tell me."

"Do you think they're wrong? They identified him through dental records, Justice."

"I'd be happier if it had been through DNA. There's still a margin of error." He looked at her. "I mean it, Felicia. I don't think he's here on a spiritual plain. Sometimes I swear he's really here. Nearby. Watching. Right before I passed out in front of Brew-haha I saw him."

"Are you sure?" she asked.

That was the hell of it, he thought. "No. I'm not sure."

"Has it occurred to you that you're sensing your father more lately because you're ready to make changes in your life? You're used to being the warrior and now you're going to be a…" She paused as if searching for the word, then grinned triumphantly. "A regular Joe. That's what you want and it makes you uncomfortable at the same time." Her smile faded. "You're the one who always told me that the only way to get over being afraid was to walk up to the fear and kick it in the balls."

He managed a chuckle. "Yes, and usually you want to know why I think fear has a gender."

"Justice, you have to believe in yourself. You have so much to offer."

He knew she was right. The problem was, not all that he offered was good. If he couldn't figure out a way to walk away from his past, he was a danger to everyone around him. He wouldn't hurt Patience or her family for anything and if he thought he might, if there was the slightest chance he could, then walking away from her was the only option.

CHAPTER FIFTEEN

PATIENCE WIPED DOWN the counter. It was ten-thirty and only a few people were in the store. Day five in the life of Brew-haha and all was going well.

There was a steady stream of customers from the moment she opened until around nine. Then things slowed until closer to lunch. There was another late-afternoon rush followed by a post-dinner surge. So far they'd had to toss people out at closing.

Just as exciting, the merchandise was selling well. Brew-haha mugs and aprons were moving briskly. She'd reordered both yesterday, and if sales kept up like this, she would have sold her projected numbers for an entire month in the first week.

She knew that some of the sales came from locals, and once they had their inventory, they wouldn't bother to buy more anytime soon. However, she'd been keeping track and nearly sixty percent of the purchases were from tourists, which was a very happy piece of news. Because tourists were forever.

The front door opened and a tall, thin blonde walked in. Patience studied her for a second before remembering.

"Hi, Noelle," she said. "Thanks for coming back."

"I wanted to see how you were doing with your new store. I came by yesterday, but you were really busy."

Patience held up her right hand with the first two fingers crossed. "So far things are going great. I'm happy." She motioned to a quiet table by the window. "Do you have a second to stay?"

"I'd like that."

Patience walked behind the counter. "What can I get you?"

"A latte, please."

A few minutes later Patience carried over two lattes and a plate of cookies. The other woman was thin enough that she wasn't sure Noelle ate things like sugar or chocolate, but her mother had raised her to always offer a snack with a beverage.

"Thanks," Noelle said, taking the mug. "I love what you've done with the store. It's inviting without being fussy." She smiled. "I'm much more a fussy type of person."

Patience smiled. "Sounds like you'd have a lot in common with my daughter. She has every stuffed animal she's ever owned." Most of them were currently curled up with Justice—a place Patience wouldn't mind being herself, she thought with a sigh.

"I can respect her commitment to the child–stuffed animal relationship," Noelle said, her blue eyes bright with amusement. She took a sip of her latte. "It's perfect."

"Thank you. The machine makes it easy. It was a

huge part of our start-up costs, but worth it. You mentioned you were thinking of opening a store yourself. Is that still going to happen?"

Noelle nodded. "I've signed a lease. I'm hoping to get my place open by mid-August." She took a breath. "It's a Christmas store. The Christmas Attic."

"I love it," Patience said. "It's perfect for this town. You'll bring in some tourists all year round and then go crazy at the holidays."

"I hope so. That's why I want to open plenty early. So I can get myself together in time for the holiday rush." She took another sip of her drink. "There's a lot to do to get started."

Patience leaned toward her. "I can't imagine what you're going through. I thought I was drowning and I barely have any inventory compared to what you'll be doing."

"I've been having lots of fun figuring out what I want to carry. There are several national and international gift shows. I've gone to a couple and was seriously overwhelmed. Now I'm talking to distributors and looking for artists. I want to have more unique items, if possible."

"Sounds ambitious."

"It is. I hope I'm up to it."

Patience hesitated, not wanting to pry. "Do you come from a retail background?"

"Not at all." Noelle hesitated. "I'm a lawyer, or I was. I grew up in Florida and moved to Los Angeles."

Lawyer to retail? Patience would bet there was a

story that went with that decision. "You have both coasts covered."

"The southern part of them."

"How did you end up here?"

"I put a pin in a map. When I opened my eyes, it was stuck in Fool's Gold, so here I am." She sipped again. "I was ready to make a change."

Which didn't give Patience much information and left her with a lot of questions. But Noelle didn't seem to want to share her entire life story. People from other places expected privacy. It took them a while to figure out that in a small town, there weren't many secrets.

"I'm glad you found us," she said instead. "And I can't wait for the store to open."

"My grandmother helped raise me and I remember she always talked about what it was like when she was little. She grew up in New England. Their house had an attic. She made it sound like a wonderful place, filled with old treasures. I want to re-create that. Sort of. You know, in an upscale, appealingly retail kind of way."

"Of course."

She studied Noelle. The other woman was pretty, if a little too pale. More ethereal, she thought, then glanced at Noelle's left hand. There wasn't a ring and she couldn't tell if she saw a slight indentation where one had been or was imagining it.

"Did you bring any family with you?" she asked.

"No. There's just me. I packed up my place in L.A. and moved it all here. I'm renting here until I get the store up and running. I was a little nervous about being in a new town, but everyone has been very friendly."

"It's a Fool's Gold thing. We're welcoming." Patience picked up her latte. "You know, there are a few new businesses in town. You and me. My friend Isabel is running her family's wedding-gown store. It's called Paper Moon. It's not a permanent move for her, but she's been thrown into the retail world, as well. We should start a support group. I'll talk to Mayor Marsha about it."

"Really? That would be great. I keep reading statistics about how many new businesses fail. I don't want to be one of them."

"Me, either," Patience said. "I'm terrified I'm going to really screw things up."

"I don't think you have to worry. I'm hearing wonderful things about your store. But if you get nervous, let me know if I can help."

"I will," Patience told her. "Thank you."

Noelle laughed. "I'm not being all that nice. I might need you to return the favor later this year."

"I'm happy to do it."

Noelle looked around. "I think I was very lucky when I picked Fool's Gold. This town is exactly what I was looking for."

"I'm glad, too," Patience said, even as she wondered what Noelle wasn't saying. There were mysteries in the other woman's past. An interesting story. No doubt she would find out what it was with time.

"All the kids are talking about summer vacation," Lillie said. "I'm excited, too, but I like school."

Justice sat on the sofa in the McGraw living room. Ava was running an errand and Patience was still at work. Today was his first day out of bed and downstairs. He was weak, but healing.

"It's good that you like school," Justice told the girl.

"That's what my mom says. Some of my friends don't like school at all. They say the tests are too hard, but I think they don't study." She bit her lower lip. "You won't tell them I said that, will you?"

"Of course not."

"Good." She smiled. "I'm going out to dinner tonight."

"I heard. With Ava and Steve."

"We're going up to the resort on the mountain. To the fancy restaurant. I have a special dress and Mom's going to do my hair."

"I want to see you before you go."

"You will," she promised.

She chatted on about a book she was reading and her upcoming summer camp. With Lillie there was always an activity planned or a place to go. She was a happy, busy kid with lots of friends running in and out of the house.

The three of them had made a good life for themselves, he thought. Found a rhythm that worked for them. But he suspected there had been tough years. Times when money had been tight and they'd had a lot of burdens.

As Lillie talked about a new movie she wanted to see, he wondered how his life would have been different if he'd had an ordinary job with regular hours and no flying bullets. If he'd been able to settle down.

He watched Lillie as she talked, her brown eyes filled with enthusiasm and intelligence. She was generous and kind, funny. So little of life's tragedies had touched her, and he didn't want that to change. He feared that while he might be able to imitate regular life, he couldn't actually *live* it. That there would always be something off inside him.

If that was the case, he couldn't risk inflicting himself on someone. But even as the thought occurred, he wondered if he was taking on too much. If, in fact, he was so used to lurking in the shadows, he'd grown fearful of sunlight. Logic told him the ghosts had long been laid to rest. Now it was up to him to make sense of his life.

Lillie turned to him. "Justice, I have a question."

"Sure. What is it?"

She regarded him thoughtfully. "Why did my dad go away?"

He reached for her small hand and took it in his. "I don't know," he told her honestly. "Because he was scared of the responsibility, I guess. His leaving wasn't about you. You were a baby at the time. You had nothing to do with what was going on."

"But if I hadn't been born, he might have stayed."

Justice felt a pain far worse than the bullet wound. "No, he wouldn't have stayed. He was always going to leave. It's just who he was." He slowly shifted until he was facing her. "You have more than one friend, right?"

She nodded, her expression solemn.

"If something happens, like a dog gets loose in the school yard, you know which friend is going to think it's funny and which one is going to worry about the dog and which one will just ignore everything."

Lillie tilted her head. "You're right. They'd all say or do something different."

"And you can predict their behavior based on what they've done in the past. You have the friend who is always late and the one who always does her homework."

"I get it." She drew in a breath. "So you're saying my dad left because he would always leave?"

"Uh-huh. He didn't leave because of you. It's what he was going to do."

"That makes sense but I still feel bad about it."

"I know," he told her. "I feel bad, too. He's missing out on a pretty great kid."

She gave him a slow smile. "You're just saying that."

"I'm not. I'm telling the truth. I'm glad I got to know you, Lillie."

"Me, too."

She leaned in and hugged him. Her arms tightened around him, sending fiery pain ripping through his midsection, but he didn't say a word. Instead he hugged her back and welcomed the feel of her affection and trust.

Ten minutes later she'd run off to get ready for her dinner out. Shortly after that, Patience arrived home.

"Sorry, sorry," she said as she hurried into the living room. "We're so busy at the store and I got to talking." She stopped and stared at him. "You're downstairs."

"I noticed that."

"Should you be? Are you pushing things?"

"I climbed down slowly. It's time for me to be up and around."

She didn't look convinced. "There's a big difference between up and around and being stupid. You're not crossing the line, are you?"

He chuckled. "No, I'm not."

She and Lillie had similar eyes. Not just in the warm brown color but also in the shape. They could both look so damned earnest.

"Because you were just shot."

"I know. I was there." He patted the sofa. "Come tell me about your day. How's the store?"

"Busy. Fun. We're getting into tourist season, which I've never paid much attention to before. While we'd get the occasional out-of-town appointment at the salon, we never catered to tourists. Pia was by today to drop off maps and festival schedules." Patience settled next to him.

"I'm worried about her," she continued.

"Pia?" He wasn't sure he'd met the woman in question.

"Yes. She had a kind of mini-meltdown a few weeks ago and now seems really scattered. She brought in the maps and schedules, then came back an hour later to deliver them again. When she saw she'd already put them out, she just stood there, staring at the display. It was weird."

"Does she have family?"

"Uh-huh. She's married with three kids."

"If you're still concerned in a few days, you should talk to her husband."

"Maybe I'll go see one of her friends instead. Charity Golden is the city planner and she and Pia are tight." She shook her head. "Sorry. You didn't want to hear all that."

"I don't mind."

"That's really nice, even if I don't believe you." She smiled at him. "We're hiring new people."

"That's good news."

"It is. My mom's handling the interviews. There are more people interested in starting their day at five-thirty in the morning than I would have thought. There's been talk about starting a support group for those of us dealing with a new business. Isabel's store isn't new, but she doesn't have much retail experience. And Noelle is opening her Christmas store in a couple of weeks. Have you met her?"

"No."

"She's really nice."

Patience kept talking, but he wasn't listening. Not to her words, anyway. He liked the sound of her voice, how she used her hands when she talked. Her eyes mirrored her emotions. From what he could tell, she was lousy at faking what she felt.

She would never make it in his business, never be one of those who could blend in, pretending for the sake of the mission. What was that old expression? She wore her heart on her sleeve.

She was tender and sweet and he wanted to get lost inside her, even if it was only for a couple of hours. Just being close to her made him more content.

"...open in August." She paused expectantly.

"Will it be a festival weekend?" he asked, having listened enough to know they were still talking about Noelle's store.

"I didn't think to check that. I should mention that to her. What a great idea." She rewarded him with a smile bright enough to power Fool's Gold for a week.

A loud crash came from upstairs.

"You okay?" Patience yelled.

"I'm fine, Mom. But a drawer came out of my dresser."

"Because she pulls them open with great enthusiasm," Patience said with a laugh as she rose. "I need to check on her."

"No problem."

"Be thinking about what you want to do about dinner. If you're feeling strong enough, we'll eat down here. Otherwise, we'll have a very delicious meal in her room."

"The kitchen is fine," he said, knowing if they went upstairs, it wouldn't be for a meal. Because he'd reached the point where it was impossible for him to be around Patience and not want her. A dilemma he had yet to solve.

"Probably for the best," she said as she headed for the stairs. "I think my mom started soup in the Crock-Pot. That could get very messy on a tray."

IT TOOK NEARLY an hour for Patience to get Lillie dressed and her hair curled, then to see her daughter and her mother out the door. When they'd driven away, she hurried back to the living room.

"I'm sorry," she said, coming to a stop in front of Justice. "You must be starving. The soup is all ready. I just have to heat some biscuits and serve the salad and we'll be good to go."

He stood slowly, his dark gaze never leaving her face. "Dinner can wait."

"But it's nearly six. Did you have a late lunch? Are you—"

He stepped around the coffee table and moved toward her. When he was close, he cupped her face in his hands and pressed his mouth to hers.

His lips claimed her with a sensual tenderness that left her equally weak and aroused. He put his hands on her waist and drew her against him.

"I don't want to hurt you," she murmured, desperate to cling to him but mindful that he was still healing. "You were shot."

"You keep saying that."

"Because it's true. You lost blood and passed out."

"I was tired."

"You weren't tired." She put her fingers on his shoulders and stared into his eyes. "Are you sure we can do this?"

Not that she wasn't interested, because she was. A single kiss and a little close proximity was plenty. Even as she stood there looking calm and concerned on the outside, on the inside she was already tingling.

Her skin was tight and hot. Her breasts ached and she felt pressure low in her belly. Classic arousal, she thought. Figures that Justice would be the one guy who could turn her on without even trying.

He moved one of his hands from her chin to the back of her head. He slipped his fingers through her hair and held her in place, then leaned in and pressed his mouth to her cheek, then her chin, then her jaw. The light, feathery touches were punctuated by soft words.

"I would very much like to try," he whispered. "If you don't mind being on top."

His lips moved against hers. She drew back slightly.

"On top, huh?"

"If you don't mind."

She'd never been one to be aggressive sexually and was a bit nervous about taking control, but this was Justice. She could trust him. Just as important, she wanted him. Needed him.

His dark gaze was steady as she took his hand and led him toward the stairs.

They made their way to the second floor. Last time their lovemaking had been about rushed passion and heat. This time the desire still threatened to suck all the air from the room, but she was more conscious, more deliberate.

She took him into her bedroom and closed the door behind them. Light still spilled in from outside. She closed the curtains, then returned to stand in front of him. She carefully unbuttoned the front of his shirt, then slid it off his shoulders.

His gunshot wounds were still bandaged, the white gauze and tape a contrast to his tanned skin.

“You were really hurt,” she murmured. “I have my doubts about this.”

“I don’t.” He reached for her hand and brought it to his groin. He was already hard.

She looked up at him and saw the fire in his eyes.

“I want you, Patience. I always have.”

“How am I supposed to resist that?” she asked, then raised herself on tiptoe and pressed her lips to his.

As their mouths moved together, she ran her hands up and down his arms. He shifted closer and pulled her against him. She parted for him and he eased his tongue into her mouth.

At the first stroke, she felt her blood heat. Liquid desire poured through her, making her weak and causing her to tremble. She needed him. She wanted to be naked in front of him, vulnerable. She wanted to give all she had, to connect with him.

She stepped back far enough to reach for his belt and then unfasten his jeans. One eyebrow rose.

“Taking charge?” he asked.

"You have a problem with that?"

"Not at all."

He stepped out of his shoes, then bent down and pulled off his socks. She undid the zipper and pushed the fabric down. His briefs went with his jeans and he stepped out of his clothes.

He was naked before her. Aroused, masculine, his erection jutting toward her. She took him in her hand and rubbed the length of him. His blue eyes closed to slits as his breath came out in a hiss.

She tugged off her T-shirt, then kicked off her own shoes. The rest of her clothes followed until she was as naked as he. She gave him a little push toward the bed.

"Maybe you'd like to assume the position."

He chuckled. "So it's going to be like that, is it?"

"I hope so."

He stretched out on the mattress, leaving enough room for her to slide in next to him. When he would have raised himself up on one elbow, she gently but inexorably pushed him onto his back.

"You can't strain anything," she told him. "You're still in recovery." She couldn't help smiling. "I get to do what I want."

"Are you taunting or bragging?"

"Both."

She sat up and surveyed the situation, trying to decide what to do first. With a very naked Justice in her bed, the options were all tempting.

She rolled over to her hands and knees, then bent down to kiss him. He parted for her, his tongue ready to dance with hers. At the same time he reached up between them and cupped her breasts in his hands. After settling her curves into the palms of his hands, he used his forefingers and thumbs to tease her nipples.

Need flowed from her breasts to that place between her legs. The ache of arousal made her moan low in her throat. She kissed him deeper. Her hair tumbled down, brushing against his face and shoulders.

He shifted one of his hands from her breast to the inside of her thigh. He moved that hand upward until his fingers reached for her swollen center and began to explore.

He found the very heart of her but then moved on. He slipped a single finger deep into her before withdrawing it. He moved down the other inner thigh before sliding it up slowly, so slowly.

She raised her head and waited.

"Patience?"

She opened her eyes and found him watching her. Before she could figure out what he wanted, he moved his fingers into place, circling against her center, making her gasp with pleasure.

He gave her a slow smile. "That's almost the best part. Watching you enjoy what I'm doing."

"It works for me, too," she whispered, finding it difficult to speak when all she wanted to do was focus on his touch.

He moved with a certainty that allowed her to give herself over to the sensations he created. The steady rhythm of his fingers against her clit sent heat spiraling through her. She rocked back and forth, moving in time with him, pressing down a little and finding it more difficult to catch her breath.

Wanting grew as she strained for her release. She bent down and kissed him, her tongue tangling with his. He slipped two fingers inside her and pressed up, slid out and repeated the motion. On his second thrust, she lost herself in her climax, her body shuddering. Muscles tensed and relaxed, her eyes sank closed.

When she'd finished, she drew back and saw him smiling.

"Good for me," he told her.

"You should feel it from this side."

She stretched out to open her nightstand drawer and pulled out a box of condoms. They were freshly purchased, which had given her a bit of embarrassment, but she'd been determined to act like a grown-up and take responsibility for protection.

He arched an eyebrow. "I see I don't have to send you back to my room."

"No, you don't."

She handed him the protection and he slipped it on; then he guided her as she straddled him. She slowly, oh, so slowly, eased herself over his erection, then sank down.

He filled her completely. She moaned softly as newly excited nerves vibrated through her body. His breath caught and he swore softly. She braced herself on her hands, he placed his fingers on her breasts and then she began to move.

They made love carefully, her body sliding over his, moving up and down. He rode with her, arching his hips and keeping pace. Her eyes locked with his as the speed increased. She was aware of her rising tension, of the way she could feel every inch of him filling her, stretching her, taking her higher and higher.

He stroked her nipples, then squeezed them gently. She moved faster, sliding up and down on his erection, taking him deeper and deeper, pushing harder, wanting more.

She was getting closer. Her breathing increased until she could only gasp and push and pump, over and over until she had no choice but to find her release.

She cried out as she came. He stiffened beneath her, his hands moving to her hips and holding her in place as he pushed in and groaned. They were still as the waves of pleasure moved through them, and then he pulled her down and kissed her.

CHAPTER SIXTEEN

JUSTICE CLOSED THE door of the warehouse and turned to Felicia. “Are you sure?” he asked. “There’s still time to add you to the deed.”

Felicia shook her head. “I don’t want to be part of the company. I appreciate the offer, but I need to be done with that part of my life. I want to find work that connects me with the community. I want what you have—a meaningful romantic relationship.”

Justice pocketed the keys and walked toward his car. He was meeting the attorney representing the seller in a few minutes and would hand them over to her. Although the keys were the least of his issues, he thought, looking at Felicia.

“What are you talking about?”

“Your relationship with Patience,” his friend said with a sigh. “You had sex with her recently. Last night or this morning. Within the last twenty-four hours. Given everyone who’s living at the house, last night makes the most sense logistically, although you could be alone in the middle of the day. If you’re both upstairs and Lillie and Ava are…” Her voice trailed off. “You weren’t asking me about logistics, were you?”

"No."

Felicia was a mystery, he thought. All women had secrets, but her mind was both a marvel and a curse.

"You want to know how I know about the sex thing."

"I'm curious," he admitted.

"You're moving differently," she said, studying him. "Your expression is more satisfied than usual. You're not as tense. The changes are subtle. I doubt anyone else would suspect."

No one else would begin to guess.

"I know," she said glumly. "I'm a freak."

"You're not." He pulled her close and hugged her, pleased the movements barely caused a twinge in his mostly healed body. "You're special."

"I don't want to be special. I want to be regular. Boring, even." She rested her forehead on his shoulder. "I see everything. It's not fun. Plus, and I say this from personal experience, being intelligent is no guarantee of happiness." She raised her head and looked at him. "I wish you'd fallen in love with me."

"No, you don't."

"No, I don't. I wish we'd fallen in love with each other. You accept me."

"You'll find someone else to accept you. What about Gideon?"

"I've been avoiding him."

"Hiding?"

She stepped back. "No. I have a strategy. It's based on avoidance."

"How is that different than hiding?"

"There are some subtleties I can't explain to your ordinary intellect."

He burst out laughing.

She was one-of-a-kind, he thought. Her past had resulted in who she was today as much as his past had molded him. That was a truth that couldn't be avoided.

"Stop avoiding Gideon."

"Why? It was a single night in Thailand. Just because it was emotionally significant to me doesn't mean it meant anything to him. Sexual intercourse starts a cascade of hormones in women. We are biologically wired to bond with a man during sex, and having an orgasm increases the effect. Men don't have the same physiological process. For them a conquest is a reason to feel pride, not a precursor to planning for a long-term relationship."

He couldn't help smiling. "You've put a lot of thought into this."

"Yes. I've been obsessing. I don't like obsessing, but I can't seem to stop."

"You're going to run into him eventually."

"Statistically, I'm very capable of living in the same town and not seeing Gideon for at least five-point-four months."

"That long," he murmured, knowing better than to tease her about the point-four part. She was nothing if not precise.

"I have until October. Unless I made a mistake in the calculation."

"And what are the odds of that?"

"Exactly."

A white Mercedes pulled into the parking lot and a woman stepped out. She was dark-haired and wearing a tight red suit. Her heels were too high, her makeup too heavy and she eyed Justice with a predatory gleam.

"Trisha Wynn," she said as she approached. "I'd heard you were yummy."

Justice took in the fine lines around her eyes and mouth and guessed she was passing for someone in her forties, but could easily be close to sixty.

"Justice Garrett. This is my friend Felicia Swift."

The lawyer gave Felicia a quick once-over, before shaking hands with both of them. Her fingers lingered over Justice's.

"Business associates," she said with satisfaction. "Nice."

Justice had never felt like prey before and wasn't sure he liked it now. He stepped back slightly.

"We've finished filling out the paperwork to begin the negotiation," he said.

Felicia fished the folder out of her bag and handed it over. "Justice is buying the property with two partners. Neither of them is here, but I've enclosed the real-estate power of attorney for both of them."

Trisha opened the folder and raised her eyebrows. "Ford Hendrix? I'd heard rumors, but I wasn't sure they were true. He was a handsome boy, if I remember correctly. When is he coming back?"

"Soon," Justice said.

"He's concerned about reuniting with his family,"

Felicia said. "The intensity of close familial bonds can be difficult as one transitions from military to civilian life."

Trisha blinked at her, then turned her attention back to Justice. "Who's the third man? Angel Whittaker. He sounds lovely."

"I don't think you could take him, ma'am."

Trisha sniffed. "First of all, do *not* call me ma'am. Second, I could certainly take him if I wanted to. I'd have you begging in fifteen minutes, only my assistant is out today and I have to get back to my office. Still..." She swept her gaze over him. "It might be worth it."

Justice held his ground without saying a word.

She held up the folder. "I'll review your offer and get back to you later today."

She smiled once, then returned to her car. Justice released a breath he hadn't known he was holding.

"That was impressive," Felicia said as Trisha drove away. "I want to be like her."

"No, you don't."

"Not the overly aggressive attitude. While I'm sure she's very sexual, it's more of a defense mechanism. I meant the flirting. The car."

"You want a Mercedes?"

"I want a car that says who I am."

"They already make those. They're called Smart cars."

She rolled her eyes. "You know what I mean. She has style."

She had teeth, Justice thought, thinking he would

make sure never to go alone to a meeting with Trisha. While he had no doubts about his ability to protect himself from the older woman, he didn't want to get into a situation where it was an issue.

Felicia glanced down at her jeans and pale yellow blouse. "Do I need a makeover?"

He held up both hands. "Not going there."

"You're right. I need to talk to a woman. Maybe Patience. She's very nice."

Finally a topic he was comfortable with. "Yes, she is."

"Do you think she's in love with you?"

Justice's relaxed mood disappeared instantly. "Why would you ask that?"

"It's a reasonable question. You've been spending time together. You're sexual partners. You stayed at her house. It's obvious you care about her and she must feel the same way. After all, she's trusting you with her child. For a single mother, that is more emotionally significant than inviting you into her bed."

Patience in love with him? He hadn't considered the possibility. She wasn't, he told himself. They were friends and there was chemistry, but anything more…

What? Anything more was out of the question? Why would Patience think that? She didn't know enough about him to realize how damaged he was, and she wasn't the type to trust easily.

"I can see by the look on your face that you hadn't considered that things might have gone further than you anticipated."

"Did she say something?" he asked.

"No, but we're not that close. I doubt she would confess her feelings to me. Besides, she knows you and I are friends and she would be concerned about my loyalties. Female friendship is based on emotional sharing rather than events."

Justice glanced around, as if looking for escape. "I care about her," he admitted. "A lot. She's special. Sweet and funny. Lillie's great and Ava's tougher than any soldier I know."

"But?"

He turned to Felicia. "You know me, probably better than anyone. Do you have to ask why it would be a mistake?"

"Yes."

He turned away and started for the car. Felicia caught up with him and put her hand on his arm.

"Your father is dead, Justice. You're not him. You've made your own way. If you were going to turn out like Bart Hanson, it would already have happened."

He glared at her. "I killed. I was a sniper. They didn't come looking for me, Felicia. I volunteered. You know what Bart was. How can you know what I willingly did and not say I'm just like him? The only difference is I stay on the right side of the law."

"Exactly. You respect the rules of society. You understand the dynamics of a community being more successful than a single individual. We all have darkness inside us. Life is about balance. That doesn't make you your father."

"You know that for sure?" he asked bitterly.

"Yes. I know it empirically and I believe it in my heart. I have faith in you. You're the one who thinks otherwise." She released his arm, but her affectionate gaze held him as firmly in place.

"She's who you came looking for," she said softly. "If you won't trust yourself, then at least trust her."

Six months ago, he would have told her she was wrong. But now he wasn't so sure. Felicia was right about Patience. She believed enough for ten men.

"MAYBE I should go back to college," Felicia said, holding her latte in both hands.

"Is there a degree you don't have?" Patience asked.

They were sitting in Brew-haha. Felicia had come in and Patience had joined her. The store was quiet, at least for now. Patience glanced toward the clock on the wall. The midmorning lull would give way to the late-morning rush, but for this moment in time, there were only a few customers.

"I was thinking of getting a teaching credential. I like kids." Felicia shrugged. "But I don't know if I'm any good with them. Do you think I could volunteer at a local school and find out?"

"You don't have very long. School's out in a couple of days."

"Oh." Felicia's green eyes turned sad. "That's right. Summer is traditionally the time for a long vacation. When I lived at the university, I worked year-round, so I didn't pay much attention to things like breaks and vacation." She frowned. "Of course, that would explain why there were suddenly fewer people in the lab."

Patience was glad she and Felicia had made friends, but she had to admit the other woman was fairly strange. Not scary, just different. She'd always assumed that being smart was an asset, but Felicia proved the cliché of "too much of a good thing."

"Won't you be spending the summer helping Justice and his friends get CDS up and running?"

"I'm only helping them organize the space and then setting up accounting books and making a schedule."

Only, Patience thought, remembering how long she'd worked to get her store open. "Something you could do over a long weekend?"

"Probably. The physical work will take longer, but the guys can do that." She sipped her latte.

"What about medical school?" Patience asked.

"I've thought about that. The thing is I'm not very good with people." She managed a slight smile. "You may have noticed."

"You have a different style," Patience said diplomatically. "Are you concerned you wouldn't be able to relate to your patients?"

"Mostly. I imagine I would start talking about their disease and then I'd forget myself and draw a technical diagram. By the end of our conversation, he or she would have either fainted or run screaming from the room." She looked at Patience. "I wish I was more like you."

Patience nearly dropped her coffee. "Me? How can

you say that? I never even got as far as community college. I went to beauty school and took night classes."

"Life isn't about getting an education," Felicia told her. "It's about the bonds we form. The connections. You have a wonderful daughter. You're close enough to your mother that the two of you share a home. My parents couldn't wait to get rid of me and I've never been able to make many friends. Especially women. My social skills have improved but..." She opened her hand, in a gesture of helplessness.

If Felicia had been anyone else, Patience would have teased her about being so beautiful. But she felt the other woman's pain and wanted to help.

But before she could say anything, the door opened and a man and a woman walked into the store. They were in their early thirties. The woman was pale, with short light brown hair and big blue eyes. She was thin and there was something about the way she walked. Her gait was slow and unsteady. The man wasn't much taller than her, but he was broad-chested and looked strong. They walked up to the counter.

The man turned to the woman. "What do you want?" he asked.

While the question was normal, the tone wasn't. There was a snide edge, a meanness.

"Maybe a latte?"

"Oh, sure. My wife always wants the most expensive thing on the menu. You'll have a coffee."

The woman flushed, then hung her head. Madeline, the twentysomething who worked the morning shift, looked from the man to his wife and back. "Is everything okay?"

"Everything is fine," the man snapped. "She'll have a small coffee. I'll have a mocha." He turned to his wife and gave her a shove. "Get out the money and pay her."

The woman trembled as she reached for her purse. The sleeve of her loose shirt fell back, exposing a huge, dark bruise.

Patience's stomach tightened as she fought back nausea. She didn't have to be a trained professional to figure out what was going on. She rose, then paused when she realized she didn't know what to do or say. If the man was abusing his wife, she should step in and say something. But what?

Before she could figure out what was the right thing, Felicia stood and walked over to the couple.

"Hi," she said, stopping beside the man.

He turned to her, looked her up and down, then gave her a leering smile. "You're a tall drink of water."

"And you're a bastard." She grabbed his wrist and twisted.

Patience couldn't see exactly what she was doing but suddenly the man was falling to his knees and screaming.

"I'm using the word *bastard* in the vernacular. I have no way of knowing if your parents were married or not," she continued.

"Get off me! Somebody call the cops."

The thin woman took a step back and looked frantically around the room. Patience wasn't sure if she was looking for help or an opportunity to escape.

"This is your *wife,*" Felicia told him. "She should be the most important person in your world. You need to treat her with respect and affection."

"She's mine and I'll do what I want with her."

Felicia twisted his arm a little more, then glanced at Patience. "Did you know that the joints in the shoulder are easily disconnected? It's a common sports injury. With the right leverage, it pops right out." She leaned closer to the man. "Would you like me to demonstrate?"

"Who the hell are you?"

Patience walked to the woman. "Hi," she said quietly. "Do you need help?"

The woman stared at her, her eyes wide.

"It's okay," Patience murmured. "You're safe here."

The woman stared at Patience for a long time, then shrugged out of her shirt. She wore a tank top underneath, but what was most startling were all the bruises on her arms and shoulders.

"I want help," the woman said, not glancing at her husband.

"Damn you, Helen," the man yelled. "I'll make you pay for this, you bitch."

"You're struggling," Felicia said, her tone conversational. "I'm not going to be able to hold you without..."

There was a loud pop; then the man began to scream.

"Hmm, he seems to have dislocated his shoulder."

Patience led Helen outside. The screams were muffled on the sidewalk. She fished her cell phone out of her jeans pocket and pressed one of her contacts.

"Charlie? It's Patience." She explained what had happened as quickly as she could.

"I'll be right there."

The few customers who had been in the store hurried out. A few seconds later, the screaming stopped. Madeline came outside.

"Felicia put his shoulder back in place. He's really sweating and crying and I think he peed himself. Do I have to clean that up?"

Patience stayed close to Helen. "I'll take care of it later."

Helen still trembled, but she didn't move from Patience's side. Less than a minute later, Charlie drove up in her truck. She was out of the cab and around to the sidewalk nearly before the engine had stopped rumbling.

She walked right up to the woman and faced her. "You okay?"

The woman nodded.

"Any internal injuries?"

"I don't think so."

"Kids?"

Tears filled Helen's eyes. "I was pregnant once. He beat me so bad I miscarried."

"Why don't you leave?"

Patience winced. She knew Charlie's question was

born from frustration, but from the little she knew about abused women, this probably wasn't the time.

But Helen surprised her by raising her head and squaring her shoulders. "I did. Twice. Then he threatened my mama. She passed nearly four months ago and I packed my bag. He put me in the hospital. I told my doctor and he said for me to be a good wife and go back home."

She turned back toward the store. "Sam has a way of convincing people he's not the problem. I am."

"Not in this town," Charlie told her.

Two police cars pulled up, with an ambulance right behind it. Mayor Marsha hurried toward them.

"I heard," the mayor said, smiling at Helen. "Hello, child. If you want to get away from this man, we can help. I know a safe house in another town. He'll never find you. But you have to want it."

Helen looked at the mayor. "I want to leave him. I want to break the cycle. I swear, I won't go back. I swear."

In a matter of minutes Helen was whisked away in a police car. Police Chief Barns drove up and got out.

"I heard," she said by way of greeting. "Did Felicia really dislocate his shoulder, then put it back?"

Patience bit her lower lip, knowing she had to tell the truth but not wanting to get her friend in trouble. "I, uh…"

Police Chief Barns smiled. "Impressive. I'm going to need to write a report. I wonder if a man can slip and dislocate his shoulder. Then Felicia was being neighborly by putting it back in place. I'll have to think on that."

She walked into the store.

In less than a half hour, nearly everyone was gone. Sam had been taken to the hospital. The police chief had her statement from Felicia, who had insisted on telling the truth. Although Patience had a feeling that the actual report would say something slightly different.

"He'll be arrested," Charlie said as they stood by her truck. "More important, if Helen wants to stay gone, she can. Mayor Marsha knows people who can make an abused woman disappear into a new life. She'll get counseling and help finding a job and an apartment. It's a chance for her to escape. Let's hope she takes it."

"Thanks for your help," Patience said.

"Happy to." Charlie looked at Felicia. "You're my kind of girl. Glad you decided to settle here."

She got in her truck and drove away.

Patience looked at Felicia. "Where'd you learn to do that?"

"I had a lot of the same physical training as the guys. I just didn't get to use it much. Until now."

Patience impulsively hugged her. "You were terrific. I didn't know what to do. I felt like I shouldn't get involved, but you got right in that guy's face."

"I hate bullies. He was a jerk." She brightened. "I wonder if he's going to sue me."

"That would mean admitting he was beaten by a

girl." Patience linked arms with her and led her back inside. "Just for the record, you *are* good with people. I'm just saying."

"CAN WE put flowers on the ribbons?" Lillie asked.

Justice glanced at Steve, who held up both hands.

"I'm hardly an expert," the older man said.

Justice wasn't, either, but he was good at solving problems. He stepped back and studied the bike. Tomorrow was the Spring Festival—yet another Fool's Gold tradition. Kids rode bikes and were pulled in wagons all decorated with flowers and ribbons and bows. The festival took place over Mother's Day so dads were supposed to do the work and the mothers were to watch and marvel. As Lillie didn't have a father, he and Steve had volunteered to help her decorate her bike.

With the help of a glue gun and fasteners, there were pastel-colored ribbons flowing from the handlebars. A big bouquet of silk flowers sat in the basket. Now the question was how to make a garland they could weave through the spokes.

Lillie sat cross-legged on the grass by the driveway. Steve wove thin strips of plastic through the spokes.

"We could glue the flowers onto this once it's secure," he said.

Lillie nodded. "That would be nice."

Justice studied her. She wasn't her usual happy self.

"What's wrong?" he asked, hoping she felt okay.

She looked at Steve. "You're my daddy's dad."

Steve froze, then nodded.

"Did you like him when he was little?"

Justice sank next to her on the grass. That wasn't the question she wanted to ask, he thought. She wanted to know why her father hadn't loved her enough to stay.

Steve turned toward her. "I wasn't there for him, Lillie. I left when your dad was small."

"Why did you go away?"

"Because I thought work was more important. Because I wasn't grown up enough to understand what I was losing and work things out with his mom. I regret what I did, but I can't change it. When I left, I taught Ned a very wrong lesson. That it's okay to leave your children."

"It's not?" she asked softly.

"No, it's not."

Justice put his arm around her. She leaned against him, watching Steve.

"I don't understand," she said. "How could you go?"

How could he go?

Steve turned away, but not before Justice saw tears in his eyes.

Justice kissed the top of Lillie's head. "You take a dance class, right?"

She looked at him. "Yes, but what does that have to do with anything?"

"Some of the other students are better than you and some are worse, right?"

"Uh-huh."

"The ones who are better can do things you can't do yet."

"They can do a lot of things I can't do. I'm scared to go up on my toes. It's going to hurt."

"Some people are better at relationships than others. Some people have a natural ability. Like dance. Others have been hurt along the way and are afraid to try. Your dad was hurt by his dad. That's not an excuse," he added quickly, knowing he was giving Ned more of a break than he deserved, but this wasn't about him. This was about Lillie.

"He's right," Steve told her. "My dad was a—" He stopped, then swallowed. "My dad wasn't a great guy, either. So I never knew what a good dad was like. I walked out on my son and my son walked out on you."

"Am I going to be like that, too?" Lillie asked, sounding worried.

"No." Justice held her tight. "You'll be like your mom, because that's what you've learned. You'll be loving and kind and you'll always be there."

Lillie considered that. "I'd rather be like my mom than my dad."

"Your dad left because of me and because of who he is," Steve said. "Not because of you. He's missing out on a great daughter. I know he's going to be sorry one day, just like I'm sorry about what I did. But I'm very grateful I've had the chance to get to know you."

"Me, too," Justice said.

Lillie hugged him, then rose and hurried to her

grandfather. She flung herself at him and he held on tight.

Justice stayed where he was, a part of what was happening and still separate.

This was something he would always remember. The warm spring morning, the bright blue sky and the half-decorated bike. But mostly what he would remember was the beautiful girl who gave her heart so easily and asked for so little in return. Ned was an asshole. Worse, he'd hurt his daughter. But Justice had been given a chance to be a part of her life.

Was he willing to put the past behind him and move on? Was he ever going to be at peace when it came to his father, or should he accept that the ghosts were a part of who he was? Accept and finally reach for that which was most precious?

CHAPTER SEVENTEEN

"Go," Ava told her daughter. "You need to see the parade. Lillie had poor Steve and Justice working on her bike for hours yesterday. Be impressed."

Patience laughed. "I promise I will be." She'd seen the scattered remains of their "art" project on the lawn. Bits of flower and twist ties. "I never thought of Justice as the help-at-home type."

"Steve said he was very good with a glue gun." Her mother's eyes twinkled. "An excellent quality in a man."

Patience knew she didn't need help falling for Justice. Just thinking about him was enough to get her heart beating faster. She'd started out determined to play it safe, which had gotten her exactly nowhere. Over time she'd learned that being around him made her feel safe, and at the same time she was stronger in his presence.

Felicia walked into the store. "What are you two doing here?" she asked. "The parade is about to start."

"I was just leaving," Patience said. "Lillie's riding and I want to see it."

Felicia looked at Ava. "She's your granddaughter. You should go, too."

"I'll be there. We're closing the store for the actual parade. Steve's saving me a seat by the fire station."

Felicia shook her head. She walked over to Patience and untied her apron.

"What are you doing?" Patience asked with a laugh.

"Taking over. Go, both of you. I'll keep the store open until the parade, then close it."

Patience was tempted. There weren't any customers, and business would be light until the parade was over. "I don't want to take advantage," she began.

"I don't mind, so you shouldn't, either."

Ava studied her. "Do you know how to work the equipment?"

Felicia smiled. "I think I can figure it out. I'm good with machines."

"I heard the same about men's shoulders," Ava said, already slipping off her apron. "You don't have to make your offer twice to me." She grabbed Patience's hand. "Come on. We both have handsome men waiting for us. We'd be fools to be late."

Patience nodded at Felicia. "Thank you. I'll be right out front and I'll save you a spot."

"I'll be there."

Patience and her mother went out onto the sidewalk in front of the store. The crowd was already three people thick in places. The area directly in front of Brewhaha had been roped off so Patience would be able to see Lillie as she went by.

"Did I tell you Lillie wouldn't let me see her bike this morning?" Patience asked. "She wants it to be a surprise."

"I'm sure Justice and Steve helped her do a lovely job."

Patience saw the anticipation in her mother's eyes as she searched the crowd.

"He said he'd be on the corner by the fire station," Ava murmured. "Oh, there he is."

Patience touched her arm. "Mom, I'm really happy for you."

Ava turned back to her. "Thank you. I'm happy, too."

"Steve's a nice guy and you've waited a long time for one of those to show up." She hesitated. "I'm glad you let him get to know you, and I'm glad he's in Lillie's life."

"Thank you for saying that. Steve made a lot of mistakes. I'm not saying he didn't, but he's learned. I believe he wants to be different now."

"He already is."

They hugged, and then Ava excused herself. Isabel strolled up, a couple of cookies in her hand. She passed one over to Patience.

"Chocolate chip," Isabel said, then took a bite.

Patience inhaled the sweet scent of chocolate and felt the warmth through the napkin. "Are these fresh out of the oven?"

Isabel nodded as she chewed. "Over there." She pointed to the crowded park where dozens of vendors had set up booths. "It's impossible to move by the booths, what with everyone buying food, but it's worth it. This town." She shook her head.

"What?" Patience asked.

"It's horrible. It sucks you in with its niceness. All friendly and caring, like they want people to stay."

Patience laughed. "You'd prefer a town that was hostile?"

"No, but I don't want to like it here."

"Because you don't want to stay."

"Right. But people are stopping in the bridal shop to say hi and make me feel welcome."

"The bastards!"

Isabel laughed. "I get your point. I shouldn't complain that I like where I'm living. But I want to be clear. I don't care how good the cookies are—I'm not staying."

"Which is too bad. I'd like having you stick around."

Isabel sighed. "I'd like that part, too. It's been fun to go to lunch and hang out. But I have a plan and it's not going to happen here."

Patience smiled. "Not even for Ford Hendrix?"

Isabel rolled her eyes. "He was so fifteen years ago. I'm completely over him."

"You say that now, but you haven't seen him. What if there's chemistry?"

"There won't be. Too much time has passed. We're different people."

Patience didn't say anything, but she was less sure.

She hadn't seen Justice in fifteen years, and there had still been plenty of chemistry between them.

Noelle joined them, a large dish of ice cream in her hands. "I never thought I would say this out loud, but OMG! Have you tried the ice cream? It's the most delicious thing ever."

"No way," Isabel said. "The cookies are spectacular."

"As if." Noelle held out a plastic spoon with some ice cream on it.

Isabel broke off a piece of cookie and handed it over. They each tasted the other's offering, and then both moaned.

"That's better," Isabel said, pointing to the ice cream. "I didn't think it was possible, but it is."

"No, yours is better," Noelle said.

They stared at each other for a second, then exchanged treats.

"So good," Isabel said, scooping ice cream.

"You're both weird," Patience said. "And blonde. As a natural brunette, I'm offended by that."

"She might be a natural blonde," Isabel told her friend. "I pay to have my hair this color. I was thinking of going red, but then I saw Felicia and frankly she's too beautiful. I don't want to compete."

Noelle smiled smugly. "I *am* a natural blonde. My mother and grandmother were, as well."

"And you're pretty," Isabel said with a sigh. "Why do I like you?"

Patience laughed.

"Is Lillie in the parade?" Isabel asked.

"Yes, she has her bike all decorated. She's riding with her friends. Apparently they've been working on a little routine together."

Isabel finished her ice cream. "Kids were one of the perks of marriage I was really looking forward to." She glanced at Noelle. "Did you know I'm recently divorced?"

"No. I'm sorry."

"It happens. I wish I could say I hate him, but I don't. We're still friends. It's all very civilized, which tells you how bad things had gotten."

"It's better than the alternative," Noelle said. "Breakups are never easy."

The way she said it made Patience wonder about her friend's past. Not that the middle of a parade route was the place to get into it.

"Ladies."

She turned and saw Justice had joined them. He moved to her and put his arm around her.

"Hi," he murmured.

The feel of his body against hers was warm and made her tingle all over. Just being around Justice brightened her day. She had it bad, she thought, accepting the inevitable. That she had totally and completely fallen for him. Foolish, perhaps, but it was done now.

"Hi, yourself." She smiled at him, then turned to her friends. "Has everyone met Justice?" She glanced back at him. "You know Isabel and Noelle?"

"Sure. Are you enjoying the festival?" he asked.

"Every part of it," Noelle told him.

"You remember that I'm meeting someone?" he asked.

"Yes," Patience told him. "And it's fine. Just make sure you see Lillie in the parade. Otherwise, she'll be crushed."

"She wouldn't be the only one. Of course I want to see her." He looked past her and then kissed the top of her head. "Angel's here. I'll see you later?"

She nodded as he stepped away. Justice was still staying at the house. He was well enough that they were running out of excuses, but she really didn't want to let him go. Once everyone was asleep, he usually slipped into her room and they made love. Everything about being with him was perfect, she thought dreamily as he cut across the parade route to the other side of the street.

"He's good," Isabel said, watching him go. "The right combination of kick-ass and sweet."

"I know," Patience said with a sigh. "He's dreamy."

Her friends laughed.

"Who's he meeting?" Noelle asked.

"I want to know, too," Isabel said. "And is this Angel person a man or a woman?"

"A man. One of his business partners. Along with Ford."

Isabel tossed her ice cream cup into the trash can by the entrance to Brew-haha. "Don't start."

"Who's Ford?" Noelle asked. "I'm never going to be able to keep these names straight."

"Ford used to live here. Isabel was insanely in love with him."

"I was fourteen," Isabel grumbled. "It was a crush. Get over it."

"Tell her about the letters," Patience teased.

"There are—" Noelle's mouth dropped open. "Oh my."

The other two turned and saw Justice standing next to a tall man with dark hair. The stranger shifted slightly so they could see his pale gray eyes and a jagged scar on his neck.

Isabel took a step back. "Is that for real? It looks like someone tried to slit his throat." She shivered. "He's scary."

Patience had to agree. Somehow she'd imagined that Angel would look more, well, angelic.

"I agree," Noelle said. "Way too dark-side for me."

"He could be a kitten on the inside," Isabel said, "but he looks like a crazed killer."

"I take it neither of you wants to be set up with him?" Patience asked with a grin.

"Not brave enough by half," Isabel admitted. "I wonder what kind of woman would be willing to take him on."

"An interesting question," Noelle said, licking chocolate off her finger. "Because you know all that intensity has to mean he's great in bed."

"WHAT THE hell is this?" Angel demanded even as he shook Justice's hand. "All this town needs are the

Munchkins from *The Wizard of Oz* and some goddamn fairy in a bubble."

"You don't like Fool's Gold?"

Angel gave his friend a slow smile. "I didn't say that. I can do cheesy, same as you."

"Then you're going to like it here. How was your trip in?"

Angel stared at him. "You gonna ask me about the weather next?"

Justice chuckled. "Sorry. I'm getting used to being around regular people. You're going to have to do the same."

"I've always been able to blend in." Angel surveyed the crowd. "What's the parade?"

"Something about Mother's Day. The Spring Festival, I think. Lillie is in it. She's ten."

Angel's shrewd expression didn't change. "Let me guess. Her mom is one of those three women across the street. The ones pretending they're not watching us."

"Yup."

Angel turned to stare at the women. They immediately began talking intently to each other, as if they hadn't noticed him at all.

"The brunette," Angel said.

"How do you figure?"

"She's looking at you, not at me. If I were a less cynical man, I would say she's in love with you." He raised his eyebrows. "How'd you let that happen?"

"I have no idea."

Justice waited for the sense of being trapped. For the

need to run. But it wasn't there. He still didn't know if he could be what Patience needed, but he was willing to admit that having her love him went a long way to healing any lingering wounds. Maybe it was wrong or selfish of him, but if Patience cared, he couldn't be all bad.

Angel glanced around, then swore under his breath. "We have to stay for the parade, don't we?"

"I helped Lillie decorate her bike."

"You couldn't have arranged the meeting for an hour from now?"

Justice slapped him on the back. "It'll be good for you."

Angel shoved his hands into his jeans pockets. "Can we at least talk about business while we're waiting?"

"Sure. What do you want to know?"

"Why you dragged me here when I had a good thing going where I was."

Justice wasn't put off by Angel's attitude. "If you liked it so much, why did you agree?"

"Hell if I know."

In the distance, they heard music.

"There's a marching band?" Angel asked, his voice incredulous.

"Probably."

Angel shook his head.

"I've found a property," Justice told him. "A warehouse with plenty of grounds. We back up on a wooded area, which is ideal for an obstacle course. I'm also looking to lease us some acreage up in the mountains for any survival training we want to do."

"We're in California," Angel grumbled. "How much survival training could anyone need?"

"The mountains are rugged."

"Yeah, but no one's trying to kill you."

Justice grinned. "You do understand we're going to be training bodyguards and working with companies on team-building exercises, right? We're not overthrowing the government."

Angel's gray eyes narrowed slightly. "I'm clear on the concept."

"Just checking."

The sound of the music got louder as the Fool's Gold high school marching band rounded the corner.

They were so young, Justice thought, watching the kids move in formation. Innocent. They were worried about things like grades and prom. He respected that, and envied them their ordinary lives. He'd known Bart Hanson wasn't like other fathers by the time he'd turned seven. By his tenth birthday, he knew that unlike criminals on TV, criminals in real life often walked or were never caught at all.

Behind the band came a group of men pulling little kids in wagons. The wagons were decorated with flowers and ribbons, the children dressed in their Sunday best. All around them women sighed and called out, waving to their families.

Angel raised his eyebrows. "Seriously?"

"You don't like it?"

"I haven't decided." Angel tilted his head, as if studying a difficult problem.

The first group of bike riders appeared. Justice spotted Lillie right away. Like her friends, she was dressed in a pink shirt and white jeans. Tiny flowers had been woven in her hair and matched the ribbons and flowers on her bike. The six girls rode around each other in slow circles and figure eights. Across the street Patience snapped pictures.

Lillie saw Justice and waved. He waved back, then pulled a small camera out of his pocket and started taking pictures himself. Beside him, Angel snorted.

"Yours?" the man on the other side of him asked.

Justice didn't recognize him, so he assumed he was a tourist.

"I have three boys," the man continued with a sigh. "Great kids. Always wanted a little girl." He lowered his voice. "My wife says no way. She's done." He gave a shrug. "It would have been nice."

The man drifted back to his wife and kids. Angel stared at Justice. "We're opening the business here?"

"Why not?"

The two men walked away from the parade. They headed toward the lake where it was quiet.

"Consuelo has agreed to be an instructor," Justice said. "She'll be teaching our students and offering classes for people in town. Self-defense, general conditioning."

Angel shook his head. "Okay, now you're screwing with me for sport. Consuelo working with the community? Teaching little old ladies how to fend off attackers?"

"From what I hear, the women in town already know how to do that. Having a change of heart?"

"I don't know. I'm more worried none of this is real and I'm in a hospital somewhere hooked up to the good drugs."

"We want you to handle the corporate work. Act as our liaison. Sell the company."

Angel stared at him. "You're kidding."

Justice grinned. "Yes, I am. Ford is more the type. We were thinking you could design the curriculum. Come up with the various exercises for the retreats."

Angel swore under his breath. "You had me going."

"I could tell."

"I could kill you, you know."

"You could try," Justice said, not worried.

"You're injured. That gives me an edge. Not that I need it."

Justice doubted anyone else would have guessed he was still recovering from getting shot. But Angel would have noticed the slight hesitation in the way he moved, the way he favored one side.

"I can't wait to see how this all plays out," Justice said. "You in Fool's Gold."

Angel shoved his hands into his jeans pockets. "I grew up in West Virginia. Coal-mining town. I know what it's like to live where everybody knows your business. Where you take care of your neighbors and pull together in hard times."

Something Justice would never have guessed. "Looking to get back to that?"

"Maybe. If it's not too late."

Justice turned to his friend. He recognized the combination of longing and resignation on the other man's face. Angel wanted to be something other than he was, but wasn't sure it was possible. Did the training run too deep? Could he fit in with people who had never seen such horrors, never had to commit them in the first place?

That *Harry Potter* author had it right. Her villain had ripped apart his soul through the act of murder. Taking another life did tear at a man's being, leaving him less than what he had been before. The question for men like Angel and himself was whether there was enough left to feel like a person.

"They don't let you live on the fringes in this place," Justice told him. "They'll hunt you down and force you to belong, whether you want to or not."

Angel turned to him. "Are you selling or warning?"

"Both. You in?"

"I REMEMBER this place," Patience said, following Justice from the car. "We used to camp up here when I was a kid." She looked at him and grinned. "The older kids came up here to park and make out."

"Did you?" he asked.

She shrugged. "No. I wasn't that wild in high school. I mean I dated, of course. There was kissing. But not full-on making out."

The air temperature was cooler up here than in town. The sky was blue and the air seemed fresher, somehow. Justice had asked Patience to help him navigate a few back roads as he searched for the right tract of land for the advanced obstacle course. The one they would build by the warehouse would work for corporate retreats and casual training, but for their more serious work, they would need something more challenging.

While he could have found his way himself, he liked having her around. Liked being with her.

She pointed to the clearing. "The land you're interested in starts over there. I remember a fence, I think. It was old back then, so it might not be standing now."

He walked next to her, shortening his stride to match hers. She grinned.

"We used to play truth or dare."

He laughed. "Which did you pick?"

"Mostly dare, which was silly considering I'm not very brave. One time the dare was to run around the camp naked, but I couldn't do it, even though there were only girls here. I kept my underwear on." Her gaze settled on his face. "You would have run naked."

"Probably."

"It's a guy thing, right?"

He stopped. She did the same.

"What?" she asked.

He touched her cheek, then her mouth, brushing his thumb across her lower lip.

She might be close to thirty, a single mother and a successful businesswoman, but she was still so damned innocent. Untouched by horror. She'd been through tough times, but the very essence of who she was remained pure. He drew back, aware there was blood on his hands. Perhaps sanctioned, perhaps necessary, but the stains would never wash out.

"Justice? Are you okay?"

"No."

He wasn't worthy. A ridiculous concept, yet completely honest. He would never be worthy, never be right. She deserved so much more. He wondered about Felicia's question. Did Patience love him? Could she? Not if she knew the truth.

"There are things in my past. Things I've done."

"I know."

"You don't. If I told you, everything would change."

She placed her hand on his chest, over his heart. "You killed people. You're right. I don't know the details and I don't have to. I know *you*."

"It can't be that simple."

She smiled. "Of course it is."

PATIENCE PICKED UP her glass of wine and took a sip. The day had been long, but happy. Her feet hurt and her back ached, but all the discomfort was worth it. She was doing forty percent more business than she'd projected. The merchandise had become a significant part of her bottom line. With the tourist season just beginning, she would have several months of excellent sales to carry her through the quieter months.

She glanced at the clock on the wall and figured

her mother would be home any minute. Justice was still out with Angel and had told Patience he would be late. Lillie was spending the night with a friend. So for now, it was just her.

She leaned back against the sofa, enjoying the quiet. There wasn't much silence in her life. Between work and her daughter and everything else she had to get done, she was running all the time.

Busy, she thought with a smile, and happy. So happy. She was in one of those perfect times, when her family was healthy and doing well. She had the store and she had Justice.

Loving him was a little scary—she knew he might not feel the same way, and even if he did, there was no guarantee, but that was okay. She liked that she'd fallen in love. It meant she'd healed enough to give her heart again. That she was willing to trust a man with her world. Even if he broke her heart, she would always have this mental health moment, and that was very satisfying.

She'd been through a lot. From her disastrous relationship with Ned, to figuring out how to be a good mom to Lillie and a good daughter and occasional caretaker for her mom, to having her dream come true. She remembered reading somewhere that luck was all about opportunity and preparation. She'd never gotten that before, but she understood it now. While Great-Aunt Becky's bequest had provided the money to start her own business, Patience had been ready. She'd taken classes and built her business plan. She knew exactly what she wanted to do, and when she had the chance, she simply had to take the steps. She was proud of herself, she thought happily.

So many of her friends were accomplished. Charlie, who excelled in what was traditionally a man's world. Annabelle, who last year had put her mind to raising enough money to buy the library a bookmobile and then had done it. Heidi, who had started with nothing and grown a goat-based empire and now sold her soaps and cheeses all over the world. Isabel, too, recovering from a divorce and still planning to fulfill her dreams.

Her new friends, Noelle and Felicia, were just as strong. She was surrounded by women who knew how to achieve their dreams. Patience was pleased to be in a place where she felt as though she had done the same.

The front door opened and her mother walked in. Ava used her cane tonight, but was still smiling happily as she stepped into the living room. She spotted the second glass of wine by the bottle and sighed.

"I raised you right, didn't I?"

Patience laughed. "Yes, you did. How was your date?"

"Lovely. We had a quiet dinner at Angelo's. If my metabolism would support it, I would have pasta every single night."

Patience was about to ask what she'd ordered when she realized there was something different about her mother. Not in her physical appearance, she thought. Ava was wearing exactly what she had been when she left, but there was a light…no, a glow. She straightened.

"What is it?" she asked as her mother approached the sofa. "What happened?"

"And here I thought I could keep a secret at least for a few days." Ava sat next to her and held out her left hand. A large diamond solitaire winked from her ring finger. "Steve proposed."

It took Patience a moment to register the meaning. Yes, Steve had been responsible so far with her daughter and her mother. But would he be forever?

"That's wonderful," she finally said, then hugged her mother. You couldn't plan love. She would hope that her mother's love would only cement the changes Steve had made in his life. "You're getting married."

Ava hugged her back, then kissed her cheek. "I can barely believe it myself. It was so romantic. We were in the back of the restaurant and the waiter brought champagne. Steve got down on one knee and everything." Tears filled her eyes. "He makes me so happy."

"I'm happy for you." Patience poured her wine and passed it over, then raised her own glass. "Congratulations, Mom. You deserve all the love in the world."

"Thank you. I'll admit I'm a little nervous. It's been a long time since I had a man in my life."

There would be a lot of changes, Patience thought. For all of them. "Have you set a date for the wedding?"

"No. We'll have a very quiet ceremony later this summer. Just family. But you and I have to talk about this house."

"Right, because it would be weird to have us all living together." Patience ignored the pang she felt at the thought of moving. “I can find some place for me and Lillie. This is your house, Mom.”

Her mother shook her head. “It’s *our* house, remember. I put you on the deed when we paid off the mortgage.”

“Yes, but—”

“No buts. Steve and I have already talked about this. We’re having a house built. One designed for me. I’ve been very lucky with the MS, but we both know there are going to be bad days. It’s silly for us to stay in a place where I can’t get to half the rooms.”

Patience nodded slowly. Her mother hadn’t been able to climb stairs for a few years now. “You’re thinking of a one-story?”

“Yes. We’ll put in a ramp and wider doors. The master bath will have a shower I can wheel into, that sort of thing. Steve has thought of everything. The kitchen counters will be lower for me so I can still reach them if I’m in my chair. Our plan is I’ll move in with him as soon as we’re married, and then we’ll move into our new house when it’s finished.”

Patience grinned. “You’re not going to live with him before the wedding?”

Ava blushed, then ducked her head. “I wasn’t sure you’d approve.”

“Why would you think that, Mom? I’m pretty sure you know there’s some sneaking around going on upstairs.”

“I have suspected. But that’s different. I’m your mother.”

"You're a beautiful, vital woman and if you want to move in with the man you love, I say go for it. Lillie won't mind that her grandparents are living together."

Ava hugged her. "I love you so much, Patience. You have always been the best part of my life."

"I love you, too, Mom." She drew back and grinned. "We can get you a fabulous dress at Paper Moon."

Her mother shuddered. "That isn't happening. I'm thinking of a pretty suit, not a wedding gown. Why don't you and I take Lillie into San Francisco when school gets out? We'll go for a couple of nights. Stay somewhere by the water and find dresses. Then we'll have the ceremony right here in the backyard."

"I love that idea."

They picked up their wine and toasted again.

"To happy endings," her mother said.

"To falling in love."

CHAPTER EIGHTEEN

PATIENCE SAT IN a booth at Jo's Bar as the sodas and iced teas were passed around. She was still feeling the glow from the previous night's announcement and was thrilled to be able to share the news with her friends.

Noelle sat by Felicia, with Isabel between them. Patience was next to Felicia.

"It's all everyone is talking about," Isabel said with a grin. "I already called your mom and invited her to come and try on gowns."

"Did she hang up on you?" Patience asked, slipping her straw into her glass of diet soda.

"Nearly. She said she wasn't interested in anything I had. I pretended to be crushed, which was fun." Isabel shook her head. "The poor woman still thinks she's getting away with only you and Lillie at the ceremony."

"Totally delusional," Patience agreed. She turned to Felicia and Noelle. "No way that will happen in this town. My mom grew up here. She knows everyone. I think a backyard wedding is a great idea. We can have the reception at Brew-haha, but as for keeping the guest list down to immediate family? No way."

"Historically, a wedding is as much a contract as

a celebration," Felicia said. "The blending of families was seen as mutually beneficial. Did you know that the female fantasy of being carried off by a handsome stranger can be traced back to times of precivilization when women were stolen by neighboring tribes? The stolen woman provided fresh DNA, which ensured healthier children."

Noelle sipped her tea. "I can't wait to see you drunk."

Felicia stared at her. "Why?"

"I'll bet you edit about half of what you say. I want to hear the whole thing. You're so fascinating."

Felicia shifted, obviously uncomfortable with the compliment. "I know I can be professorial."

"A little, but it's fun." Noelle looked at Patience. "Let me know if you need any help getting things ready for the wedding. I'm at a slow stage with my business. I have the lease signed, but there's about three weeks' worth of remodeling that has to be done. I've started ordering my inventory, but some items are going to take six weeks. So I have time to run errands or whatever."

"Thanks," Patience said. "I'll let you know. First my mom has to face reality. If she's getting married in town, she's going to have a guest list pushing two hundred people. I can't wait!"

"It's just plain romantic," Noelle said with a sigh. "Finding love later in life."

"It gives us all hope." Isabel sipped her drink. "So, Patience, was Justice different than what you remembered?"

"His basic character is the same. He's still sweet and funny."

Felicia frowned. "Justice?"

"I know there are other sides to him, but I don't see them as much."

"Unless these two are keeping secrets," Isabel said, "you're going to have to have a relationship for all of us. My marriage disaster isn't anything I want to risk repeating."

"I'm recovering from a broken engagement," Noelle said.

They all looked at her.

"I'm sorry," Felicia said. "I didn't know."

"I hadn't said anything to anyone. It sounds so sad. A broken engagement. Like it got dropped on the floor or something."

Felicia picked up her drink. "I can't bond on this subject. I haven't been in any kind of romantic relationship and my sexual encounters have all been extremely short. I'm considering the possibility that I have responsibility in that beyond the barrier of my intelligence."

"That you're avoiding men who might want more from you?" Patience asked.

"Yes, and that I'm not putting myself in the appropriate social situations. I say I want to fall in love and have a family, but until I moved here, I hadn't done anything to facilitate that occurring."

Isabel leaned into Felicia. "We've all been idiots.

Don't beat yourself up about it. You see what you've been doing and now you can correct the problem."

"I'm not always successful at self-correcting."

"None of us are," Noelle told her. "But that doesn't mean we shouldn't keep on trying."

"Do you know what you're doing?" Lillie asked.

Her tone was gentle and her gaze warm and affectionate, but Justice still felt the sting of her words.

"I'm trying," he muttered, carefully combing her hair.

This wasn't supposed to happen, he thought grimly. One of the staff had called in sick, so Ava had gone in to help at the store. Patience had phoned and promised she would be back in time to get Lillie ready, but she was—he glanced at the clock—twenty minutes late. Apparently the last day of school was a big deal for a ten-year-old, so Justice had stepped in to fill the breach, so to speak. Or in this case, try to figure out how to make a fancy braid look right.

"I can show you on a doll," Lillie offered.

He sectioned the hair, as he'd been shown and tried to manipulate it the way he'd seen Patience do it a hundred times. Her fingers flew through the process. It had looked so easy.

"If you and Mom get married, you need to think about having a boy," Lillie told him. "You'd like that and you wouldn't have to worry about his hair."

He dropped his hands and stared at her, at her pretty face, at the affection in her eyes. He heard the acceptance in her words. She'd taken him into her heart, much as he suspected her mother had.

"Lillie," he began, not sure what to say.

She flung herself at him, hanging on tight. He hugged her back, barely aware of the twinge in his midsection.

"You'd be a good dad," she whispered in his ear.

The front door flew open.

"I know, I know," Patience said as she hurried inside. "I was watching the clock. Then I turned around and I was late. I ran the whole way."

She was flushed and panting, proof of her point. She hurried toward them, then paused. "You look so grown-up. When did that happen?"

Lillie smoothed the front of her pink-and-white dress and smiled. "Mom, we can talk about me growing up later. I need to get to school."

"Right. French braid."

Patience took the comb from Justice and smoothed her daughter's hair. Seconds later her fingers were moving in rapid sequence. More quickly than he could have thought possible, it was done and she'd tied a pink ribbon on the end.

Patience rose and headed for the stairs. "Wait right there. I have something for you."

Lillie turned to Justice. "Do you know what it is?"

"I don't."

"Mom gives the best presents. Just wait until Christmas. You won't believe what you find under the tree."

Christmas. He'd never had much reason to acknowledge the holiday. He'd usually been working and often out of the country. He would guess that in Fool's Gold the season was celebrated with gusto and festivals.

There would be snow, he thought. Traditions. It would be a time of memories and belonging. Did he want that? Could he let go of his past and be a part of something that lasted?

Patience raced down the stairs and handed her daughter a pale silver box. The fancy script said Jenel's Gems in the corner.

Lillie's eyes widened. "For me?"

Patience hugged her. "I'm so proud of you. You're a good student. You're interested and curious and you work hard. This isn't all about your grades, though. This is because you're a wonderful daughter and I love you so very much."

Lillie's eyes filled with tears. She held on to her mom and mumbled, "I love you, too."

He watched them, both in the moment and separated from it. He'd never had anything like this, he thought. He was sure his mother had been tender with him when he was young, but by the time Justice was six, Bart didn't allow any signs of affection. He didn't want to "weaken the boy," as he put it.

What his father had never seen was the power and strength in love.

Lillie straightened then she opened the box. Inside was a gold butterfly charm on a delicate chain. She gasped.

"Do you like it?" Patience asked. "I saw it and thought of you. Here, let me put it on you."

Lillie turned.

Patience slipped the necklace over her daughter's head, then fastened it. Lillie ran toward the downstairs bathroom.

"I want to see! I want to see!"

Patience smiled at him. "Her birthday's in a couple of months and she doesn't know it yet, but I'm going to let her pierce her ears. I already bought the butterfly posts for her."

He touched her cheek. "You're a good mom."

"I hope so. Thanks for helping with all this. Her last day of school crept up on me. I'm totally not prepared."

"You've had a few things going on."

Lillie returned and threw her arms around both of them. "I love it, Mom. I really love it!"

"I'm glad."

Justice squeezed her tightly before letting her go. They all stood.

"Okay," Patience said. "Eleven-thirty. We'll all be there." She looked at him.

He nodded. "I'll be there on time. I promise. We'll take pictures."

Lillie beamed. "There's not a ceremony or anything. It's not like next year when I graduate. But there will be cookies."

Patience bent down and kissed her daughter's cheek. Lillie moved to Justice, her body language expectant.

It took him a second to realize what she wanted—

the same kiss on the cheek. He bent forward and lightly touched his mouth to her smooth skin. When he straightened, she danced away.

"Bye. See you at eleven-thirty."

"Bye," Patience called after her. When the door closed, she turned to Justice. "Okay, I have to get back to the store. You know where the school is and everything?"

He nodded.

She kissed him on the mouth, and then she was gone, too.

He was left standing alone, apparently the only one aware of what had just happened.

"YOU'RE NOT listening," Felicia said.

With any other woman, the words would be a complaint, but with Felicia it was simply a statement of fact.

"I know you find the topic of the business interesting," she continued. "So your inattention must have another source." She raised her eyebrows. "Patience?"

They were at the dining table of the small, furnished town house Felicia had rented. Papers were spread in front of him, but he hadn't read any of them.

"Patience," he agreed.

"It wasn't a significant guess for me. She's been on your mind a lot lately."

"It's not just her. It's Lillie, too. And Ava, although less her. She'll be moving out to live with Steve." He rose and walked to the window, then turned back. "I can't sleep anymore. I can't stop thinking about them. Lillie's going to be eleven. I don't know anything about eleven-year-old girls. But she hugged me and wanted me to kiss her on the cheek."

"She loves you. You're a natural father figure. Did you think she wouldn't bond with you?"

"I didn't think about it one way or the other. I was focused on Patience. I like Lillie. I'd do anything for her. But what if I hurt her? I could hurt them both." He felt his hands curl into fists and had to consciously relax his fingers.

"How can I know I'm good enough? How can I be sure he's gone?" He shook his head. "I know my father is dead. You don't have to remind me. That's not what I mean."

She stood and crossed to him. "I know what you mean. You're afraid that who he was is a result of biology and that you've inherited his, for lack of a better word, evilness."

"I can't risk it."

She pressed her palm against his chest, over his heart. "You love them."

He closed his eyes, then opened them again. "I don't want to put them in danger."

"Love can't do that."

"It can."

"Your father didn't love anyone. Not even himself. But you're not him. You never were. As for the rest of it, this is Fool's Gold, not an op. You walked away from that life, Justice. More significant, you came here on purpose."

He covered her hand with his. "I didn't know where else to go. I had to see Patience again. But I wasn't supposed to stay."

"You've been drawn to this place since you left. You belong here. You have something special, something that can't be manufactured." Her expression turned sad. "Something so many of us want."

He squeezed her fingers. "You'll find the right guy."

"I hope you're correct. I want to and I'm afraid. I've never had such mixed emotions. Sometimes the desire is stronger and sometimes the fear. I've tried to create a formula to predict my emotions, but I'm unable to."

He released her and stepped back. "Maybe that's part of the magic of being human."

She smiled. "I agree. There is an element of magic. And chemistry. While I can detail the process and even the hormones involved, I can't tell you why one person will cause the reaction and another won't. You were never interested in me that way."

"No." He pulled her close. "Life would have been easier if I had been."

"For both of us."

They held each other for a few seconds, and then she moved away.

"Although I was angry at the time, I'm glad we never had sexual relations," she told him. "Not only because it could have damaged our friendship but because it might have been…" She hesitated.

"Gross" he offered.

She laughed. "Yes. Gross." Her humor faded. "Justice, you will never truly be free of your past. But if you let that fear win, then so does your father. I know the man you are. I've seen you under nearly every circumstance possible. I know who you are when you're exhausted and wounded and hopeless. I would trust you with my life. If I had a child, I would trust you with that child's life. Whoever your father was has no bearing on who you have become. You're a good man. Patience deserves a good man."

He wanted to believe her. Wanted the promise of long years with Patience. Lillie's offhanded comment about having a son had lodged in his brain. He would like that. He would also like a little girl. Children and a home. And a lifetime with Patience.

Felicia was right. He'd never forgotten her, had always thought about the girl he'd known so long ago. Stupid maybe, but true. So he'd come and she was even more than he'd imagined.

He wanted to give her all he had, to plan a future with her, to enjoy the rhythm of life in this ridiculous town. All that stood between this moment and that future was his father. Oh, and Patience, he thought with a smile. He had to convince her to say yes.

It was a simple choice. The past or the future. The wide-open bright light of promise or the small, dark corner of shame. Yes, a simple choice, but not an easy one. Because to pick the light meant having faith in himself.

"I can't lose her," he said.

Felicia sighed. "That's so romantic."

He glanced at his watch. "I have to go. Can we pick this up later?"

"Yes. Go."

JENEL'S GEMS WAS an elegant store with more rings than Justice had ever seen in one place. Not that he could remember ever being in a jewelry store before. He hadn't known about this one until he'd seen the box Lillie's present had come in.

He stared down at the display of twinkling diamonds and felt his chest tighten. How was he supposed to decide?

"Good morning."

A tall, pretty blonde walked in from the rear of the store and smiled at him. "I'm Jenel. How can I help?"

"I'm, uh, Justice Garrett. I want to buy an engagement ring."

Her smile widened. "Based on your slightly panicked expression, I'm going to guess this is a decision made recently?"

"Just now. But it's right. I won't change my mind."

"Good to know, although we do have a return policy." She studied him. "Who's the lucky lady? Just so you know, I'm very good at keeping secrets. Knowing the future bride helps me guide you toward the rings she would like most."

"Patience McGraw."

Jenel's blue eyes lit up. "I know Patience. She's wonderful and her daughter is adorable. I'm so happy for both of you. Don't you love her new store? The logo is charming and so creative." Jenel sighed. "This is great news. All right. You need to take a few deep breaths and then we'll look at rings. Do you have anything in mind?"

She pointed to a padded stool. He sank down and looked at the display in front of him.

"I have no idea. Something nice. A ring she'd like."

"Patience isn't especially flashy, and with the work she does, a large solitaire might get in the way. Having said that, every girl loves a little flash with her bling. And it's very satisfying to have a sparkly engagement ring."

She pulled out several rings and put them on a padded, velvet tray. "These are simple solitaire diamonds. Classic and elegant. You can go any number of ways with the band. Platinum, gold or something with diamonds. I would urge you to consider the latter because she probably won't wear her engagement ring all the time. Especially at work. So diamonds in a wedding band are a nice touch."

He swallowed hard, muttered, "Sure," then knew he was totally out of his league. He needed help, and fast. Then he saw it. A ring that seemed to sparkle more than the rest.

"That one," he said, pointing to one in the case.

Jenel nodded. "Nice. It's one of my favorites, too. One and a half carats, it's a modified cushion-cut diamond with a double row of bead-set diamonds surrounding it. There are also some diamonds on the band, as you can see."

Little of what she said made sense to him. What he saw was a large, somewhat square diamond surrounded by smaller diamonds. The whole thing was held up by a V structure.

She returned the other rings and pulled out the one he liked, along with several bands with diamonds.

"With this style, they can nestle together, and she'll have a flat ring for work."

He knew this was the moment where he decided to let go of the past and believe in his future. Together he and Patience could make it. He loved her. He'd probably loved her for the past fifteen years. Felicia was right—Patience was the reason he'd come back to Fool's Gold. Now that he'd found her again, he never wanted to let her go.

He looked at Jenel. "That's the one."

"It's beautiful, but if Patience doesn't like it, I'll happily exchange it for something else."

His phone rang. He glanced at the screen and saw Patience's name and number.

"Excuse me," he said, and stood. "Hello?"

"Justice?" The sound was more of a sob than an actual word. Patience sucked in breath. "Justice?"

He could hear the tears in her voice. The panic. His body went very, very still.

"What's wrong? Tell me what happened?"

"I don't know. I don't *know*. It's L-Lillie. At school.

A man c-came. He had a gun and he took her. Justice, please." She began to cry.

In less time than it took him to absorb the words, he began the process of disconnecting from all that was around him. There was only the moment and the mission. He didn't know what had happened or why, but he knew how it was going to end.

"You're at the school?" he asked.

"Yes, but Police Chief Barns wants me to go home."

"I'll be right there."

CHAPTER NINETEEN

"I DON'T understand."

Patience didn't know how many times she'd said the words, but they remained the truth. She didn't understand. How could she? Things like this didn't happen in real life. They were the stuff of crime shows and movies. She lived in Fool's Gold. There was no way a man walked in to an elementary school and kidnapped her daughter.

Only it had happened and Lillie was gone.

Fear was cold and dark and clung to her like a giant leech. She couldn't breathe, couldn't think. She wanted to scream she would do anything, give all she had, if only Lillie would come home.

She stood in her kitchen, shaking and fighting tears. Felicia was with her, as was Police Chief Barns. There were other people, too, but she couldn't focus on them right now. Not when it was so hard to breathe.

"Why?" she asked.

Felicia put her hands on her shoulders. "You're in shock. You need to keep your breathing steady and even. I'll get you some water. I don't know why, but offering water is what we do and drinking it is surprisingly helpful."

Chief Barns shook her head. "I'm with you, Patience. None of this makes sense. We have a roadblock in place and are contacting state authorities. Every person in my department is out looking for Lillie. We're interviewing her teacher. What we know is that a man walked into the classroom and took Lillie. He wanted her specifically. Can you think of a reason why? It's not your ex-husband, is it?"

"Ned? I haven't had contact with him in years."

"Is there anyone new in your life?"

"Just Justice and he would never—"

"What did the kidnapper look like?"

Patience turned toward the speaker and saw Justice walking into the kitchen. She rushed to him and threw herself at him.

"You have to help," she said, tears pouring down her cheeks.

"I will." He lightly kissed her. "I'll get her back, Patience. No matter what it takes, I will find her and bring her home."

There was certainty in his eyes. A promise. She knew she could trust him with her child and was able to draw in a breath.

Chief Barns flipped open her small notebook and began to read from it.

"About five-eleven. Graying hair, brown eyes. Mid-to-late fifties. Black or dark jeans, a black T-shirt."

Patience felt Justice tense.

"Did he have a scar on his cheek? His left cheek? Almost like a question mark?"

The police chief stared at him. "How did you know?"

Justice ignored her and turned to Felicia. "It's Bart. We need to set up a command post and fast. Help the police. They're out of their league on this one."

Patience watched wide-eyed as Felicia crossed to the police chief and started talking about phones and computers and personnel. Then his words sank in.

"You know who took her?"

Justice's expression tightened. "I do. I'm sorry. This is my fault."

"What? Why?" Bart. He'd said Bart. Why was that name familiar?

"It's my father."

"But he's dead. You said he died."

"I thought he was. That's what we were told. There was a fire." He shook his head. "It doesn't matter now. I've sensed he was nearby. I told myself I was imagining things, but I wasn't."

Justice wasn't making sense. How could his father not be dead? Why would he have taken Lillie? She pressed her hands to her stomach and wanted to be able to scream her fear and frustration. *Take me.* That was the answer. She should have been the one, not Lillie.

She stood in the center of her living room as people moved around her. They all had purpose and all she could do was be afraid. Ava and Steve raced in.

Patience went to her mother and they held on to each other.

"I don't understand," her mother said over and over again.

Patience told her what she knew, which wasn't much, and they clung to each other. Less than fifteen minutes later, the phone rang.

"We're not ready," Felicia said. "I can't trace the call or tap in to it."

Ava straightened. "We'll use the phone in my office. It has a speakerphone."

Patience realized everyone was waiting for her to answer. She walked into her mother's office, both eager and reluctant to hear whatever Bart Hanson had to say. She felt more tears on her cheeks and pushed the speaker button.

"Hello?"

"You must be the mother. He's there, isn't he? My boy?"

"I want to talk to Lillie," Patience said, her voice more firm than she would have expected. "I want to talk to my daughter right now."

There was a short, humorless laugh. "You think you can boss me around? I don't think so. You can't talk to your daughter, but you can *hear* her."

There was a moment of silence, followed by a short scream of terror. Patience lunged for the phone. The room spun, but she refused to give in to weakness.

"Stop it!" she screamed. "Stop it!"

The screams ended and there was only a soft whimpering sound.

Patience hung on to the desk. Arms came around

her. She wasn't sure who held her and she didn't care. She needed to crawl through the phone lines and get to her daughter.

Justice moved closer. "You know this isn't about Patience or her daughter."

"No, it's not, son. It's about you. It's always been about you. I've waited a long time to find you, and now I have."

Patience was mindful of both Chief Barns and Felicia in the living room, frantically talking on their cell phones. The part of her brain that was still rational wondered if they were trying to trace the call. To find Bart so they could rescue Lillie.

She realized Steve was the one hanging on to her. She wanted to tell him she was fine, but she knew she wasn't. She would never be fine again.

"Take me," she whispered. Maybe she could talk Bart into an exchange. He could do whatever he wanted to her.

"Let her go," Justice said. "I'm ready to take her place."

Bart chuckled. "Where's the fun in that? You come find me, and then maybe I'll let her go and maybe I won't. I waited a long time for you to show your hand, son. A long time."

The phone went dead.

Patience screamed and reached for it. Steve held her back.

"What does he mean?" Ava asked. "About you showing your hand."

"He waited for me to care about someone," Justice said flatly. "He's been out there watching. He took Lillie to hurt me." He turned to Patience. "I'm sorry."

FELICIA HELD OUT the bulletproof vest. Justice pushed it away.

"You think getting dead changes anything?" she asked, her green eyes cool. "That Lillie will be safer with you bleeding out? You have to be alive to get her away from him."

He couldn't deny the logic of her argument. Of course, his father could take him out with a head shot, but that was a problem he would deal with if it became an issue.

He stripped to the waist and slipped on the vest, then pulled on his shirt. Bart would probably guess he was wearing one, but there was no need to advertise the fact.

Less than thirty minutes had passed since his father had hung up. In that time equipment and backup had arrived. There was a large map of the town and the surrounding areas on the wall. The police were setting up a phone and computer system. One of the police officers had been sent to CDS for a sniper rifle.

"Hell of a time for Angel to be out of town," Justice muttered. "I could have used the help tracking him."

Felicia sighed. "I'd offer, but I know you'd refuse."

"I need you here, handling this. Chief Barns does a good job, but she has no experience with a man like Bart."

"They're calling in the feds."

"By the time they get here, it will all be over."

Felicia grabbed his arm. "You can't let him beat you. He'll try to get in your head. That's the only way he wins. You're not him. You've never been him."

"I'm going to kill my father today, Felicia. What does that make me, if not like him?"

"You're doing what you have to. You're saving a child. You take no pleasure in the act."

She was right about that. But he also knew the price he would pay. He wouldn't hesitate, wouldn't second-guess himself. He'd killed before, but this was different. Killing Bart meant crossing a line, and once he did, there was no way back.

He tucked in his shirt, then took the earpiece she held out. Once it was in place, they tested it to make sure it worked.

The police would follow, but he would be the one to go in. No one on the Fool's Gold police force was trained to deal with a situation like this. He hoped they never had to again.

"Do you have any idea where he is?" she asked.

Together they crossed to the map.

The school had already been marked, along with Patience's house. Justice sensed they couldn't believe the actual motive. That his father wanted retribution. As a sixteen-year-old kid, Justice had chosen the police over his father. Bart had spent nearly twenty years looking for payback. He wanted his son to find him.

Justice scanned the map. "Not by the casino," he

said. "There are too many people." He studied the roads out of town. Lillie wasn't drugged, so Bart was dealing with a terrified little girl. Even tied up, she would slow his progress. He wouldn't have gone far.

Then he saw it. The road he and Patience had taken to look at property. The clearing where they'd talked. Where she'd said she knew there were secrets and accepted him anyway.

His gut churned as he realized Bart had been there that day. Had been there the whole time.

"Here," he said, pointing to an old road leading up into the mountains.

"That's a fire road," the police chief said.

"I got it." A woman in uniform jogged into the house. She held Justice's rifle in one hand and a box of ammo in her other.

He took the rifle and checked it. "I'm ready."

He crossed to Patience, who stood with her mother and Steve. She was pale and trembling. Her brown eyes filled with tears as he approached.

"I'll get her," he said. "I will bring Lillie home to you. I give you my word."

She flung her arms around him. He hung on tight, knowing this was the last time. That when he returned, he wouldn't be who he was at this moment.

"I love you," he whispered, then turned and walked out. As he went, he touched his earpiece to activate the unit. "Felicia?"

"I'm here."

While everyone back at the house would be on the

same frequency, only Felicia would talk to him. Right now he didn't need any more voices in his head.

BART'S TRUCK WAS parked less than fifty feet off the highway, on the fire road. Not fifty feet from where Justice and Patience had gone only a few days before. Justice pulled in behind him, taking the extra second to block his escape.

He carefully hid his keys under a pile of leaves, then started up the road until he saw the broken branches that flagged his father's path.

"I'm here," he said quietly to Felicia. He gave the coordinates. "Tell the others to stay back. If he gets spooked, he'll react badly."

"Will do."

He moved quietly, even knowing there was no point. That Bart was expecting him. But his training couldn't be ignored. Ten minutes later, he was in a clearing. Lillie lay curled up at the base of a large tree. She was blindfolded and tied, but alive.

"Lillie, it's Justice," he called, loading his rifle. "I'm here."

She struggled to sit up. When she turned, he saw the gag in her mouth and the blood on her arm. Blood from where Bart had cut her.

Hatred burned hot and bright inside Justice. Then he pushed it down to the darkest part of his being. No emotions, he reminded himself. This was business—what he'd been trained to do. He was a man who killed and he would do it again. Today.

"I knew you were weak enough to come after the girl."

His father's voice came from the woods. Justice ignored him.

"Whatever happens, Lillie, I want you to listen for my instructions, okay? You need to do exactly what I say as soon as I say it. Do you understand?"

She nodded frantically.

"Your mom and I love you very much," he said, his voice slightly softer. "You're going to be okay."

"Aw, that's so sweet," Bart said. He appeared by Lillie and jerked the girl to her feet. "You love her and now you're going to watch her die."

Lillie screamed, the sound muffled by the gag. Justice stayed in his head, disconnected from all except what he had to do.

His father was older. Grayer, but still strong, with a straight back and cold eyes.

"Why aren't you dead, old man?"

"I should be. They thought I was. You did, too, and you should have known better."

"How'd you do it?"

"Fake my death? Easy. There was a man in prison just my size. I made friends with him, convinced him to escape with me. Got the dentist to forge the dental records. I was declared dead. And here I am."

"You killed him, too." It wasn't a question.

"The dentist? Sure. Why not? Killing's the best part. He thought he was going to make a shitload of money off my little trick." Bart kissed the top of Lillie's head.

"To be honest, I can't decide what I should do. Kill her first and let you watch, or kill you first. Then you'd die knowing you didn't protect her from whatever I decide to do."

Justice knew his father wasn't interested in young girls, at least not sexually. Lillie would be spared that. But if Bart made good on his word, then Lillie would die and not quickly. Bart had always enjoyed the process.

"A quality problem," his father said with a cackle.

"I'm getting all this," Felicia said in a low voice. "So are the others. They're moving in. They only need a few more minutes."

Justice knew they wouldn't be here soon enough. He wasn't sure anyone was a trained sharpshooter, and with Lillie so close, she could easily be hit.

Justice took aim.

Bart picked up the girl and held her in front of him like a shield. Lillie screamed. He lowered the gun and Bart lowered the girl.

"You see how this is going to be," his father told him. "I'm glad of that. I thought you were too far gone to play the game. What were you thinking, son? It was one thing when you were in the military. You belonged there. But this town? With folks like her?" He shook Lillie. "You can't. It's just not right."

Justice watched and waited. Bart would make a mistake. He had to.

"You've got too much of me in you, boy."

"You're right about that," Justice said. "You fooled them all and you found me. How'd you do it?"

"You got your picture in the paper, boy. Guarding some fat-cat banker in Europe. From there I got your name. Justice. What the hell?"

"One of the marshals suggested it. I like it."

His father glared at him. "You're my son and you'll take my name. You hear me?"

"I want nothing from you."

Bart was getting angry. The tactic had risks, but Justice knew how fast he could fire. At this distance, taking out Bart was a sure thing. It was all going to be about the timing.

"You never were right in the head," his father said angrily. "Siding with the cops. That was wrong. You had too much of your mother in you. Too much of her weakness. I tried to beat it out of you, but I wasn't hard enough on you. Damn you, boy."

Bart stepped to the side. For a second, he released his hold on Lillie. The girl spun.

"Lillie, get down!"

The shout filled the quiet, but Justice hadn't been the one to call out. Before he even got his rifle in position, a shot rang out and Bart dropped to the ground.

Not knowing who had intervened, Justice was already moving. He crossed the clearing and grabbed Lillie.

"It's me," he told her, peeling away the blindfold, even as he carried her into the woods and away from Bart. "You're okay now."

He removed the gag next and she gasped for air, then started to cry.

A tall, dark-haired man stepped out from behind a tree. Ford Hendrix shrugged. "I had the better shot," he said. "So I took it. Hope you don't mind."

CHAPTER TWENTY

PATIENCE WATCHED HER daughter sleep. For the first two nights, her daughter had slept fitfully, but now she was more relaxed and settled.

The past couple of days had been a blur. Once Lillie had been rescued, there had been a whirlwind of conversations with the police and counselors. She'd been checked out by her doctor and hailed a hero by the town.

Patience slipped out of the room and returned to the living room. She'd finally convinced Ava and Steve it was okay for them to leave. Patience knew she would be sleeping in Lillie's room for however long it took for her daughter to feel safe.

From what she could tell, Lillie was healing. Patience wished she could say the same for herself. Every time she closed her eyes, she was back in the horror of what had happened. She was so tired of talking about the kidnapping, yet nearly every daylight hour brought another concerned friend or neighbor stopping by with food and good wishes.

The front door opened and Justice walked in. She crossed to him knowing he would hold her and make all the scary parts go away. He'd been there for her constantly, stepping between her and the authorities, directing everyone. He'd been the one Lillie wanted to talk to.

"How's she doing?" he asked, stroking her hair.

"Better. She's really asleep and she seems calmer." She managed a slight smile. "I think she's enjoying being a celebrity. Everyone is calling her a hero."

"She was very brave."

"I know. I'm glad school's out. She doesn't have to deal with telling the same story over and over again. By the time summer camp starts on Monday, most kids will be done talking about it." She looked up at him. "You missed dinner."

"Didn't you get my message? I had a meeting."

"I did get the message. And I saved you some mac and cheese. It's homemade and really delicious."

"The casserole brigade."

"You can mock it all you want, but this town comes through for people. Based on the rate casseroles are flowing into my freezer, I won't have to cook for at least a month. I kind of like that."

He touched her hair, then the side of her face. His blue gaze seemed to be studying her. "How are you holding up?"

"I'm okay. I go from terrified to numb and back about fifteen times an hour."

"That's normal. It will get better. The mind heals."

"How are *you* doing?"

He shrugged. “Fine. I wasn’t the one who took Bart out.”

No, that had been Ford Hendrix. Patience couldn’t believe he’d simply arrived in town, heard what was happening and gone off to help.

“You would have,” she said, knowing it was true. “You would have killed your father to protect Lillie.”

“Don’t make it sound like more than it was. Bart should have died years ago.”

“Still.”

He dropped his hands to her shoulders. “I’m not a hero. Don’t make me into one. Bart was an evil man. I’m glad he’s gone.”

She was, too. Maybe it was wrong, but she was willing to live with the flaw.

“You saved us and I’ll never forget that.” She grabbed his hand. “Come on. Let me feed you. We’ll both feel better after you eat.”

She expected him to smile or make a joke. But he did neither and he didn’t move.

“I can’t do this,” he told her.

“What? Did you eat already? That’s fine. The casserole will…”

His dark eyes had a distant expression. As if he was really somewhere else. And then she knew. He wasn’t talking about dinner. He was talking about leaving her.

“No,” she said, careful to keep her voice low so she wouldn’t wake Lillie. So she wouldn’t cry out, because once she started, she would never stop. It was too soon, she thought desperately. She didn't have anything left to get through him leaving. "No, you can't. You can't."

She knew she was pleading, that when it came to the man in front of her, she had no pride. "You said you loved me."

"I meant it. I do love you, and Lillie. But I can't risk hurting you."

"You won't."

"I will." He lowered his arms to his sides. "Somehow, somewhere, I'll drop my guard."

"You're not your father. You're nothing like him." She had to convince him. He had to understand; otherwise, he would go and she didn't think she could survive that.

"I won't take the chance."

She felt tears forming. She would have sworn she was cried out, but obviously not. Pain tore through her, making her want to fall to the floor. She folded her arms across her chest, holding herself together as best she could.

"We need you," she whispered. "Doesn't that mean anything? I love you and Lillie loves you and we need you."

He stiffened, as if he'd been struck. Or stabbed. She wanted to be grateful for his obvious pain, but she was suffering too much herself.

"Justice, don't. Please, you can't walk away. This is where you belong, with us. We're a family."

He drew her against him. For a second, she thought

she'd won. She allowed relief to relax her as she breathed in the scent of him.

He drew back and stared into her eyes. "I will love you forever," he told her.

Anger joined pain. She hung on to the rage because it was strong and right now she needed that strength.

"You're lying," she said coldly. "If you loved me you would stay."

"It's not that simple," he told her, then turned and walked out of her life.

"WHAT WAS I thinking?" Ford asked as he leaned back against the sofa in Justice's suite and sipped his beer.

When his friend had arrived, Justice had taken a break from packing. When they were done, Justice would throw his suitcases in his car and leave town. It didn't matter that it was ten at night. He liked the dark. And he needed to be gone. Now that he'd told Patience the truth, he owed it to her to disappear. He didn't want her to have to worry about running into him.

Justice picked up his own beer and sat across from his friend. "You grew up here. What did you expect?"

A muscle in Ford's jaw twitched. "Not a hero's welcome. I can't step foot outside without someone running up and welcoming me home. Old ladies are hugging me and I swear one of them pinched my butt. My mother checked on me five times last night. Do you know what it's like to come awake and find your *mother* hovering over the bed? I'm thirty-three years old, for God's sake. She needs to leave me alone."

Under other circumstances, he would have found his friend's pain amusing. Just not tonight. Not when he'd left Patience earlier that evening, had lingered outside long enough to hear her start to cry and to know he was the cause of her pain.

He wanted to make it better. He wanted to tell her he wasn't worth it. Only why should she believe him? All he'd done since arriving was screw up her life. He'd allowed her to believe in him. He'd fallen in love with her and let her think it was safe to love him back. Because of him, her daughter had been kidnapped by a madman.

Ford took another swallow of his beer. "She wants to help me find an apartment," he said with a shudder. "I've been on my own for, what, fourteen or fifteen years, I've been all over the world, I've been to war and my mother thinks I need help finding an apartment."

"She loves you."

"She's smothering me. This has got to stop."

For the first time since the kidnapping, Justice managed a smile. "It's been forty-eight hours, bro. You need to suck it up."

Ford gave him the finger. "She's one of the many reasons I didn't want to come back. Having to deal with her and my sisters." He swore. "They're growing up to be like her. Dakota and Montana have both offered me a place to stay. Only Nevada seems to get that I might not want to be treated like a runaway ten-year-old."

"Life is pain."

Ford looked at him over the bottle. "You're not very sympathetic."

"I have my own troubles."

"Why? You're a hero, too. You took on your old man and won."

"You shot him."

"We can't all be lucky." Ford's dark eyes studied him thoughtfully. "Well, hell. You're leaving."

"I can't stay."

"Sure you can, but you don't want to." He frowned. "No way. I thought people were just talking, but they're telling the truth, aren't they? About Patience. You know, they're saying she's in love with you."

Justice tightened his grip on his bottle of beer. "I know," he said, trying not to flinch. "It's my fault. I let her think things could work out."

"Instead you're going to run."

Justice looked at his friend. "You saw my father. You know better than most what kind of man does that. You've seen what I'm capable of. How thin a line separates us. Would you risk it?"

Ford put down his beer and raised his arms so he could link his fingers behind his head. "I don't know," he admitted. "I guess it depends on how bad you want it. Being with her, I mean. You're the most controlled guy I know. You're cool in a fight, deadly in an op. You're not ruled by emotion. Bart lived on hate. It ate him up until there was no humanity left. You're not like that."

"I could be."

"You could. That's up to you. Do you love her?"

A question Justice didn't want to answer. But he was also unwilling to deny his feelings for Patience. He nodded.

"Then think long and hard before you walk away. Once it's done, it can't be undone. There's no going back. From what I hear, Patience is a sensible woman. She raised a kid, started a business. She's not going to be made a fool of twice. When she's over you, it's finished."

PATIENCE LEFT WORK at her usual time. It was warm and bright and she couldn't figure out how the sun could look so happy. As she walked toward her house, she noticed the children playing in the park and the flowers in the planter boxes in front of the various businesses.

Life had gone on. Justice had left two days before and life continued. Look at her. She kept on breathing, kept on moving. She got through her shift, restocked shelves, took Lillie shopping to get ready for camp, cooked dinner and even chuckled at a well-meaning joke or two. She could fake being alive, but on the inside, she was long past dead.

When Ned had left, she'd assumed that was the worst thing that would ever happen to her. Abandoned by her husband. That she would be a single parent with a baby daughter.

She remembered the days had been hard, but more so because she was embarrassed—a failure at marriage. She'd known everyone was feeling sorry for her, and that was difficult. But nothing compared to Justice walking away.

She didn't care what anyone else was thinking. She didn't care if people talked or pointed or even laughed. What she cared about was the hole where her heart used to be, the ache that hadn't finished growing, let alone started fading. She hated the questions in Lillie's eyes and the sympathy in her mother's. She wanted it to be a year from now, so she could be over him.

She would never stop loving him—she accepted that. She'd given her heart fully to Justice. Even the most secret places she'd kept from Ned, she'd handed over to Justice. He'd believed in her and encouraged her. He was good and gentle and funny and kind. He was an honorable man, and a case could be made that he had left her for honorable reasons. But that didn't make the situation any easier to stand.

"There you are!" Felicia hurried up to her, breathing fast. "You left work a few minutes early and I was afraid I wasn't going to catch you. Come on."

Before Patience could protest, Felicia was leading her down a familiar street. "We're going to Isabel's house."

"We are? Why?"

"She needs to, uh, speak to you about something. It's important."

Patience nodded. In the past few days she'd neglected her friends. She simply didn't have the strength. But maybe talking about someone else's problems would help, she thought. Distract her for a few minutes.

Isabel had grown up in a low, one-story ranch house. The kind that sprawled in all directions. Back in school, it had been one of the newer houses in town, with a modern kitchen and big rooms off long hallways. There was a garage to one side and a small apartment above it.

Felicia herded Patience up the walkway. The door opened before they reached it and Isabel stepped onto the long porch.

"How are you doing?" she asked, her voice and expression sympathetic.

"Not great, but I'll survive."

Isabel moved close and hugged her, then put her arm around her and led her inside.

It took Patience a second to adjust to the dimness of the living room. When she did, she stared blankly at the dozen or so women sitting on sofas and standing around, talking.

Noelle was there, along with Pia and Charlie, Annabelle, with her baby in her arms, and an even more pregnant Heidi. Evie Stryker was talking to Liz Hendrix. Montana, Dakota and Nevada were clustered together, but looked up when she walked in.

Patience stared at them all. "I don't understand."

Jo walked in from the kitchen. She had a pitcher of what looked like margaritas in one hand and a full blender in the other.

"Virgin drinks in here for those of you breeding,"

she said, waving the pitcher. "The good stuff's in the blender. Don't get it mixed up."

Jo looked at Patience. "Hey. It sucks, huh? Justice leaving. Don't worry. We'll get you good and drunk. We'll call him names and tomorrow you'll have a hangover. It's the beginning of the healing process."

Then Patience understood. This was what the women in town did for each other. They showed up when times were hard and men were stupid. They ate ice cream and chips and drank margaritas. They told stories of their own breakups and helped each other through the pain. She'd been at countless evenings like this. Honestly, she'd never expected to have to have one of her own. Knowing her friends were looking out for her made her feel both better and worse. While she appreciated the love, she didn't like the cause. Because when this was all over, Justice would still be gone.

Charlie crossed to her and hugged her. "I can beat him up for you," she said. "He has skills, but he's still injured and I have righteousness on my side."

"Don't hurt him," Patience told her friend. "That's how bad it is. I don't want you to hurt him."

Isabel joined the hug and then everyone else was close, holding her and offering help. Somewhere along the way, she started to cry.

THE FRENCH ALPS in late spring were pretty much the way everyone imagined them, Justice thought as he waited on the narrow streets of the village. There was still snow on the mountain peaks, lambs and calves in the fields and flowers everywhere else.

He stood outside the cheese shop, listening to the conversations around him. The older French couple discussed what to serve for dinner. The two German women were more interested in the hike they would take that afternoon. The air smelled of freshly baked bread and melted chocolate. There were no cars, no jet engines, just the everyday sounds of a simpler life.

Justice had been here before. In the village, with the family. They always requested him when they came to stay in the old family home. There were two children, a boy and a girl, and Justice had known them for several years. He liked the children, enjoyed the duty.

He worked a twelve-hour shift, six days on. He had a room in the large old house. The staff treated him well. Although there was always the threat of danger, he wasn't in a war zone and he'd found the assignments easy.

Until today. Until the sound of Johann laughing reminded him too much of another child, a girl, also finding joy in life. Until the way Greta smiled at her husband made him think of Patience.

A black Mercedes pulled up at the end of the street. Two men in dark suits got out. Justice immediately started toward them, cataloging as he walked, prepared to pull the gun out of his chest holster if necessary. Then he recognized the man who ran the bank and his brother and waved at them. He returned to his post by the cheese shop and waited while the family shopped.

He would have taken on any assailants. Would have killed if necessary. It was part of the job. Although he'd planned to leave the work behind, to open CDS instead, he wouldn't. Staying in Fool's Gold would be too difficult. Although Angel and Ford were refusing to accept his decision. They still insisted he would be back. Time would prove them wrong, he thought.

Greta came out with a shopping bag over one arm. "They are arguing about cheese," she said with a laugh. "Johann is being very stubborn today." Her smile faded. "Your eyes are sad, Justice. I think you have left a woman behind, yes?"

He nodded.

"She has your heart, then. And you feel the loss."

"Thank you for your concern, but I'm fine."

"Fine. An American word with no meaning." She wrinkled her nose. "While my husband tells me I'm a great beauty, I see the truth in the mirror. You're not here because of your affection for us. You are here for the job, yes? But is it where you should be? Do *you* see truth in the mirror?"

"Trying to get rid of me?"

"You know I trust you with the lives of my children. I would like you to stay always. When you're around I feel safe. Klaus is the same. But you are not…" She frowned. "What is the word? Irreplaceable."

She moved closer and lowered her voice. "Do you love her?"

He nodded.

"Did she ask you to leave or did you make the decision for her?"

"How did you—"

"Men," she said, rolling her eyes. "Why do you think you know best? It was like that with Klaus. What he did was too dangerous. He wouldn't presume to invite me to share his life. He could be killed at any time. How he went on and on. Yet here we are, twelve years later. Do I feel the fear? Of course. Are there nights I can't sleep? Ya. But I love him and I have my children with him. The future will be here and then we will know what is to happen." Her expression turned shrewd. "I am disappointed that you would give up so easily."

"I didn't give up. I made the difficult decision."

"Is it what she wanted?"

He didn't answer.

Greta sighed. "I thought not. Foolish, foolish man."

She shook her head and returned to the cheese shop.

Justice watched her go, knowing she was wrong. He couldn't…couldn't…

The truth slammed into him like an angry bull. He swore under his breath as he glanced around and realized what he'd done. What he'd lost. By walking away he'd allowed his father to win. Even from the grave, Bart kept him from the only thing that was important—the people he loved.

When had suffering become so damned noble?

GETTING FROM THE French Alps to Fool's Gold with little notice wasn't easy. Justice took a train to Paris and from there got on a flight to New York. He had a six-hour layover, waiting for a seat to San Francisco, where he rented a car, arriving in the still-sleeping town after thirty hours of travel.

It was nearly five in the morning. He drove through the quiet streets, his heart pounding, his palms slick with sweat. He hadn't called or given any warning; he was just going to show up and hope for the best. It had only been two weeks. Patience couldn't have fallen out of love with him that quickly, could she? He still had a chance.

He would convince her, he told himself. He would explain how he'd been wrong, thinking he should walk away to protect her. He would beg if he had to, make her see that he would spend the rest of his life making sure she was happy and safe and loved.

He parked in front of her house and walked toward the front door. The house was dark and he swore as he realized it was far too early for him to be knocking on the door and disturbing everyone. After what they'd gone through with his father, he would only upset them. He needed to wait until…

He turned suddenly and started to run. Patience wasn't in bed asleep; she was at Brew-haha. She always took the morning shift.

He raced through the quiet streets of town. His still-healing wound ached, but he didn't care. He rounded the corner and saw the glow of the bright lights spilling onto the sidewalk.

One of Patience's friends—Charlie, he thought—walked out with a to-go coffee. She was with a man. They both glanced at him; then Charlie nudged the guy and whispered something. He hurried past them.

Inside the store, there was a big crowd. Several police officers sat at tables. A few businesspeople waited in line and a couple of old ladies were huddled together in the corner.

But he only cared about Patience. She was working the cash register, her smile bright as she talked to her customers. Only he saw past the pretend enthusiasm to the shadows under her eyes and the way her mouth trembled a little at the corners.

He'd hurt her, he thought sadly. Broken her heart. What had he been thinking?

He crossed to her. She glanced up and saw him. Her hands froze and a couple of dollar bills fluttered to the floor.

"Justice," she breathed.

There was a lot he wanted to say. He wanted to tell her how he'd been wrong to leave, how he'd been so damned scared of hurting her and Lillie. He wanted to explain he hadn't had faith. That he'd thought his father's hatred was strong, only now he knew love was so much stronger. He needed her to know he was going to work with Ford and Angel to start up CDS and that she would never have to worry about him going away again.

Instead he stopped in front of her, cupped her chin in his hands and kissed her.

"I'm sorry," he murmured. "I love you, Patience. I was wrong and I hope you can forgive me. I love you."

The store went completely silent. He could hear his heart pounding in his ears. Her brown eyes widened slightly.

"You're back."

"I'm back and I want to stay. If you'll have me. I want to marry you."

Someone behind them sighed.

"He's very handsome," one of the old ladies said.

"He's an idiot."

"Still. I'll bet he's hot in bed."

"She should marry him."

"I think she will."

Patience smiled. "You want to take this somewhere a little more private?"

"That would be nice." He kissed her again. "Are you going to marry me?"

"Probably."

He grinned. "When will you decide?"

"After I find out if you're hot in bed."

He leaned close, his lips brushing against her ear. "I am."

She shivered, then threw herself at him. "I missed you so much."

"I missed you, too. I was really an idiot."

"A man who knows when he's wrong and does a

halfway decent apology. I may have to marry you after all."

She glanced past him and smiled. "We're going to be a little shorthanded this morning."

Just then Felicia stumbled into the store. She looked sleepy but determined.

"Morning," she said with a yawn. "Mayor Marsha called and said I should come in and help." She spotted him. "Justice. You're back. Good. You wouldn't have been happy anywhere else."

"You have the statistical analysis to back that up?" he asked.

"No. It's actually a guess on my part, but a good one."

Patience wrapped her arms around his waist as they walked out of the store.

"How do you suppose Mayor Marsha knew you'd be back?" she asked.

"I have no idea."

"She's very mysterious. I think she has superpowers." She leaned into him. "Thank you for coming back."

"Thank you for forgiving me. I have a lot to tell you."

She looked up at him. "I want to hear all of it," she told him. "Especially the parts where you say you're wrong. But later, okay? For now, let's go home and tell Lillie that we're going to be a forever family."

They walked the quiet streets of Fool's Gold together. All around them lights came on as people rose to start their day. Once at the house, they went inside and up the stairs. Lillie woke as soon as they stepped into her room.

She took one look at them and started to laugh. “I *knew* it!” she crowed. “I knew you’d be back.”

She flung herself at him. He reached for her and held on. Then Patience was in his arms, too. They were together. His own forever family.

* * * * *

New York Times bestselling author

SUSAN MALLERY

welcomes readers back to Fool's Gold, where a one-time fling could become the real thing...

Felicia Swift never dreamed she'd hear a deep, sexy voice from her past in tiny Fool's Gold, California. The last time Gideon Boylan whispered in her ear was half a world away…on the morning after the hottest night of her life. Her freaky smarts have limited her close friendships, and romance, but she came to Fool's Gold looking for ordinary. Gorgeous, brooding Gideon is anything but that.

Black ops taught Gideon that love could be deadly. Now he pretends to fit in while keeping everyone at arm's length. Felicia wants more than he can give—a home, family, love—but she has a lot to learn about men…and Gideon needs to be the man to teach her.

As these two misfits discover that passion isn't the only thing they have in common, they just might figure out that two of a kind should never be split apart.

On sale June 26, 2013, wherever books are sold!

Be sure to connect with us at:

Harlequin.com/Newsletters

Facebook.com/HarlequinBooks

Twitter.com/HarlequinBooks

PHSM768CS

The "First Lady of the West,"
#1 *New York Times* bestselling author

LINDA LAEL MILLER

welcomes you home to Parable, Montana—where love awaits

With his father's rodeo legacy to continue and a prosperous spread to run, Walker Parrish has no time to dwell on wrecked relationships. But country-and-western sweetheart Casey Elder is out of the spotlight and back in Parable, Montana. And Walker can't ignore that his "act now, think later" passion for Casey has had consequences. Two teenage consequences!

Keeping her children's paternity under wraps has always been part of Casey's plan to give them normal, uncomplicated lives. Now the best way to hold her family together seems to be to let Walker be a part of it—as her husband of convenience. Or will some secrets—like Casey's desire to be the rancher's wife in every way—unravel, with unforeseen results?

Available wherever books are sold!

Be sure to connect with us at:

Harlequin.com/Newsletters
Facebook.com/HarlequinBooks
Twitter.com/HarlequinBooks

PHLM765

From *New York Times* bestselling author

Susan Andersen

a classic tale of a good girl, a bad boy and the chemistry they can't resist...

Jane thinks nothing can make her lose her cool. But the princess of propriety blows a gasket the night she meets the contractor restoring the Wolcott mansion. Devlin Kavanagh's rugged sex appeal may buckle her knees, but the man is out of control! Jane had to deal with theatrics growing up—she won't tolerate them in someone hired to work on the house she and her two best friends have inherited.

Dev could renovate the mansion in his sleep. But ever since the prissy owner spotted him jet-lagged and hit hard by a couple of welcome-home drinks, she's been on his case. Yet there's something about her. Jane hides behind conservative clothes and a frosty manner, but her seductive blue eyes and leopard-print heels hint at a woman just dying to cut loose!

Available wherever books are sold!

Be sure to connect with us at:

Harlequin.com/Newsletters
Facebook.com/HarlequinBooks
Twitter.com/HarlequinBooks

PHSA784